ANNA CASEY'S
PLACE IN THE WORLD

ANNA CASEY'S PLACE IN THE WORLD

Adrian Fogelin

PEACHTREE
ATLANTA

PJR
A Peachtree Junior Publication

Published by
PEACHTREE PUBLISHERS, LTD.
1700 Chattahoochee Avenue
Atlanta, Georgia 30318-2112

www.peachtree-online.com

Jacket and book design by Loraine M. Balcsik
Book composition by Melanie M. McMahon

Manufactured in the United States of America

10 9 8 7 6 5 4 3 2

Library of Congress Cataloging-in-Publication Data

Fogelin, Adrian.
    Anna Casey's place in the world / Adrian Fogelin ; illustrations by Suzy Schultz.-- 1st ed.
        p. cm.
    Summary: Anna, a twelve year old girl with strong survival instincts, tries to adjust to life in a Florida foster home in a strange neighborhood with an overly tidy single woman and Eb, another foster child who is not at all sure he wants to stay there.
    ISBN 1-56145-249-1 (alk. paper)
    [1. Foster home care--Fiction. 2. Homeless persons--Fiction. 3. Florida--Fiction.] I. Schultz, Suzy, ill.
II. Title.
    PZ7.F72635 An 2001
    [Fic]--dc21   2001002261

For my parents,
Maria B. and Carl E. Fogelin,
who taught me the meaning of home.

Thanks to Peachtree editors Vicky Holifield and Sarah Helyar Smith,
who helped make Anna the girl she is today.

And thanks, as always, to Helen Bradford, Mary Z. Cox,
Richard Dempsey, Noanne Gwynn, Taylor Phillips,
and Linda Sturgeon—The Wednesday Night Writers.

CONTENTS

1—The Explorer. 1

2—First You Get a Stone. 10

3—This Way Be Monsters 21

4—In the Bone Museum 31

5—Boots Just Like That. 42

6—Show Us Your Stuff 51

7—Out There Flappin'. 62

8—Fireworks 72

9—Kings of the Race-A-Rama 84

10—Listening 94

11—"Earth to Sam Miller". 98

12—The Most Dangerous Thing in the Woods 104

13—The Big Itch. 112

14—More Homeless Than Ever 119

15—Maybe Rabies 128

16—Long Distance. 141

17—Nursing Mr. Miller 147

18—The Einstein of the Dog World 156

19—Ninety-Nine Point Nine Percent. 164

20—The Sand Below 172

21—To Move a Forest 181

22—The Last View of Eb 188

23—The Skeleton of the Earth 199

24—Anna Casey's Place in the World 204

Chapter One

THE EXPLORER

Mrs. Riley hadn't even started the car when the purse on the seat beside her beeped. "Shoot," she said. She pulled out the pager, checked the number, and said "Shoot" again. "I have to make a quick call, kids. Eb, Anna, talk, you two. Get acquainted." Then she dashed up the steps to the agency.

Sitting in the back, all I could see of the boy was his skinny neck and his short, bristle haircut. I undid my seat belt, slid up, and rested my arms on the seat. "Hi, Eb. So, you're ten?"

He was all scooched up against the door, staring at the Band-Aids on his knees. His legs were spaghetti-thin.

"You don't look ten," I said.

"And you don't look twelve," he shot back, still staring at his knees.

"I guess we're both small for our ages."

No answer.

"Do you think we'll like our new home?"

"No." He wouldn't look at me.

I hung over the seat a little more. He turned toward the window. "Maybe we will," I said, talking to the back of his head. "If we do, and everything works out so that we stay, I mean *really* stay, I'm going to get a cat."

I caught a quick glimpse of blue eyes, then he was looking out the window again. After a long pause he asked, "Why a cat?"

"I like cats. Don't you?"

"Never had one."

"I had a cat named Buck when I lived with my grandmother. When she died we moved to my aunt and uncle's—Buck and I did, I mean."

"Where's old Buck now?"

"He got hit by a car the second day we were there."

"He did?" Eb was still looking away, but I saw his ears lift, the way they do when someone smiles. "Was he like...squished?"

"Yeah."

Up went the ears again. "Cool."

I slid back in my seat. *Cool? No cat for him. Forget it. Any cat we get will be mine. But first I have to be sure that I'm staying, because cats don't like moving around.* When we lived at my grandmother's, Buck spent mornings on one windowsill, afternoons on another. That's enough change for a cat. And that's why I never got another one. All the places I'd lived in the last four years? It wouldn't have been fair to the cat.

Suddenly electronic burps and bleeps started coming from the front seat. Eb must have slipped some kind of video game out of the pocket of his baggy shorts. "Die, dark lord!" he cackled, and the toy in his lap hissed like a bug zapper.

"I hope we do get to stay," I said softly, talking to myself, not him.

But his voice came back over the seat. "You can stay. Not me." There was a sizzle as he fried another lord of darkness. "Anyway, I'm allergic to cats."

The driver's door opened, and Mrs. Riley tossed her purse back in. "Is everybody ready? Seat belts on!"

I did my belt, then picked up the pack from the seat beside me and hugged it. My suitcase was in the trunk, but my explorer's pack stays with me, always. I keep all my important stuff in it: my notebook, postcards, pocketknife, waterproof matches, my family picture, my

Boy Scouts of America Explorer's Manual—not that I'm a boy. But I *have* done some exploring.

I've seen quite a bit for twelve, lived lots of places with aunts and uncles and cousins. But relatives aren't like parents. They don't have to keep you if they get divorced, or if they need your room for a new baby, or if their arthritis gets bad. They just pass you along until, one day, you run out of relatives. Then you have to go with someone like Mrs. Riley. Mrs. Riley is a social worker for the State of Florida. I was one of her cases. So was Eb.

"We're getting close now," said Mrs. Riley. "Would you mind putting that game away, Eb?"

The chirping and beeping went on until Eb yelled, "Yes! Total annihilation!"

"Anna, dear?" Mrs. Riley gave me a smile in the rearview mirror. "Take your hat off so Miss Dupree can see what a pretty girl you are."

I slid my denim hat off, set it on top of my pack, and rested my chin on its wide, floppy brim. My uncle used to call it his bush hat. He let me keep it when he saw that I wore it every minute I wasn't in bed.

"Now kids," said Mrs. Riley, "Miss Dupree is a first-time foster mother, and a personal friend of mine, so you two will be extra nice, won't you?"

I nodded.

She turned to Eb for nod number two, but he was all slumped down, as if turning the game off had turned him off too.

We rode in silence until Mrs. Riley announced, "Here's your new neighborhood." I closed my eyes and held my breath for luck. Then I looked.

The houses in our new neighborhood were small, yards crammed with dogs and bicycles, birdbaths and huge old trees. A telephone pole with a basketball hoop nailed to it cast its shadow across the chalk drawings in the road.

"It certainly looks as if there are plenty of kids," Mrs. Riley observed. "How wonderful!"

Eb pulled his head down between his shoulders like a turtle.

We slowed in front of a white house with green shutters. No toys or bicycles littered its perfect lawn. The shrubs that guarded the door looked as if they had come out of a giant ice cream scoop. Just as Mrs. Riley turned in, I saw a small, pointy face peeking between a pair of curtains. Miss Dupree was waiting for us.

This could be better than relatives. Miss Dupree had chosen to become a foster mother. That meant she wanted us. Well, maybe not us specifically. But she must have wanted kids. It was a start.

As the front door opened, Mrs. Riley sang out, "Good morning, Miss Dupree." With a hand on each of our backs, she marched us up the walk. "Here they are! Anna Casey and Eb Gramlich." She introduced us as if we were movie stars, then gave each of us an extra little shove. "Kids, this is your new foster mother, Miss Dupree."

Miss Dupree patted our shoulders the way you'd pat a dog you were afraid was going to jump up, and then she folded her arms. She looked scared. Like Eb and me, Miss Dupree was small. Her brown hair was short and fluffy. She wore eyeglasses so thick, she seemed to peer at us from underwater. She looked Eb over first. Maybe she was wondering why he wore a long-sleeved shirt when it was so hot. Maybe she wondered how anyone could be that skinny. "Your name is Eb?"

When he didn't answer, I rushed in. "That's right, It's Eb."

Her eyebrows went up.

"I know," I said, "it takes some getting used to. E plus B. Eb. It doesn't seem like enough, does it? It's more like a hiccup than a name." I knew I was blabbering. I was pretty nervous.

"It's nice to meet you, Eb," she said.

Eb stared at his sneakers.

Then she turned to me. "So, this is Anna."

I smiled my class-picture smile, lips closed to hide my chipped front tooth. Whatever she had hoped for, it didn't seem to be a kid with too many freckles and mouse-colored hair, a girl in a hand-me-down blouse two sizes too big. But that was okay. I'd grow on her.

Mrs. Riley got our paperwork out of the car. "Emergency numbers are up front." She pushed her half glasses up on her nose and opened the folder labeled Gramlich, E. "As I told you on the phone, Eb has a little problem with asthma, but it's being managed." She turned to Eb. "You know what to do for your asthma, don't you, Eb?"

Eb's arms hung at his sides.

"Don't worry," I told Miss Dupree. "I'm sure he knows."

Mrs. Riley opened the trunk of her car. As I dragged my suitcase up the walk, I heard her say in a low voice, "Anita, I want to thank you again for taking the boy on such short notice. We just *had* to get him out of there."

Seeing me, she went back to her official voice. "Be good, you two. If there's a problem, here's a number where you can reach me." She gave each of us a business card and a kiss on the cheek. She engulfed Miss Dupree in a hug. "Relax, Anita. You'll do just fine." I put my hat back on as soon as she drove away.

"Come, children, let me show you your new home." Miss Dupree sounded fake-happy, with scared underneath. I kept smiling and Eb kept frowning, but it didn't matter. Our new foster mother darted up the steps and held the door without actually looking at either of us.

The entry room was tiny, with nothing in it but artificial flowers on a small table, an empty coat rack, and the strong smell of fresheners and deodorizers and cleaning products all trying to outdo each other.

"You can hang your hat up, Anna."

"No thank you, Miss Dupree. I'll keep it with me. It's my lucky hat."

"Hats are for outside, Anna. Hang it up, please."

My hat drooped on the rack. It was an old hat, and it looked lonely hanging there all by itself. Compared to the light wall-to-wall carpet, it seemed dirty. I looked down at my worn sandals and Eb's junky high-tops. *What if our shoes leave marks?* I worried.

We walked through the living room and into the kitchen, which was where Miss Dupree seemed to want to start the tour. "This is the kitchen," she said.

Eb rolled his eyes.

"It's nice," I said.

It *was* nice, but terminally clean. The glossy white table had never had a glass of orange juice spilled on it, I bet, or eraser crumbs from someone changing answers on a homework assignment. The only things on the counter were the dish soap, a bowl of potpourri, and a can of Super-Kill bug spray.

We cut back through the living room. "And this is my office," she said, opening a door. Inside, a video camera was trained on a chair in front of a blue backdrop. A computer sat on a desk. "I run a dating service called 'Perfect Match,'" she said. "It's for busy professionals who want to fall in love but need a little help scheduling it." On the wall behind her was a map of the United States with pins stuck in it.

I moved in for a closer look. "What's the map for?" I asked. Maps are my hobby.

"Some of my clients want to locate people they've lost track of. High school sweethearts, mostly. The pins are successful finds." She put a hand on my shoulder and steered me out of the room. "Everything in a business like mine is confidential, I'm afraid, so this room is off limits." She closed the door with a little click.

"This is the living room. Yes, Eb," she added before he had a chance to roll his eyes again. "The living room. I do some business in here too."

The room looked a lot like a doctor's office. All the furniture was white. On the coffee table, next to magazines arranged in neat rows, were two thick photo albums, one pink, one blue. Each said Likely Prospects on its cover. "I greet clients in here," she said, "serve them coffee, give them a first look at potential partners." She ran a hand over the cover of Likely Prospects, pink. "But most of the time the three of us can use it for sitting around or watching TV." I tried to imagine the three of us sitting around. It wasn't easy.

"Now Anna, I hope you'll like the next room." Miss Dupree looked excited. "I decorated it just for you." She flung open a door.

The room was nonstop pink—the walls, the bed, the curtains. Even the top of the trash can had a ruffle that matched the paint. It was really, really ugly.

"Well, Anna?" She held her breath a moment. "Do you like it?"

The color made my stomach hurt. The ruffles were stupid. It was totally the wrong kind of room for an explorer. But she had fixed it just for me. "It's great, Miss Dupree," I said. "Super, really."

She relaxed and smiled. "I'm so glad you like it. Now Eb, I apologize. I wasn't expecting two. Your room is not as nice as Anna's, but we can work on it." She led us up a dark flight of narrow stairs.

"Wow!" I said as we stepped into a tiny room tucked under the roof. An air conditioner hummed in one of the two small windows in its sloping walls. I ran over to the other window, which framed a huge old tree. "You're so lucky, Eb! You could climb right through this window into the tree."

"I've been meaning to get some of those branches trimmed back," Miss Dupree fussed. "But of course, Anna is kidding, Eb. That would be too dangerous."

"Not for a good tree-climber. See that branch? I'd have to stretch, but I could get to it." Then I remembered the ruffly pink room. Maybe Miss Dupree didn't want a good tree-climber. I sat down quietly on the edge of the bed and looked around.

It seemed as if all the interesting things that weren't allowed downstairs were up in the attic. Mysterious trunks and boxes were stacked on one side of the room. My hat would have felt right at home hanging with the other old hats on the rack in the corner. I flopped back on the bed, which was soft and deep and feathery. "Where'd you get all this great stuff?" I asked.

"It belonged to my mother," she said. "She never threw out a thing."

Lucky for you, I thought. And lucky for Eb. He was going to have this room. He should have been jumping for joy, but he hadn't budged from the top of the stairs.

"What happened to your mom?" he asked. "Did she croak?"

"Yes, she died several years ago."

Eb eyed the leaning boxes as if Miss Dupree's dead mother was in one of them.

"It's dusty up here," he said. "It's giving me an asthma attack. I'll sleep on the couch." He clomped back down the steps.

Miss Dupree hurried after him. I wanted to explore the attic room, but I followed them.

Back in the living room, Miss Dupree glanced at her all-white couch, then at the grubby boy who thought he was going to sleep on it.

"Hey, Eb," I said. "I'll trade rooms with you."

"But Anna," Miss Dupree cut in, "I fixed the pink room just for you." She took a second look at her couch. "You're sure you wouldn't mind?"

And that's how I got the treasure room and Eb got the one with the frilly garbage can.

I grabbed my suitcase before he could change his mind. As I dragged it up the stairs, it thumped against the edges and almost pulled my arm out of the socket. Not that there was much in it, just the usual socks and underwear plus some old clothes from my twin cousins, Jenny and Janice. What made it heavy was the stones.

The first thing I did was line them up on the windowsill, in order. Stone number one, a chunk of Maine granite, belonged to my grandmother originally. She lived in Maine all her life until she got married. When I asked her why she kept it, she said, "When you leave a place, you need something to help you remember."

Grandma died when I was eight—one of the top worst things that ever happened to me. After the funeral I ran down to the pond behind her house and grabbed a rock from the bank. It was nice and flat. My cousin Janice wanted to skip it across the pond, but I put it in my pocket. I've done the same thing in each place since—picked up a stone to help me remember.

Massachusetts, New Jersey, Virginia, North Carolina. Each stone came from a little further south, like I'd been tumbling down the map. My last stop was at the top edge of Florida, just south of the Georgia line. Now here I was in Tallahassee. My Tallahassee stone just had to be the last one. If I kept going, I'd fall right off the map.

Once my stones were arranged on the windowsill, I sat down cross-legged on the bed and undid the buckles on my pack. I slipped out the framed photograph that sat on top.

This picture came with me every time I moved to a new place. In it was a man with longish hair and a pretty woman with freckles, like mine. The baby on her hip had one sock on and one bare foot. All three of them were smiling. The one-sock baby was me, Anna. The two smiling grownups were my parents, Josh and Mindy Casey. Sitting on my new bed, I smiled back. This was the last picture ever taken of them.

I looked deeper into the picture. Swimming in the lake behind my parents and me were most of the relatives I'd lived with since the accident. There was Aunt Linda, who raised canaries in cages in her basement, and Aunt Betsy and Uncle Harry. They used to sit me in a chair in the corner when they thought I was getting too wild. The two pairs of feet sticking out of the water belonged to Jenny and Janice. They were doing underwater handstands. Off to one side I could see the back of Grandma's head. Just her white rubber bathing cap was sticking out of the water. I wished I had a better picture. One where she didn't look so much like a lightbulb.

I missed every one of them. Especially Aunt Eva and Uncle Charles, the last ones to have me. They were in the picture too, standing ankle-deep in the water, holding hands and laughing. The picture was taken before they were married. My cousins, Mark and Macy, hadn't been born. And now my Aunt Eva and Uncle Charles weren't married anymore, and all of us were scattered, me the farthest.

I put my picture on the table by the bed and took out my explorer's notebook. I opened it and wrote my new address and the date at the top of a fresh page.

Uncle Charles used to say he joined the Navy to see the world. I was seeing the world too. One neighborhood at a time.

Chapter Two

FIRST YOU GET A STONE

Miss Dupree shuttled between our rooms. She seemed eager to help me unpack. But there were only a few things in my suitcase, just enough to fill one drawer of her mother's chest of drawers. "You'll need some new clothes before school starts," she said. "I've been looking forward to having a girl to dress."

"Oh, I'm not one of those girls who likes a lot of clothes," I said. The truth was, my aunt and uncle were always too busy fighting to think about kids' clothes. I couldn't tell Miss Dupree that.

But if I was giving Miss Dupree second thoughts about being a foster mother, Eb was giving her thirds and fourths. She was handing out tuna sandwiches and glasses of milk for lunch when he announced, "Milk gives me a rash. A big ugly one all over my back."

She picked his glass back up like she didn't know what to do with it.

"I love milk," I said. "I'll drink his too."

She put the second glass down in front of me and got Eb some water. She looked from Eb to me to Eb. A phone rang in another room. "Excuse me," she said, and scurried out of the kitchen. A moment later we heard a door close.

"Saved by the bell," Eb said.

"Would you *try* to be nice?" I hissed. "You're scaring her." I took a big bite out of my sandwich and a big gulp from each of the glasses.

"I don't know about you, Eb, but I don't want to find out where you go if you flunk at being a foster child."

I heard chirps and burps. Eb was playing his game under the edge of the table. "No games at the table," I snapped. I must have sounded tougher than Mrs. Riley. The sounds stopped immediately. "Thank you." My grandmother had taught me that mealtime is for eating and conversation. There was no TV. No picking things up with our fingers. No reaching across. To eat with my grandmother you had to be civilized.

Later, when I was being shuffled from house to house, I learned that being sit-down civilized was kind of rare. In the last place I lived, the fights between my aunt and uncle got so bad that for supper my cousins and I ate bowls of cold cereal on the couch. We turned the TV up to cover the shouting.

But it was easy to see that Miss Dupree was civilized. Very. I took another gulp from each glass. "What would you like to do after lunch?" I asked.

Eb stared at the floor like there was a message there, written in the gold splotches on the white linoleum.

I had finished the first glass of milk and was almost done with the second one. Eb still hadn't touched his sandwich or his water. He was still staring at the floor. "Eat, Eb."

"Not hungry." I could hear him scuffing his sneaker back and forth.

"Eat anyway."

He picked up half a sandwich and took a baby bite. His foot kept scraping the floor.

"And quit scuffing."

By the time I had finished my sandwich, half of Eb's, and both glasses of milk, I could hardly breathe.

Miss Dupree's office door was still closed.

I carried our plates and glasses to the sink. "I'll wash, you dry."

"But you ate most."

I pointed to the neatly folded dishtowel on the rack.

After I scrubbed our plates with a soapy sponge and rinsed them, Eb dragged the towel over them for about half a second. I opened a cupboard to put them away. "Look, Eb!" Sparkling glasses and stacks of plates were lined up in neat rows. "At my aunt's house there were hardly ever any clean dishes," I said. "If you wanted something, you had to hunt around. One time I found three plates under the sofa."

"So?" said Eb, like he knew all about plates under sofas.

"This is the way it was at my grandmother's," I whispered, opening another cupboard. "Listen, Eb, we have to put things back in the exact right spot. We can't make stains or scuff the floor. And *please*, don't do or say anything gross, understand?"

He dropped the towel on the counter, opened his mouth wide, and belched. Then he went back to his chair and stared at the spot where his plate had been. I left him sitting and walked to the office door. I knocked and called out, "Excuse me, Miss Dupree, may Eb and I go outside?"

She said something to the person on the phone, then stuck her head out the door. "I suppose that would be all right." She looked hesitant. "But don't leave the neighborhood, okay? And don't be gone long. We need to get to know each other. It *is* your first day."

"Yes ma'am."

I went back for Eb, but he wouldn't budge.

"You can't just sit there all day. Come on. Let's go outside."

He crossed his arms. "I *hate* outside."

I tried to look into his eyes. "That's dumb, Eb. Outside is where the whole world is." He twisted away. "Fine," I said. "Stay here then. I'm going to get a stone." I was walking away when I heard Eb's chair scrape.

"How come you need a stone?"

"Tell you later." I grabbed my hat.

"Jeez, it's hot," Eb said as soon as we'd stepped out the door.

"That's because you're wearing long sleeves. Want to go back and change your shirt?"

"Nah, that's okay," he said, tugging the cuffs down as if he was hiding something.

"Suit yourself." I put my hat on.

"Ben!" yelled a little boy who was standing in the middle of the road right in front of the house. "Ben, I wanna come too!" He wore his bike helmet backwards; his bike lay on the tar. "Please…I promise I won't tell."

Three bigger boys sped down the street on bikes. Two had shovels on their shoulders. The third had a gallon jug of water swinging from his handlebars.

The little boy stamped his foot. "Ben!"

The boy with the water jug turned back. He dragged his sneaker until he stopped, then flicked his brown hair out of his eyes. He looked older than me, and cute. "You're too little, Cody," he said.

"Am not." The little boy kicked a tire on the bike that lay on the ground. "I'm six going on seven."

A second boy, one with red hair, turned back. "Oooh," he said, "six going on seven." He pedaled in a big circle around Cody and Ben. "How many fingers is that?"

"I'm too old to do fingers." Cody kicked his bike again.

"Yeah?" The redhead let go of his handlebars and held up both hands. "Well, when you're this many you can come with us, okay? You *can* count to ten, can't you?"

Ben turned on him. "Don't rub it in, Clay."

"Yeah, Clay. Don't rub it in," Cody echoed. "You're not so big yourself."

"Am too." The redhead reared his bike up on one wheel. "I'm eleven, Cody. I'm plenty old."

The third biker, a short, stocky kid, had stopped at the end of the street. He stood with his bike between his legs. "Hey! You guys coming?"

Ben lifted Cody's helmet, ruffed his sandy hair, then set the helmet on the right way. As he and the redheaded boy rode away he called back, "We'll do something later, okay?"

"I hate later!" Cody stamped his foot. "I'm coming too!"

"You'll be sorry if you do," said Clay, turning around in his seat. "*Real* sorry." The three boys bumped across the strip of grass at the end of the road, cut through some trees, and disappeared.

I grabbed Eb's arm. "Let's follow them."

"No way. You heard what he said."

"Aren't you curious about where they're going?"

"No. I'd sort of like to go on breathing."

"*I* know where they're going." The little boy stood his bike up. "The Race-A-Rama."

"What's the Race-A-Rama?" I asked him.

Cody shrugged. "I dunno. That's just what they call it, the Race-A-Rama. They're making it with shovels." He turned the bike so it pointed away from the Race-A-Rama, ran with it, then jumped on. As soon as he had some speed he took his hands off the handlebars and his feet off the pedals. "No hands, no feet, see?" He had to grab the handlebars quick to make the turn at the corner.

"Come on, Eb, it'd be an adventure."

"You call getting killed an adventure? That Clay guy wasn't kidding around. Anyway, I thought we were supposed to be looking for a stone." He began walking in the direction Cody had gone, but we had barely left the driveway when he bent down and picked up a piece of gravel. "Here you go."

"No, Eb. It can't be just any old stone. It has to be special. A specimen." I like the word *specimen*. It sounds scientific.

"A stone's a stone." Eb threw the gravel as hard as he could. It poinged off a mailbox. "Why do you need one anyway?"

"I pick one up in each place I live, to remind me. The way things are going, I might need this one right away."

"You know, it's really hot out here." Eb flopped down on the curb. With his legs straight out, the skin around the Band-Aids on his knees puckered. "How many stones do you have so far?"

"Eight." I sat down beside him. In the bright light, I could see little blue veins in his eyelids and in his cheeks. He needed to get out in the sun more.

"You mean you got kicked out of eight places?"

"One of the stones belonged to my grandmother."

"Seven places. Big difference. Where were you before here?"

"My aunt and uncle's. They split up. They couldn't keep me after that. It wasn't my fault."

He leaned back on his arms. "One of 'em could've kept you."

"No. My Uncle Charles travels all the time for work. Aunt Eva's only my aunt by marriage. She has enough to worry about taking care of my cousins and the dog and all."

"She kept the dog and kicked you out?" He shook his head and laughed. "Nice."

"How come *you* got kicked out?"

"Who says I got kicked out?" Eb sat up straight and squeezed his skinny thighs with both hands. "I didn't get kicked out!"

"Calm down. I didn't mean anything." I hugged my knees and looked at the toes of my sandals. "But if you didn't get kicked out, how come you're here?"

"We lost our trailer and had to move in with Eddie. Then things got weird." Eb swallowed. "I won't be here for long, though. I'm just a temporary placement. As soon as Lisa gets us another place and dumps Eddie, she'll come get me."

"Who's Lisa?"

"My mom, of course."

"You call her Lisa?"

"That's her name."

"Who's Eddie, your dad?"

"My dad?" he sputtered. "No way. Eddie's just some guy. Come on." He stood up again. "Let's get your rock." At the corner he jumped up to smack a stop sign. "Hope she comes soon. That pink room is gonna make me puke."

"Too bad you have asthma."

"My asthma was okay." He ducked his head. "It was all the dead-lady stuff. Dead people creep me out."

∽

We walked and walked, but aside from gravel, which doesn't count because it always comes from somewhere else, we didn't see one single stone. When Eb started to whine, "It's really, really, really, really, really hot out here," we circled back. As we turned onto Miss Dupree's street we passed a woman picking up trash from the edge of the road with a long pair of metal tongs. She was big like Uncle Charles. Not fat, just tall and strong looking. She wore army boots with purple socks folded over the tops and khaki shorts with half a dozen bulging pockets. Her blond hair was gathered into a ponytail with a garbage twist tie. Printed on the canvas sack slung over her shoulder was a drawing of the western hemisphere and the words, Be Kind to Your Mother, Recycle.

"I've never seen a place with no rocks before," I said to Eb.

"Rocks?" The woman straightened up. "A few miles that way you'd find rocks." She pointed with the tongs. "The southern foothills of the Appalachian mountain range end just north of here. Where we're standing was once the edge of a shallow sea." She picked up a Big Mac wrapper and stuffed it in her sack, then pointed the other way. "From here south is nothing but sand. Miles and miles of ancient dunes. Most places they're covered with trees, but they're sand dunes nonetheless." She trotted down the street chasing a plastic bag. "The only naturally occurring rock here is the karst," she called over her shoulder. "And most of that's buried."

"Karst? What's that?" I asked. "What does it look like?"

Miss Dupree opened her front door. "Kids? I was beginning to worry. You two have been gone so long." As we followed her inside I looked back at the woman picking up trash. I wanted to ask her about the karst, but Miss Dupree hustled us inside. "That woman you were talking to is a bit, well…strange. She's out there every single day picking up trash. Hang your hat, Anna."

"Do you know anything about karst?" I asked, hanging my hat on the same hook as before.

"Is he a county commissioner?"

"No, it's some kind of rock. Have you ever seen it?"

"I'm afraid I don't know much about rocks. They all look kind of alike to me." Then she brightened. "Follow me," she said. "I have a surprise for you two."

Coloring books and crayons had been set out on the kitchen table. I was afraid Eb would say coloring was for babies and hurt her feelings again. Instead he sat down and picked up a blue crayon and a book with a spaceship on the cover.

While we colored, Miss Dupree sat at the other end of the table, paying bills. I could see that she was watching us, stealing peeks when she thought we weren't looking.

Eb propped his chin up in his hand. At first I thought he was bored, but then I looked at what he was doing. He was filling in the spaces with all different colors, shading each part. His space aliens began to pop right off the page.

When we finished, Miss Dupree used cat magnets to hang our pictures on the refrigerator.

"Cats!" I said. "Miss Dupree, do you like cats?"

"I like pictures of cats. Real cats shed." She straightened our pictures and stepped back. "I've never had any kid drawings to put up before," she said. "They look great."

"Mine's okay," I said. "I stayed in the lines and everything, but Eb's is fantastic." When Miss Dupree agreed, Eb acted like he didn't hear. All he had to do was say "thanks," but he didn't seem to know the word.

She made us put the crayons back in the box, then handed Eb a sponge to wipe the table. In water letters he wrote MISS DUPREE IS A.... I grabbed the sponge and erased it fast.

I don't think Miss Dupree saw. She had her head in the freezer. "Who likes pizza?"

"We love pizza!" I said, not giving Eb a chance to say a thing about rashes. "Pepperoni's the best," I added, reading the lid of the box she pulled out.

She looked at Eb's skuzzy knees. "Showers first?"

"What?" he squawked.

"Good idea," I said. I had to push him. The pink bedroom had its own bathroom. Eb used the shower in there. I used the one next to Miss Dupree's room. Rows of bottles stood on the shelf in her shower, liquid soaps and scrubs, each for a different body part. I screwed the lid off each one, sniffed it, and tried a tiny dab. After my shower I asked Miss Dupree if I could wear my hat. She let me, because my hair was wet and she didn't want me to catch a cold in the air-conditioning. With my hat on, I felt better.

The Band-Aids were off when Eb came out for supper. His knees were scabby, and on his left arm, just below the T-shirt sleeve, were five dark bruises. "What happened to you?" I asked.

He hid his arms behind his back. "Nothing." Miss Dupree pursed her lips but didn't say anything. She already seemed to know about it.

The timer on the stove dinged, and Miss Dupree pulled our pizza out. "Looks great," I said. While Eb and I wolfed down pepperoni pizza, Miss Dupree ate salad and a little yogurt.

After the dishes we watched TV. I was glad Eb had taken a shower. I didn't have to worry when he plopped down on the all-white couch and demanded *Star Trek: Voyager*.

Miss Dupree checked the TV guide. "It doesn't come on until ten. I'm sorry, but that's past your bedtime."

"I don't have a bedtime," he said. "Lisa says I know when I'm tired."

Miss Dupree folded her hands in her lap. "I make the rules here, and Eb, I'm not your mother."

"You sure aren't," he said. And that was the end of the discussion.

On the dot of nine Miss Dupree said, "Time for bed."

"Man...," Eb whined. "Nobody goes to bed this early, not even babies." I noticed that he didn't fight hard. We had been sitting on the sofa being polite for two hours.

But then we had a whole new problem. We didn't know how to say good night to our foster mother, and she didn't know how to say good night to us. When she leaned toward Eb, he held up his hands. "No displays of affection, please. Hug allergy. Don't touch the kid." He disappeared into his pink bedroom.

Stranded on the couch, Miss Dupree and I just sat there silently, watching a commercial, each waiting for the other to make the first move. There were two little TVs on her eyeglasses. Finally I said, "Thanks for having us. It was a good supper."

"Good night, Anna," she called as I walked toward the attic stairs. "Sweet dreams."

I hesitated on the steps. *Sweet dreams.*... Grandma used to say that before she turned out the light.

"The same to you, Miss Dupree."

$\sim$

I lay awake in my new bed, in my new house, and it was dark and quiet. By moonlight, the stones on the windowsill cast long black shadows. The boxes and trunks crouched in the corners. In my last place I shared a room with my cousin, Macy. She had a night-light. I always thought it was babyish, but I wished I had Macy's night-light now.

I heard the long, low whistle of a passing train. Some people think it's a sad sound, but it made me feel better. My grandmother's house was near the tracks. No other houses were nearby, no kids. It was just the two of us, my Grandma and me—and the trains. When I was little, she would make up bedtime stories about where passengers were going. The man with the basket on his lap was taking a puppy to his granddaughter. Sometimes the puppy would escape and everyone had to chase it around the car. Another passenger was on his way to California to find gold. Another was going to Alaska to visit the Eskimos. Then there was the woman in the big red hat—but by then I would be asleep.

I told Grandma stories, too, about all the places I was going to go, places I had found in the *National Geographics* on the shelf in the hall. "I'm going to Borneo."

"Good," she answered. "Send me a postcard."

"Grandma...they don't have postcards. They don't even have clothes in Borneo."

I was too old for stories now, and still too young to go to Borneo. I needed to stay put for a while, so I could get through middle school and high school and not be the new kid all the time. The tree's shadow twisted across my bed. But would Miss Dupree let me stay, or would she ask Mrs. Riley if she could trade me for some other girl who was—I don't know—prettier maybe? One who liked the color pink and drawers full of new clothes?

Itchy tears filled my eyes, but I wiped them away with the sleeve of my nightgown.

Sometimes you just have to tell yourself that everything will be fine, so I did.

It was kind of like a night-light.

Chapter Three

THIS WAY BE MONSTERS

Who made you God?" Eb asked as I held him by the shoulders and walked him to the middle of the street. "Stand here," I said.

"What if I don't want to stand here?"

"It'll only take a second," I said. "I've got to get our bearings."

I used to have a compass in my pack, but it belonged to my uncle. I knew another way to find directions using a watch, but I didn't have a watch either. Luckily, my Explorer's Manual told how to make a shadow compass. All I needed for that was a four-foot pole. Eb was the pole.

I sat on the curb and opened my notebook on my knees. In the early morning light Eb's slanty shadow fell across his grubby high-tops and stretched all the way to the curb. I drew two crossed lines with arrows on the ends and wrote N, S, E, W. Eb's shadow pointed west. "You can move now," I said, starting to draw the map.

Eb's shadow fell across the page. "What're you doing?" He sat down next to me.

"Making a map. I do it every place I live." I flopped the notebook onto his knees. "See? This rectangle is Miss Dupree's house. These lines are the road. The crossed lines are the compass rose. North always points up."

Eb stared at the few little lines on the page. "This is a map?"

"Just the start. There's a lot more to do."

Eb stared as if his eyes had gotten stuck.

"You want to add anything to it before we start walking?" I had asked the question just to get him unstuck, so I was surprised when he held out his hand for the pen.

He drew slowly at first, gripping the pen tightly. His nails were bitten back to the pink. As he drew, floops and loops and curlicues began to decorate the two crossed lines. The pen picked up speed.

When I leaned over to watch, my hair brushed his arm. He pulled away. "Sorry." I held my hair back with one hand. The pen point raced on. "That's fantastic, Eb."

The pen hovered, then dropped on the opposite page. Eb drew a wavy line.

"What's that going to be?"

The darting pen made sharp points.

"What are those? Teeth? Claws?"

Eyes came next, then a long spiny tail.

"It's a sea serpent!"

THIS WAY BE MONSTERS, he wrote. He handed me the pen and shifted the notebook back to my lap.

"This is great, Eb! You can really draw."

He squeezed his hands between his knees. "I saw that sea serpent thing on an old map in my Social Studies book."

"You are an artist, Eb. From now on, you're doing the pictures."

His neck and ears got red.

"Come on," I said. "This way. We need to find the railroad tracks."

"How come?"

"We're locating the major features of the area."

"But why?"

"I already told you, for the map." I walked quickly, headed in the general direction that the whistle had come from, northeast by the compass rose.

"Why do we need a map?" he kept asking. But every time we came to a new street, he squatted, opened the notebook on the ground, and added the street to the drawing. I could tell right away that his map wasn't going to be accurate. The roads were however long Eb felt like making them, but if making the map kept Eb walking, that was good enough for now. I would tell him later about counting his steps and converting to the scale of the map.

We read the next sign—Roberts Avenue. Roberts was a busy street with a bus stop on the other side. Maybe it was one of the boundaries of the neighborhood Miss Dupree had told us not to leave, but she hadn't spelled it out. And what was the difference between one side of the street and the other? In some parts of the world twelve year olds get married—a totally gross idea. I'm only saying that a person old enough to get married—in some parts of the world—will do okay crossing a street.

But Eb didn't want to cross. "We've walked enough. It's too hot out here," he complained. "We're not going to find the tracks. And even if we do, big deal."

I didn't see any cars coming, so I hurried across the street. Eb followed.

A black woman holding a little girl by the hand was waiting at the bus sign. "Excuse me," I said. "Is there a railroad track near here?"

She turned and pointed. "Through the woods."

"You see, Eb? We're getting close."

"You kids be careful now," the woman called after us. "Watch out for snakes."

"Snakes?" Eb stopped, but I grabbed his arm. I couldn't see a path, but people had definitely been in the woods because, at least near the edge, there was a lot of trash. I guess the woman who had told us about the karst didn't get down this way to pick things up. As we walked deeper in, the paper trash died out, but we passed some tires and a wrecked tricycle.

We were out of sight of the road when we came on a green velvet armchair. It was just sitting out there among the trees, and next to it was a chest of drawers with a Styrofoam cup on top. "There's coffee in it," said Eb, peering into the cup. He slid a drawer open. "Jeez, look at this!" The drawer was full of clothes. On top of one neatly folded pile was a gray T-shirt that said Mitchell's Concrete on it in maroon letters. Nestled among the clothes was a knife, a jar of peanut butter, and a loaf of bread in a plastic bag.

Eb picked up the cup of coffee and his eyes got wide. "It's still warm," he whispered. Holding the cup, he turned in a circle, staring off into the trees. "You think someone's...watching?"

Just then, we heard a scuffling in the leaves, as if someone were coming toward us, feet dragging. The hair on my arms stood up. *Shush...shush.* No one was there. *Shush...* The cup slipped out of Eb's hand and fell in the drawer, spilling coffee all over the clean clothes. *Shush...shush.* The noise was louder now, closer. Eb opened his mouth but nothing came out. He clutched my notebook to his chest and took off.

But I stayed. There had to be a logical explanation. *SHUSH... SHUSH.* "Hey!" I yelled. "Wait for me!"

I followed the flash of Eb's skinny white legs as he ran between the trees. Branches whipped my face and arms. We never slowed until we were back in the safe sunlight of the street.

"You two see a snake?" the woman called as her bus pulled up. "Told y'all to be careful." She lifted the little girl up the bus steps.

Eb fell in the grass next to the bus stop. His short hair spiked up in front. "Man, that was scary," he wheezed. He fished the inhaler out of his pocket and breathed in a puff of medicine. "It sounded like a zombie was coming after us," he squeaked, letting his breath out slowly.

The bus pulled away with a loud *swoosh.* Eb had just opened the notebook, when he glanced up. "Hey. Bet it was an armadillo. They scuff in the leaves like that. Lisa and me had them around the trailer all the time." He blinked hard. I acted like I didn't notice.

We stared into the woods while we caught our breath. We could see the junked tires and the tricycle with its wheel up in the air. The woods were trashy, not scary.

"The coffee wasn't all *that* hot," Eb said.

"Might've been a while since someone was actually there."

Eb had a twig jammed into a sneaker lace. He didn't bother to pull it out. "I wasn't super-scared," he said, standing up.

"Me either." We walked along the edge of the road skirting the woods. Now that we were out of it, the woods looked ordinary, just a bunch of trees. "We could cut through again at a different spot," I said.

"Okay with me," he said.

So we went back in.

We hadn't gone far when we saw the polished silver rails between the trees and smelled the pitchy tar of the ties. I ran ahead and hopped up onto one rail. The worn-down soles on my sandals were slick, so I had to step carefully. Eb caught up and stepped up onto the other rail. We held our arms out for balance and walked the rails for a while. Heat from the gravel bed rose up our legs.

"Wonder where these tracks go," Eb said.

"We could follow them and find out."

"Yeah, right." Eb carefully put one foot in front of the other.

"My grandmother told me that there used to be men who lived along the railroad tracks. The hobos would sneak onto the freight trains when they wanted to go somewhere. They'd make camps by the tracks called hobo jungles."

"Bet that coffee belonged to a hobo." Eb ran a couple of steps on the rail.

"I don't think there are hobos anymore. The trains got too fast for them to jump on and off." My grandmother had told me that when I said I'd like to ride the trains like a hobo.

"*Somebody* was drinking that coffee." Eb slipped off, then stepped back up. "Wish I hadn't spilled it in his drawer. It must be hard to wash your clothes if you live in the woods." He squatted on the rail. "Hey look, there's plenty of rocks here."

"It's still just gravel. I'm going to wait 'til we find some of that karst, whatever it is."

Eb squinted, then shaded his eyes. "Is that a train?"

Way down the track, a pinprick of light shimmered. We heard a warning *clang-clang-clang* from the nearest crossing.

"Let's see who stays the longest," Eb said. "First one to jump is a chicken."

As the light grew, I could feel the *ca-thunk* of the cars through the soles of my shoes. "Come on, Eb." It seemed as if Eb was scared of things that couldn't hurt him, like boxes in the dark corners of the attic, or sneaking over to the Race-A-Rama, but fearless about things that could. He stood there grinning at the oncoming train.

I grabbed his arm. By the time I dragged him off the track the train was close. Even though we were back from the track, the engineer blasted our eardrums with the whistle and shook his fist as the engine passed. The hot wind flipped the brim of my hat back and lifted the hair off my neck. The legs of Eb's shorts flapped.

Behind the engine were flatcars loaded with logs, then swaying boxcars with flashes of sky in between. *Someday,* I thought, *instead of being taken or sent, I'll choose the place I want to go. I'll ride the train like the woman in my grandmother's stories, the one in the red hat.*

When I looked over, Eb had his arms out, his head thrown back. He was yelling. His words were swallowed by the pounding of the train, but when he quit yelling, he smiled.

～

Two tall, skinny girls, one white, one black, were running along the side of our street when we got back. The woman who collected trash was there too, picking things up with her tongs.

"Hi, Miss Johnette," said the white girl, stopping, but still running in place.

"Hey, Miss Johnette," said the black girl, doing the same. "You out here pickin' up trash again? Nobody's paying you, right?"

"I'm just trying to keep the planet clean, Jemmie."

The girl rolled her eyes. "Looks like you've got your work cut out for you."

Miss Johnette grinned. "Luckily, earth is one of the smaller planets." She set her sack down to look at a plant growing right up against the cement.

"That's just a weed," the white girl said.

"A weed's a plant nobody likes, and I like this plant." Miss Johnette ran a finger over the lacy leaves. "It's a partridge pea. It has pretty flowers in the late summer."

"Flowers?" The girl tucked a strand of hair behind her ear, then bent down for a closer look. "What color flowers?"

"Yellow."

"Bet someone mows it down before it gets any kind of flower," the black girl said, and then she took off running. "See ya, Miss Johnette. See ya, Cass," she called.

"Would you wait up?" the white girl yelled. "Bye, Miss Johnette. Bye, you two."

I didn't think she'd noticed us, but she gave Eb and me a wave.

She had just caught up with her friend, Jemmie, when the three boys we'd seen the day before came pedaling up the street.

The cute boy said, "Give me a ride, slaves."

He coasted between the two girls and put a hand on each of their shoulders. The girls squealed, "Ben!" but kept on running.

"Ah, this is the life." He took his feet off the pedals and leaned back. "Can't you two go no faster?"

"Get your lazy butt off of that bike and run, Ben Floyd, an' we'll show you faster," Jemmie said.

As the girls towed Ben, the two other boys circled around and around them. "Hey, Justin," the redheaded boy called to the heavy-set kid. "What's with the tape on your sneakers? You trying to be cool?"

"I'm naturally cool, Clay," said Justin. The silver tape on his sneakers flashed as he pedaled.

"Then why the tape?"

"My shoes were falling apart." Justin swerved around the corner, and the others followed.

I listened to their fading voices, wishing I was going with them.

"I'm hungry," Eb whined. "I want to go in."

We turned toward Miss Dupree's house. That's when he noticed a second car in the driveway. "Lisa!" he shouted. He ran a couple of steps, then stopped.

"Is that your mom's car?"

"No. Just looks like it." He kicked the curb hard.

"Ouch!" said Miss Johnette. "I'll bet that hurt."

Eb kicked the curb harder, then sat down beside her and buried his head in his arms.

"Eb?" I sat next to him, being careful not to touch. "Come on, Eb, don't cry."

"I'm not crying." He kept his head down.

I watched his shoulders shake. There was nothing I could do.

The woman watched too. I guess she didn't know what to do either. "We keep running into each other, so we may as well introduce ourselves. I'm Johnette Walker," she said. "Miss Johnette."

"I'm Anna Casey."

She ducked to take a look at me under the brim of my hat. "Pleased to meet you, Anna Casey." We reached over Eb's back and shook hands.

She let go of my hand and ran her fingers along the knobs of Eb's spine. "And who's this?"

"Eb Gramlich," Eb said into his lap. He sat back up, shrugging away from her hand. He rubbed his nose on the back of his wrist, then wiped his wrist on his shirt. "Miss Dupree says you're nuts."

When she threw her head back and laughed, I could see all her teeth, even the ones at the very back. Miss Johnette laughed from her belly, like a man. She slapped her knees, then gave Eb a friendly whack on the shoulder.

"Hey, don't touch the merchandise," he said.

She didn't seem to care about the invisible wall Eb had around him. "It's nice to meet you both." She stood up. "I live in the first white house around the corner, the one with the stone wall. I'll be home all afternoon if you want to stop by and see my bone collection." She slung her sack over her shoulder and walked away whistling.

"Bone collection?" Eb called out to her. "What do you mean, bone collection?"

~

The man seated on the couch with Miss Dupree was showing her his necktie. "Yes," she said, touching it with one finger. "Excellent choice. A dark tie with a narrow stripe has such a look of power." While the man admired his own tie, she made a little fluttery motion toward the kitchen with one hand. She wanted us to go away.

Eb ignored the hint. "I'm starving."

"And I'm with a client, Eb. You two get yourselves a snack, okay?"

I shoved him through the kitchen door.

"All I did was ask for food," he whined loudly.

I grabbed his arms, stood him in front of the refrigerator, and opened it. "Pick something."

He stuck his head inside and looked around. "Nothing to eat." He closed the door and fell into a chair.

"Excuse me?" I opened the refrigerator again. "There's yogurt and tofu and English muffins. There's cut-up fruit and cottage cheese."

"Like I said. Nothing to eat." He put his feet up on a second chair.

I yanked the chair out from under his dirty sneakers, then checked the cupboards. "How about popcorn?"

"Yeah, I guess."

I heated some oil in a pan and added popcorn. When the first kernel popped, I put on the lid.

The popcorn had just finished popping when Miss Dupree came into the kitchen. "That smells so good," she said.

When I dumped the popcorn into a bowl, just two unpopped kernels lay in the bottom of the pan. "Hey, look. Only two old maids."

"Anna!" said Miss Dupree. "That is not a nice expression."

It took me a second to figure out *what* wasn't a nice expression. "Oh, I'm sorry. My grandmother used to call them that." I watched

29

her eat, one piece of popcorn at a time. She didn't look old, but she acted kind of old, and she was definitely single.

"That fat man with the ugly tie?" Eb said, his mouth full of popcorn. "Who'd want to date him?"

"Oh, I'm sure there's someone out there for him," she answered. "There's a Mr. or Ms. Right for everyone. Sometimes it just takes a little work to find them." When she took off her glasses and wiped the lenses, her eyes looked dreamy. Without the glasses her eyes were bigger and prettier.

"So, where's *your* Mr. Right?" Eb asked.

"What?" She looked up, startled.

"I mean, with all these Mr. Rights coming and going all the time, why don't you pick one out for yourself? You do get first crack at them."

She put her glasses back on. Her eyes became small and rabbitty again. "That would not be professional," she murmured. She looked as if she'd been slapped.

Chapter Four

IN THE BONE MUSEUM

W e finished our popcorn fast. I snatched my hat off the rack, and then we were back outside. "Eb, why'd you have to ask her about Mr. Right? That was mean."

He shoved his hands in his pockets. "Who mentioned old maids?"

"I wasn't trying to hurt her feelings. You were. She's going to kick us out for sure."

"Like I care. If I get kicked out, Lisa'll have to come get me."

"She will? So far she hasn't even called."

"For your information, she can't. Eddie's phone's disconnected. But you'll see, she'll come soon."

"Well, that takes care of you, but I don't have a mother to come get me. Would you at least *try* to be nice?" With nothing else to do, we headed over to Miss Johnette's to see the bones.

"Bet this is the house," Eb said. The stone wall Miss Johnette had mentioned looked as if it was there to hold the garden in. Flowers stood head high. The air buzzed with bees. Butterflies flitted from flower to flower. It looked as if anything that could crawl or hop or fly had made its way to Miss Johnette's. At the far end of the garden path were steps and a purple front door. Limbs of a huge oak tree in the backyard arched over the roof. I started up the path, but Eb grabbed my arm and jerked me back.

"Spider!"

Stretched across the path between the stems of two sunflowers was an enormous spiderweb with a huge spider straddling the middle.

"Come on, Eb. We can go under it."

Eb held back. "No way." Holding back was his specialty. "I don't want some spider sinking its fangs into my neck."

I got as far as the web and stopped. The spider was really big, but kind of pretty too, all speckled with silver, with interesting tufts of black hair on its knees. "Hello?" I called out.

"Anna?" Miss Johnette's voice came from inside the house. "Don't be shy. Come on in."

"But there's this spider…"

When Miss Johnette opened the door she had a rock in one hand, a magnifying glass in the other. "That's my guard-spider, Charlotte. She keeps away door-to-door salesmen. Just duck under."

So I ducked.

"How about you, Eb?" she asked. "You coming?"

"Nuh-uh. I don't want some spider sucking on my neck."

She laughed. "If you were a fly you'd have to worry about getting sucked on. But you're way too big to be Charlotte's meal."

He inched toward us. "You could knock that web down easy, with a stick."

"Just duck, okay?"

Eb got down on his knees and crawled under.

"It's a miracle," Miss Johnette said as he stood back up. "Eb made it through alive. Let me check your neck." She peered at him through her magnifying glass.

"Very funny," he said.

She held the door for us. "Now, don't mind the mess."

Mess? I thought as I stepped inside. *What mess?* "Look!" I squeezed Eb's arm. "Look, specimens! Specimens everywhere!" There were rocks on windowsills and nests on shelves; there were seashells and fossils and bones—lots of bones. "This isn't a mess. This is a museum!" I said. "It's perfect."

"Why, thank you, Anna." She gave me a huge smile. "Folks use all kinds of words to describe my house. Perfect isn't usually one of them."

"There's no air-conditioning," Eb said.

I ran my finger over a piece of rock that had fossilized fish skeletons in it, then pulled back. You weren't supposed to touch in a museum.

"Go ahead," Miss Johnette said. "Pick it up."

"Everybody has air-conditioning," Eb persisted.

Miss Johnette greeted the news with her usual big laugh. "Not everybody, Eb."

"Aborigines don't," I said, looking around for the *National Geographic*s. She had to have some.

"Well, Americans do," Eb shot back. "Don't you sweat?"

"Sure." Miss Johnette fell into a stuffed chair upholstered in a zebra-striped print and threw one leg over the arm.

"So is sweating, like, a hobby of yours?" he asked.

She laughed again. "No. But I like to breathe real air. I like to hear the birds. We have barred owls in the neighborhood. I have a hunch they roost in that big tree behind your house. In the night they call out, 'Who cooks for you? Who cooks for you all?' I wouldn't want to miss that."

"So, where are the bones?" Eb asked.

Miss Johnette and I looked at each other. She spread her arms. "Open your eyes, boy-child." There were bones everywhere. Any place Aunt Eva would have put an ashtray or a knickknack, Miss Johnette had put a skull.

"Oh," he sniffed, looking around at the bone-cluttered shelves. "I thought you meant skeletons. You know, like Halloween."

"Oh, *human* skeletons. Coming right up." Miss Johnette climbed out of the chair and opened a closet. A skeleton—a human skeleton—swung out, arms flailing. "Eb, meet Edgar." Edgar's bony heels rattled against the wooden door.

"Whoa!" Eb jumped back. "This is totally creepy. How'd ya get him? Rob a grave?"

She knuckle-rubbed the top of his head. "You have a great imagination in there, Eb. Sorry to let you down, but Edgar's a mail-order skeleton from Edmund Scientific."

He slid half a step closer. "So, *they* dug him up."

"No, they made him."

"Made him?" Eb rapped on one of Edgar's kneecaps with his knuckle. "Plastic." He gave the door a shove that set the bony man dancing. "What's so spooky about plastic?" He acted like Edgar was some worthless prize out of a gumball machine.

"All the other bones are real." Miss Johnette pointed out a large skull. "Who do you think this one belonged to?" The skull was as broad as an adult's hand with the fingers spread. You could have fit a lemon through each of the eye sockets.

Eb touched the beaky point at the front of the skull and shrugged. "A giant bird?"

"Good guess, but it belonged to a sea turtle."

"Is it heavy?" I asked.

"You tell me."

"Oh my gosh!" When I lifted it, the lower jaw still sat on the table.

"Put your eyes back in your head, Anna Casey. You didn't break it. The muscles and tendons that hold bones together don't last." She pointed to a skull on a shelf. "What about that one?" Except for the beak it was no larger than her thumbnail.

"*That* one's a bird," Eb said.

"Give the kid a prize!" She clapped, as if he had just said something extra smart. "It is a bird, a pine warbler."

"What did it die of?" I asked.

She lowered her voice. "A sudden, fatal blow to the head."

"You mean you whacked it?" Eb whispered.

"It sort of whacked itself. It was migrating through Tallahassee, minding its own business, when it flew into the Department of Environmental Protection building. Ironic, huh?"

"Must be a pretty dumb bird if it flew into a building," Eb said.

"Not dumb, just confused. The DEP's windows are like mirrors. Birds fly into them because all they see is sky."

"Why don't you have a whole shelf full of pine warbler skulls then?" Eb asked.

"She doesn't need a hundred to know what they look like," I said.

"Do you have a job?" Eb asked, ignoring me.

"Believe it or not, I do. I introduce unsuspecting high school kids to spiders." She walked her fingertips up his arm, imitating a spider. "I'm a biology teacher."

"Is that why you have all these dead things?" Eb poked at a beetle to see if it would move.

"You've got it backwards." She took a larger beetle off a high shelf and set it down in front of Eb. "I teach biology because I love all these dead things. I've been collecting since I was five years old."

"Some hobby, collecting dead things." Eb arranged the two lifeless beetles head to head, like they were fighting.

"When I was a kid I collected live things too. I had dozens of aquariums."

"Do you have any now?" I asked. I was sort of hoping for an alligator in the bathtub or a closetful of Mexican fruit bats.

"I don't collect them much any more. Live things do better if you leave them where you find them. I do have one nice live thing in the kitchen, though." Eb and I followed her.

But the live thing wasn't a wombat or a Tasmanian devil. On a blanket by the stove lay a big yellow dog. His face and paws were frosty white. He didn't get up when he saw us, but his tail whacked the floor, *thump, thump.*

"Hey, Gregor." Miss Johnette squatted to scratch his ear. "This is Eb and Anna." The dog looked up at us with milky eyes. "Kids, this is Gregor Mendel."

I knelt down to pat him. "I never met a dog with a last name before."

"He's named after a famous botanist. Gregor Mendel was one of the first men to think that every living thing must have a code book built into it to make it the way it is."

"Genes?"

"You hear that, Greg? Anna Casey knows about genes. I swear, these are two smart kids." Gregor's eyelids drooped as she patted him. "Greg used to go with me on all my field trips. Now he's half blind and he has arthritis in his hips. You're a retired biologist now, aren't you, Greg?"

"If you ever want help on a field trip, I'll go," I said.

"It's pretty sweaty work."

"I don't mind."

"Anna likes to sweat," Eb said, kneeling down beside the dog. Gregor put his head in Eb's lap. "Jeez, he stinks." But Eb stroked the old dog gently.

"I'm famished. How about you two?" She stood and opened a cupboard. "Oreos?"

"Food!" Eb shouted. "Just pass the package."

Miss Johnette tore open the bag. "Help yourselves."

"Double Stuf," said Eb approvingly. He took six cookies.

"Healthy appetite," Miss Johnette said. She took a handful herself. "So, Anna, you want to come collecting with me sometime?"

"I'd love to. I have a rock collection."

"Eight rocks." Eb twisted the top off an Oreo. "Some collection." He snuck the top to Gregor, then scraped the icing off the bottom cookie with his teeth.

"I'd like to get a piece of that karst you were talking about," I told her.

"Sure. I know just the place," she said, taking the top off her cookie too. "The Econfina River. We'll go canoeing there sometime, okay? What do you say, Eb? You want to come along?"

"Thanks, but no thanks."

Eb had eaten a whole stack of Oreos when he announced, "Time to get back to air-conditioned comfort. Let's go, Anna."

Walking home, I was already wondering how soon we could go back to the bone museum. When we got to Miss Dupree's, Eb sat right down at the kitchen table and began to draw Gregor Mendel in my explorer's notebook.

"Miss Johnette is the coolest adult I've ever met," I said.

"She's weird," he said. "I mean, she's nice and all, but she is seriously weird."

"She is not."

"Is too." He shaded Gregor's fur. "Good snacks, though. We should go back sometime."

~

It was late afternoon when Mrs. Riley stopped in. "I just wanted to see how the three of you were getting along," she said. She talked to each of us separately: first Eb, then me, then Miss Dupree. Her conversation with Eb lasted about a minute and a half. And from what I could hear in the living room, she did all the talking. When it was my turn I sat down with her at the kitchen table. Before she even asked I said, "Everything's great. I like Miss Dupree. I like my room. The food is great. Eb is great. And the neighborhood—"

"Anna." Mrs. Riley put a hand on my arm. "Anna, you don't have to like everything. You're in a new place. You must miss being with people you know."

I felt my eyes prickle. "I kind of miss my cousins. But I like it here. I like it a lot." I told her about Miss Johnette.

"I know her," said Mrs. Riley. "My granddaughter had her for biology. Johnette Walker is a very good teacher."

I would have to remind Eb. Miss Johnette wasn't *weird*—she was a teacher.

When it was Miss Dupree's turn, Eb and I sat on the white couch. "Should you be looking at that?" I whispered. Eb was flipping through the pink Likely Prospects book. But in a second I forgot all about supervising Eb. Behind the closed kitchen door, Miss Dupree had just said, "Anna." *What about Anna?* Unfortunately, Miss Dupree was hard to hear even when you were in the same room with her.

Eb poked me in the thigh with the corner of the album, pointed out a photo of a woman, then barked like a dog.

"Eb, I'm trying to hear!"

"But you've got to look. This one's a real oinker."

Luckily Mrs. Riley had a clear, no-nonsense voice that cut across Eb's comments. "We feel fairly sure that this will be a short-term placement," she said.

For who, Eb or me?

"We prefer kinship care whenever possible," she continued.

What the heck is kinship care?

"There is an aunt who would be appropriate."

Oh, that kind of kin. She couldn't mean me. I was out of kin. "Hey, Eb," I whispered. "Do you have an aunt you could live with?"

"No!" He threw his arms out as if he'd been shot. "I'm *not* going to live with Aunt Terry. I'd rather eat dirt and die."

"I'll be in touch," said Mrs. Riley, as the women came out of the kitchen. "Bye, kids." She waved at us and let herself out.

Miss Dupree paused in front of the couch. "Eb, what are you doing?"

"Nothing." He slid the Likely Prospects album back onto the coffee table.

"Those books are there for clients only. The information in them is confidential. I thought I told you that."

"'Likely Prospects,'" Eb grumbled as she went back into the kitchen. "'Likely Rejects' if you ask me. Half the women weigh about nine thousand pounds."

~

Miss Dupree served baked chicken and peas for supper. The chicken was dry. The peas were wrinkly. Since Eb just picked at his food, I had to stuff myself again. If this kept up, I would look like one of Eb's likely rejects in no time.

When I went up to bed, I turned off the noisy air conditioner first thing. Then I forced open the window by the tree, which wasn't easy. I bet it hadn't been open for eons. At first I only stuck my head out. That was all I meant to do, really. The ground was a long, long way down, but there, right in front of me, was that branch Miss Dupree wanted to cut, the one that came too close to the house. I reached out and grabbed it with one hand, just to see if I could. Suspended between the tree and the house, I didn't have a choice. Pushing off the sill with both feet, I launched myself toward the tree. The fingers of my other hand barely grazed the bark. I twisted hard and made another grab.

I hung by both hands, swinging. My heart galloped. A breeze fluttered my nightgown. The nightgown was my cousin's, so it was too long. All that cloth got in the way when I kicked my legs up, but I managed to wrap myself around the limb. Slowly, I pulled myself up so I sat on top of the branch. In a minute my heart got quiet. Sitting in the tree I felt safe like a little kid feels safe sitting in someone's lap. The leaves at the top whispered that I should climb higher. I didn't, because of Miss Dupree. All I did was look up, hoping to see an owl in the branches above me. Only the moon looked down. I scooted over closer to the window and crawled back inside, but I left the window open so I would hear the owls if they came.

~

I woke up and couldn't think where I was. My heart banged in my chest like it was running around, looking. Then I remembered—I was alone in the attic at Miss Dupree's. A thread of light showed under the edge of the door. Downstairs someone was up. I climbed down the narrow steps, holding up my nightie so I wouldn't trip. I tiptoed across the living room and peeked through the open kitchen door.

Only the small light above the stove was lit. In the shadowy kitchen Miss Dupree was perched with her feet up on the chair. She had pulled her nightshirt down over her knees to make a sort of tent. Just her bare toes showed. A glass of milk sat on the table in front of her. Staring at the dark kitchen window, she hummed a sad-sounding melody.

"Miss Dupree?" I called softly.

She jumped, then peered through the dark doorway. "Anna. Are you awake too? Come sit with me. Get yourself some milk."

I poured myself a glass and sat down across from her.

"Having a hard time sleeping?" she asked.

I shrugged. "You?"

She shrugged back, and for a while we just drank our milk.

"Miss Dupree, can I ask you something?"

"Of course."

"What made you want to be a foster mother?"

I would never have asked that question in the day. By day she seemed anxious, always a little worried. And if I had asked, I bet her daytime answer would have been one she had worked out ahead. But in the quiet kitchen, with the refrigerator purring and the lights low, she seemed to be thinking it over.

"Why did I want to be a foster mother?" She folded her arms on her bent knees and rested her cheek against them for a moment, thinking. "Mrs. Riley suggested it. Her daughter Janie and I were best friends in high school. I hadn't seen either of them for a long time, then one day I ran into Mrs. Riley at the grocery store. The first thing she asked was how many kids I had. Janie and I had always talked about how we wanted to have great big families." She smiled like she was remembering the children she used to make up. "When I told her I didn't have any, she said that there were lots of kids who needed good homes and just a little help until they found their own place in the world. Then she showed me the pictures of Janie's three girls. I thought it over for a long time and decided I'd give it a try."

I felt like I was standing at the dangerous edge of something. "How do you like it so far?"

"I like it. I like to hear your voices in the house."

It was a small beginning, liking the noise we made. It was small, but it was something.

"I'm worried about Eb, though. He always seems so angry."

"Angry?" I asked. "Wait, don't move a muscle. I'll be right back." Nightgown held high, I sprinted up the stairs two at a time. I was back in a flash with my explorer's notebook. "Here, look at these drawings. Eb did them."

She smiled at the grinning sea serpent and the portrait of Gregor by the stove.

"Eb isn't always angry," I said. "He's just a little knotted up."

"We'll have to unknot him then, won't we? What do you say, Anna, shall we give it a try?"

"Sure. Here's to unknotting Eb!" I said, and we clicked our glasses together. After we finished our milk we rinsed and dried the glasses and put them away. Walking me to the foot of the stairs, Miss Dupree rested her hand on my shoulder. I pretended like I didn't notice. That's the best thing to do with shy people.

"Sweet dreams," she called after me.

I climbed the steps thinking, *sweet dreams*. Grandma said it, and now Miss Dupree said it. It had to mean something.

Chapter Five

BOOTS JUST LIKE THAT

The next day was Saturday. Miss Dupree slept in. Since it was summer, it was like any other day to Eb and me. We ate cold cereal. I made him help me clean up.

"Again?" he said.

When the dishes were done I told him we were going outside.

"Why?" he asked. "Why can't we watch cartoons for a change?"

I left a note for Miss Dupree. "Let's go."

Actually, Eb seemed to be getting used to the outside. He liked drawing in my notebook. In a strange way he even seemed to like the bugs and the heat. They gave him a chance to complain. But he had only opened the door a crack when he closed it again. "Kid alert."

"Let me look." I opened it and peeked out. Eb was right. The street was full of kids—the boys who had been riding bicycles the first day and the two girl runners. If we went out right now, maybe we would meet them. I dragged Eb out the door, but no one even looked at us.

"Heads up!" Ben yelled, tossing a basketball. The tape on Justin's sneakers flashed as he jumped for it, but Jemmie snagged the ball instead.

"I swear," she said, bouncing it from one hand to the other, "you boys are so slack. We're gonna whip your butts. Right, Cass?" She popped the ball over to her friend.

Cass caught it on her fingertips and the girls sprinted out ahead, passing the ball back and forth between them as they ran. When Ben managed to catch up, he grabbed the back of Cass's shirt and hung on.

"Hey, play fair," Jemmie yelled.

Ben let go and stood in the middle of the street. "We'll show you two when we get to the ball court," he said.

"You just do that," Cass said, passing to Jemmie.

Jemmie dribbled the ball ahead of her as she ran. "Try to get there before church tomorrow, okay? Come on, Cass."

The boys ran a short distance, then gave up. "Hey, guys!" yelled the redhead. "Let's go get the bikes."

We could hear them for a while after they disappeared around the corner. Then it was just the two of us, the invisible kids.

"What now?" Eb asked.

"There's plenty we haven't seen yet, places to put on the map." I was thinking of one place in particular. I just started walking. Eb followed, but when we got to the spot where the boys had cut through the trees the other day, he stopped dead.

"Oh, no. I'm not going in there. You heard those guys."

"They're gone, Eb. Those two girls are whipping their butts right now."

He walked in a little way, trying to see what was beyond the trees. "Maybe there are other guys working on the Race-A-Rama. You don't know everything, Anna."

"I'll go without you. Give me the notebook."

Eb hid it behind his back. "But you can't draw as good as I can."

"I guess you'll have to come along, then." I walked away.

"I don't know about this." Eb followed slowly.

The skinny path through the trees, made by bike tires and boys' feet, opened out in a broad, mowed area beneath power lines, with tall, shaggy grass, a wire fence, and a road beyond that.

All we saw at first was the grass and blackberry brambles, and birds on the wires. Then Eb pointed. "Over there. What're those?"

As we got closer, we could see that the low sand hills weren't natural.

"Speed ramps," I said. "For jumping bikes. They've got a whole racecourse out here."

The Race-A-Rama went on forever. I ran up a ramp and stopped at the edge of a hole. Miss Johnette had said the karst was buried. I looked for it at the bottom of the hole, but all I saw was sand. "Eb, this pit must be three feet deep. It looks like it was dug with a steam shovel."

"Big deal," Eb said. "A hole." He looked over his shoulder toward the trees, as if marauders on bikes would descend on us at any moment. "Can we go now?"

"Aren't you even impressed, Eb?" The course the boys had built was scarred with tire tracks and skid marks. "It's amazing!" I said. "Colossal! It's like the pyramids."

"Yeah, it's great. Let's go, okay?" He glanced toward the trees again.

I ran to the edge of another pit. "Hey, Eb!" I dropped to my knees. My hat tumbled into the hole. When it landed it looked small and far away. "Eb, you've got to see this."

"Let me guess. Another hole?"

"Not just another hole." I hung my legs over the side and jumped into the pit to retrieve my hat. "Wow." Arms stretched, I couldn't touch either wall. My head would have been even with the ground except that the sand that had been dug out formed two enormous mounds on either side of the hole. After standing in the sun it felt cool and damp in the pit. Even the air smelled different. I lay down on the bottom and looked up at the sky. I imagined a bike flying over.

Instead I saw Eb's face and the toes of his sneakers. "Can we go now?" Grains of sand dribbled down the steep side.

"Oh, okay." I stood back up and brushed off the sand. "Can you give me a hand?" As he dragged me out of the pit, more sand spilled down the side.

"You know they'll kill us if they catch us," he said. Then he noticed our shoe prints in the sand. "We're dead meat," he breathed. "They'll see our prints and come after us."

He insisted on kicking sand over our tracks.

"We're just gonna make new ones walking out," I said.

"Not if we take our shoes off."

Each of us had one shoe off when Eb grabbed my arm.

"What now?" I asked.

"Over there. Look over there!"

A man stood at the edge of the field. "Static!" He threw back his head and shouted at the sky. "All I hear is static!" He was tall and skinny. Long hair poked out from under his baseball cap, and a tangled silver beard hung down over his chest. "Static and Chinese! Beam me something in English, why don't you?" He shook a fist at the clouds. "And nighttimes, I'd like a little rest, if it's all the same to you."

"Who's he talking to?" I whispered.

"Forget that, look at the shirt."

It was just a gray T-shirt, with maroon letters on the front, half-covered by beard. "Mitchell's Concrete," I read, piecing it together. "Eb, it's the shirt from the chest of drawers!"

He slapped a hand over my mouth. "Would you shut up!"

A bird flew by the man, then skimmed over our heads. It was odd the way he swung his whole body to keep his eyes on the bird. His clenched fist was still raised when he saw us. He stopped and stared without moving, eyes fixed on Eb and me. The breeze pushed his baggy pants back against his toothpick legs. Slowly, he opened his fist and took a lurching step toward us.

I snatched up my sandal. "Run!" I yelled, and we took off. The sneaker Eb held by the lace smacked his leg as he ran. My hat blew off. I swooped back, grabbed it, and kept on running. We didn't stop until we reached the street.

"What about our shoe prints?" I asked.

"You go back. I'm not going," he panted. "Not while *he's* there." Eb put on his other sneaker.

"Where do you think he came from?" I asked. "It was like he just appeared."

Eb stood and raised his hand high. "I come in peace. Take me to your leader." He jammed his hands into the pockets of his shorts, and we started back toward Miss Dupree's. "At least he got his shirt clean. I didn't see any coffee on it."

"But who do you think he is, Eb? And how come he lives in the woods? I mean, he must have family somewhere."

"Maybe not. You don't."

~

After lunch I had a hard time getting Eb back outside. His preference was definitely sofa and TV. Luckily Miss Dupree had a client coming, so she needed the living room. "If you stay inside, you'll have to play in Eb's room," she told us. "Quietly, okay?"

"You don't want to spend the afternoon in the pink room, do you, Eb?" I whispered. "Let's go. We'll find something to do."

He stalled out on the front step. "No way. It's like a million degrees out here."

Just then, Miss Johnette came around the corner, whistling. "Hey there, Eb. Hi, Anna."

"Where's your garbage sack?" Eb asked.

"Left it at home. I'm walking over to Goodwill. You two want to come?"

"Sure," I said. Eb hesitated, then we both fell in step with her.

"Why are we going to Goodwill?" Eb asked as we tramped toward Roberts Avenue.

"I need some jeans."

"Jeans? Let's go to the mall." Eb's eyes lit up, like there was a chance we'd hop in Miss Johnette's car and spend the afternoon in air-conditioned luxury.

"Why? There are plenty of jeans to choose from at Goodwill. They only cost four bucks apiece, and they've already had the stiff washed out of them."

"But they're used," Eb said, trotting to keep up. "Somebody's already had their privates in them."

"Doesn't matter to me as long as their privates are out of there when I put them on." She rubbed his bristly head. "Anything you use over is one less thing to make, Eb."

"Big deal," Eb said, "one pair of pants."

"Big deal," she said, imitating him. "There's just so much stuff to go around, Eb. Only so much water, minerals, air. Animals and plants need these things too. It's a crowded planet, Eb. The less we use, the better."

We passed a place called the USA store. "Super-size drinks. Icy cold," Eb said, reading a sign on the window. "One of those would sure hit the spot. Hint, hint." When Miss Johnette kept on walking, he ran to catch up. "Hey, we could share!"

There wasn't a speck of shade as we turned onto Mabry and crossed the track. Heat licked our legs. Eb had sweated through his T-shirt. "This is crazy," he mumbled.

Miss Johnette gave him a playful shove. "Come on wimp-boy. Goodwill's air-conditioned."

As Eb staggered through the door of the Goodwill, he croaked, "Eb Gramlich, lost in the desert for three days, crawls into the oasis."

Eb's oasis was packed with clothes, old dishes, plastic flowers, shoes with scuffed toes, and bicycles with ratty streamers on their handle grips.

Miss Johnette went straight to the men's section to look at jeans. Eb found a bin of comics and a recliner. "You two take your time," he said as he settled into the chair. "I'll just sit here 'til it gets cool out."

I slid hangers along a rack, looking through a row of fancy dresses. "Try on anything you want," Miss Johnette called. She held a pair of jeans up to her waist.

As I zipped up the first dress, I pretended that I was going to a prom. Would Ben prefer the blue satin or the pink one with sequins on the sleeves?

Miss Johnette tried on eight pairs of jeans before finding one with legs loose enough to fit over army boots. By then I had decided on the dress with sequins. But would Ben like it? I needed a male opinion.

I walked over to the recliner. "Do you like this dress, Eb?"

"It's okay," he mumbled without looking up. Miss Johnette was already in line, waiting to pay, and he was in the middle of a Spiderman comic. He wasn't going to waste a second looking at some dumb dress.

I was waving a sleeve between his eyes and the comic to make him look when a man came out of the back room. "Eb!" I dropped my voice to a whisper. "Eb, it's him!" The man in the Mitchell's Concrete shirt walked toward us, carrying a chair. As he shuffled between the racks, he rocked from one foot to the other, like Frankenstein, brushing the hanging clothes on either side. *Bang!* He dropped the chair right next to Eb's recliner.

Eb swallowed hard. The comic slipped from his fingers.

The man leaned over the recliner and stared at Eb. "What're you lookin' at?" He didn't smile. He didn't even blink.

The cash register rang. "I don't need a bag for those," Miss Johnette said. She ambled over with her new jeans hanging on her arm. "Don't you look pretty, Anna? Golly, it's been years since I owned a dress. Turn around, let me get a look at you." I turned slowly. When I faced the man again he was staring at Miss Johnette's feet.

"I had boots like that," he said softly. "Boots just like that, when I was in Nam."

"You did?" said Miss Johnette, but he didn't answer. Instead, he lurched back across the room, setting the clothes on the racks swinging again.

"Don't mind him," said the woman at the checkout. "He slips gears every now and then, but he's harmless."

I went back in the dressing room and took off the prom dress. *He doesn't look harmless,* I thought as I put my damp T-shirt back on. *There's something creepy about him.*

"You two want a popsicle?" Miss Johnette asked as we walked back home.

Eb definitely wanted one until he saw the bikes—Ben's, Clay's, and Justin's—all leaned against the front of the USA store. The basketball lay on the sidewalk. He stopped in the middle of the parking lot. "They're all in there," he hissed.

"That's okay," I told him. "We'll just get our popsicles and go."

The lure of popsicles started him walking again. I wanted a popsicle, but mostly I hoped that something would happen so we would actually meet the neighborhood kids. Maybe I would go over to the freezer and Cass would be there already and maybe she would say, "Aren't you the girl I saw the other day when I was talking to Miss Johnette?"

The bell on the door tinkled and the Indian man behind the counter looked up. "Why, Miss Johnette! How are you this lovely day?" The kids who were scattered in the aisles looked up too.

"I'm fine, Mr. G." Miss Johnette clamped a hand on the back of each of our necks and walked us to the counter. We must have looked like a couple of cats swinging by their scruffs. "This is Eb Gramlich and Anna Casey. Kids, this is Mr. G."

"A great pleasure," he said, pressing his palms together. "Have you two met the others?" He looked out over the aisles of snack foods and car care products. "Children?" He clapped his hands. "Come, come!" This wasn't the way it was supposed to go. It was supposed to just happen. It was like Mr. G. was ordering them to meet us.

For a moment, they all just stood where they were, then Cass grabbed Jemmie by the back pocket. "Come on out of there. Mr. G. wants us for something." Jemmie had as much of herself in the freezer case as she could get, short of standing on the frozen fish sticks.

"Clay? Justin?" Mr G. called. Clay and Justin stopped fighting over which flavor Combos to buy and walked over to the counter with one bag of Cheddar, one of Pizzeria. "Ben? Come, come."

They stood together, the five of them facing the two of us. Eb slid closer to me. No one said a word. "Now you must all shake hands," said Mr. G. "Who is first? Ben?"

"Hi." He ducked his head and his hair fell across his eyes. Just as he stuck out his hand I thought about the sequined dress…the prom. My face felt hot. *Oh, great,* I thought. *I'm blushing, and my hand is all sweaty.*

"Very good," exclaimed Mr. G. "And this is Clay, Justin, Jemmie, and Cass." We all had to shake hands. "And this is Anna and Eb."

"Eb?" said Clay. "How do you spell it?"

"Like it sounds," said Eb. "E-B."

"That's not a name. You need more letters."

"Why?" asked Mr. G. "You call me by one letter only."

"Your real name *is* longer," Clay said. "Only no one can pronounce it."

"And perhaps it is the same with Eb, but no matter. What matters is this," said Mr. G., holding out his hands. "Eb and Anna are children." The hand closest to us dipped, as if he were weighing us. "And you also are children." He dipped his other hand. "They are here." Dip. "And you also are here." Dip. "And now." He clasped his hands lacing his fingers together. "All of you will be friends…like this." But the other kids were already sliding back down the aisles.

"Eb and Anna live right around the corner from me," Miss Johnette called after them, "in the white house with the green shutters, the one with the lawn that looks like Astroturf. You guys should go over and see them sometime." When no one answered she said "Great!" like everyone had said they'd knock on our door the first chance they got. She pointed us toward the freezers at the back of the store. "Now, what do you two want?"

Eb and I grabbed the first two popsicles at the front of the case and slunk out. They both turned out to be papaya.

50

Chapter Six

SHOW US YOUR STUFF

W e were sitting on the curb by the mailbox—just sitting, not doing anything. My notebook was on Eb's knees. Not that he was drawing in it. He just seemed to like carrying it around with him. "What I want to know is why we're out here so early," he said.

I didn't know, even though it had been my idea. I just felt kind of low, on account of the eggs. Miss Dupree had made scrambled eggs for breakfast out of some fake stuff that came in a carton. "No cholesterol," she said. Anyone could see that Eb needed a little cholesterol.

"My uncle used to make these great omelets," I said, looking at the way the knobs on Eb's spine stuck out when he leaned forward. "He would crack the eggs two at a time, and then he'd add onions and cheese. Heart-Attack-on-Toast, he called it. They dripped with cheese and butter."

"Lisa makes killer eggs too," he said. "She fries them in bacon grease."

"Oh, Eb!" I imitated Miss Dupree. "Think of the cholesterol!" But neither of us laughed. It wasn't the greasy eggs we missed. It was the people who used to cook them for us. I didn't know whether a fake-egg eater like Miss Dupree could ever feel like family. I wanted her to—I definitely wanted her to. But it was hard. I had to be so careful around her, do everything right. I felt like I was holding my breath.

"So, we're out here to talk about omelets," Eb said.

"No, we're out here so that something can happen to us."

"Yeah, right," he flung his legs out straight. "If we sit real still some dog might pee on our legs."

"Not like that. Something good. An adventure."

"What is it with you and adventures? We might get hit with a Frisbee, or catch the morning paper, or—" Suddenly, we heard runners coming toward us. We couldn't see them yet, but whoever they were, they were moving fast, and they were about to turn the corner.

"Pick it up, girl," someone called. The slap of sneakers on pavement got faster.

It had to be Cass and Jemmie. I didn't want them to see me after the dumb introductions in the USA store, but there was no time to hide.

Jemmie, in a bright red crop-top and gold hoop earrings, streaked around the corner with Cass half a step behind. Cass's loose T-shirt said Tallahassee Trail Blazers. Her stubby ponytail stuck straight out.

"Hey," said Jemmie, slowing as she neared us. "You're Anna and Eb, right? You about to go to the dentist, or something? You look pitiful."

"We're waiting for a dog to pee on our legs," Eb said.

Cass laughed and flopped down on the curb beside him. She leaned back on her arms. "You shouldn't have to wait long in this neighborhood."

Jemmie ran in place. "Don't you go gettin' comfortable, Cass Bodine. It'll be hot enough to fry an egg in another hour. Let's go." It was funny that she mentioned an egg, since we had just been talking about them. Aunt Eva, who claimed to be psychic, would have called it a sign.

"Are you two related to Miss Dupree?" Cass asked.

"We're just staying with her a while," I said.

Standing straight-legged, Jemmie bobbed down and slapped the ground with her palms. "Staying with her?" Her blue nails were as long as talons. She hadn't had them when we shook hands. "How come?"

"I'm in foster care with Miss Dupree," I said. Mrs. Riley had warned me to let Eb speak for himself.

"Where are your parents?" Jemmie asked.

I hesitated. If I wanted to be friends with these girls, I had to tell them. So I said it right out to get it over with. "I'm an orphan."

Jemmie shot up like I'd slammed a door on her finger. Both girls stared. That always happened when I told people. First they got shocked. Then they pulled back, as if being an orphan was contagious. After that they usually found an excuse to get away.

But Cass put her arm around my shoulders, as if my parents had just died.

Jemmie squatted on her heels. "My dad died a couple of years ago, so I sort of know how you feel. Hey, maybe Miss Dupree'll adopt you."

"Maybe."

"Fat chance," Eb mumbled.

"How about you, Eb?" Jemmie poked him in the arm with a blue nail. "You an orphan too?"

"Not me. My mom'll be by to pick me up as soon as she can."

Cass sprang to her feet. "You two want to come with us? We're going to the school to run."

"I hate running," Eb said.

"Come, come." Jemmie clapped her hands, imitating Mr. G. "You watch. No need to run." She folded her hands. "And we will all be friends like this."

Eb walked to the school. And I mean walked. He didn't trot, he didn't jog, he just put one foot in front of the other. Jemmie and Cass ran around him in circles.

"Hey, old man," Jemmie called as she dashed by. "You're so slow you're wearin' me out."

They ran to the corner and back to Eb, to the corner and back. I'm a pretty fast runner so I tried to keep up, but it was hopeless. Any time they got near me, they asked questions about orphanhood. "Were you ever in one of those creepy orphanages where they hardly give you anything to eat?" Cass asked. "We read about it in a book called *Jane Eyre.* I'll lend it to you."

"You think she wants to read about bad stuff happening to orphans?" Jemmie said. "I mean, she *is* one."

Cass blushed. "Sorry." She ran next to me for a few steps. "But the book ends up fine. Jane marries Mr. Rochester. Something like that could happen to you too."

"Girl." Jemmie gave Cass's arm a slap. "She doesn't have one single idea what you're talkin' about. Ask her something practical, like does she have any brothers or sisters?"

Cass looked hopeful. "Do you?"

"No."

"Too bad." She tucked a loose strand of hair behind her ear. "Sometimes they're a pain, though."

We were way ahead of Eb when I saw the man from Goodwill walking toward us. I wheeled around and ran back. "Eb!" I whispered, but Eb had seen him too.

Muttering softly, the man watched the ground. Half of his shirt collar was folded under. His left leg seemed to be locked at the knee so the toe of that shoe dragged. The way he walked looked scary at first, but it had to hurt to walk like that. He could never have chased us across the field; he couldn't run.

Cass and Jemmie ran out in the street to pass him.

Eb and I were still on the sidewalk. I said, "Come on, Eb," but he wouldn't go. Instead, he stopped. He looked the way he had standing on the track waiting for the train. I couldn't budge him.

When the man saw the toes of Eb's shoes, he stopped too. Slowly, his gaze ran up Eb's bug-bitten shins, over his knobby knees, his shorts, his manatee T-shirt. He stared, unblinking, into Eb's eyes. "Password, soldier."

Eb hugged my notebook.

The man ran his tongue over his cracked lips. "Password."

"Uh..." Eb blinked twice. "Armadillo?"

"That's armadillo, *sir!* And look sharp."

Eb stuck his chest out. "Armadillo, *sir!*"

The man nodded. "At ease, soldier." He stepped off the sidewalk into the grass. "Proceed."

~

"What took you two so long?" Cass leaned with her palms against a pecan tree, stretching the muscles in the backs of her legs.

"Bet Eb decided to crawl," said Jemmie, putting her palms against the tree too. I copied the girls. The three of us leaned and stretched.

Eb sat. "Wish I'd brought my Game Boy." He picked at his knee until the scab fell off, then watched to see if it would bleed.

"Forget games." Jemmie put her hands on her hips and twisted from the waist. "Run with us."

He opened the notebook and began to draw. "You said I could watch, remember?"

"Running's more fun." She and Cass sat on the ground. Each girl folded one leg back and stretched the other leg out in front, then they leaned forward until their chests touched the ground. I tried it. All I could do was look at my knee.

Eb made sure they noticed. "What's the matter, Anna? Out of shape?"

I threw my hat at him.

"Thanks," he said, and he put it on.

The three of us stepped onto the track. Cass and Jemmie took off. "Come on, Anna," Cass called. I wasn't halfway around the track when they passed me. "You're doing fine," Cass said as they went by.

Jemmie called out, "You sure you don't want to run, Eb-man?"

He ignored her.

She had passed him, but stopped and jogged backward, clapping her hands. "Come, come."

"No!" He pulled the brim of my hat down.

Jemmie hovered at the edge of the track, dancing from foot to foot. "Oh, come on, Eb. Get out here, show us your stuff!"

"Buzz off."

Leaving the track, she trotted over to him and dropped to a squat.

Cass slowed down to run beside me. "Now she's gonna pester him to death."

"It won't do any good." I tried to smile and breathe at the same time. I liked Cass. She wasn't pretty like Jemmie. Her face was plain but friendly, and she had even more freckles than I did.

Cass nodded like she knew something I didn't. "Oh, she'll get him out here all right. She's stubborn." Eb turned his head away like Jemmie was trying to make him swallow medicine.

"Eb's...pretty stubborn...himself," I gasped.

"Won't help. Jemmie won't take no for an answer."

"Then...we have a...problem. No is Eb's *only* answer."

Eb shook his head violently, but Jemmie was still talking. "Oh, she'll wear him down," Cass said.

"You don't know Eb. Eb can out-stubborn...anyone." Jemmie stood up and turned away. "See what I mean?"

"I don't know Eb," Cass said. "But I *do* know Jemmie."

And in a moment, Eb jumped to his feet. He drove his knuckles into his hips. "Fine!" he shouted at her back.

Jemmie threw him a you-talking-to-me? look over her shoulder. Then she grabbed his arm and swung him toward the track. "After you, Eb-man."

He looked stiff as he walked up to the gate, muscles tight. One second he was walking slowly, the next his white knees were pumping, his sneakers hammering the track. As Eb churned his way around the course, it looked as if he was going really fast, but Jemmie, who loped along beside him had time to study her nails as she ran. She was barely exerting herself.

He made it around the track just once before stumbling back through the gate and off into the grass. The rest of us followed. As soon as he hit the shade he toppled. He lay on his back, chest heaving. "Hope…you're happy," he wheezed. "You went and gave me…an asthma attack." He sat up, fumbled for the inhaler in his pocket, inhaled a puff, and flopped over again, pulling my hat over his eyes.

Cass and I exchanged worried glances. Eb's lungs were whistling like a squeak toy. "You all right?" Cass knee-walked a little closer. "You looked pretty good out there running," she said.

Eb lifted the brim and opened one eye. "Yeah, right."

"No, I mean it." She brushed her bangs away from her eyes. "You have potential."

"No, I don't," he wheezed. "I have anti-potential. I…I can't do anything right. Not even…breathe."

Jemmie lay down on her belly beside him. "You'll be okay. There are plenty of athletes with asthma. You just have to overcome it."

Eb closed his eyes.

"Well, you could at least try!" She held out a hand to examine her blue nails again.

"Oh, show Anna your Flo-Jo nails," said Cass. She grabbed Jemmie's hand and turned it toward me. "My sister did them." Jemmie's nails were blue daggers with little stars on them.

"Cool. Why do you call them Flo-Jo nails?"

"Girl, you never heard of Flo-Jo? She was just one of the most famous African-American track stars ever." Jemmie laid her hands flat on the ground so I could get a good look at them. "She used to do her nails for races to make herself look fierce."

"Jemmie looks just like her," said Cass.

"They're kind of a drag, though." Jemmie raked her nails across my palm. "It's hard to do anything with them on."

Eb let out a long wheeze. "Hey, I'm dying down here."

"Don't be such a baby," Jemmie said. "Stay calm and breathe slow. In through your nose…out through your mouth. In through your nose—"

"Shut up! I said I'm dying."

"Baby!" Jemmie said.

Eb said something back to her. He was mumbling, but I knew what he had said. The girls did too. Cass turned pale. Jemmie raised up on her knees and leaned over him like she was going to rip his heart out with her fierce Flo-Jo nails. "Boy? Did you call me the N-word?" Eb squeezed his eyes shut. "Now, where'd you get an ugly word like that?"

"A lot of people say it."

"Yeah? Like who?"

"My mother's boyfriend, Eddie. He says it all the time."

"Not to me he wouldn't."

"You apologize," Cass said, crowding him from the other side.

Eb threw an arm over his face, crushing the brim of my hat.

"You know, Eb, you have a lotta mean in you," Jemmie said.

"So do you," he answered. "Making people run when they don't want to."

"Don't you worry," Jemmie said, pulling the lace on her sneaker extra tight. "I won't be asking you to do anything again. Not in this lifetime."

We walked home in silence. "See you later," I said as Cass and Jemmie trotted up the sidewalk to Jemmie's house.

"Listen," I said as soon as they were inside. "Maybe *you* don't want any friends, but I do. No one is coming to get me."

Eb mouth twisted. "You don't see anyone coming for me, do you?"

He shoved my explorer's notebook at me, dropped my hat on the ground, and marched off.

We still weren't speaking when we got to the house. I just wanted to get to my attic room and be alone. And Eb? Eb could stare at pink walls for the rest of his life for all I cared.

~

I never even made it to the stairs. Miss Dupree had been waiting for us. "We need to spend some time together," she said. "I know, let's bake a cake." She made it sound as if she had just thought of the cake idea, but when we got to the kitchen, I saw a recipe book, open to white cake, lying on the table. Bowls and pans and measuring spoons had been carefully set out too.

"Girl stuff," Eb said, and in a moment we heard the door of the pink room slam.

So there I was, having to cover for him again. "He needs to rest. He just had an asthma attack."

"An asthma attack?" Miss Dupree whipped open the drawer where she had put our folders. "I'll call the doctor."

"He's okay. Jemmie talked him out of it."

"Eb is my responsibility." She held his folder in her arms. "You're sure he's all right?"

"I'm sure." I wasn't exactly sure, but he seemed okay. I was tired of thinking about Eb. "Let's make the cake. It'll be fun."

But it wasn't fun the way Miss Dupree did it. First, she had me read the recipe out loud, which I thought was a sneaky way to find out if I was a good reader. She complimented my reading, but she hated the way I measured. I scooped up the first teaspoon of baking powder.

"No, no," she said. "You have to level the teaspoon with a knife."

It was like the recipe was the Ten Commandments. We had to follow every step exactly.

"Could we add some lemon juice?" I asked.

"White cake doesn't call for lemon juice."

It seemed to me to be calling for something. I mean, white cake. What flavor is white? My grandmother used to cook with a pinch of this and a dash of that. "You stir it up and then you judge," she would say. To judge we'd stick a finger in the batter and taste it. If I had done that, Miss Dupree would have had a cow, but how else could you tell what a cake needed?

When every perfectly measured ingredient was in the bowl, I began to stir. The recipe called for three hundred strokes. My grandmother always put the bowl on her hip and walked around the kitchen while she stirred. She'd look out the window; she'd hum. Thinking of Grandma I kind of lost count. I stirred until there were no lumps and stopped. "What flavor icing are we making?"

"Vanilla. You need thirty-seven more strokes."

I watched the creamy batter fold around the spoon. One…two…three. *White cake, white icing. What could be more boring?* Five…six. Then I saw the box of food coloring on the shelf. "Can I add one thing, Miss Dupree?" I asked. "Just one little thing, please? You won't even taste it and it'll make our first cake together special."

"Our first cake *should* be special," she said. I could tell she was wavering. "And this mystery ingredient of yours won't change the flavor?"

"Trust me. It'll taste just as white as ever. Please?"

When she heard our cake would be just the same—only special—she agreed.

Everything went wrong after that. First, the box of food coloring was on a top shelf. I had to stand on a chair to reach it, which meant my dirty sandals made actual contact with the seat of her clean chair. Then I picked the wrong color. I knew she liked pink. But I grabbed the little blue squeeze bottle.

"Blue?" she asked. She said the word "blue" like it tasted bad.

I'll make the blue so pale, I thought, *she'll have to like it.* I took the cap off and gave the bottle a little squeeze. *Squoosh.* Every bit of the blue coloring jetted right into the batter.

"Don't worry," I said, picking up the wooden spoon. "It'll look okay when it's mixed in." Seven…eight…nine. The food coloring formed a dark, ugly tornado.

After the thirty-seven strokes, the batter was as blue as midnight. The spoon was blue. The plastic bowl was blue. "I'm so sorry, Miss Dupree."

She tried to smile. "We'll hide it with white icing. It'll be fine."

Iced in white, it looked like a normal, respectable cake. But after supper, when Miss Dupree cut it, the Anna mistake blared out.

"Navy blue cake!" said Eb. "Cool." I could tell he was trying to get back on my good side. "What kind is it?"

"It's a blue moon cake," I said, more to Miss Dupree than to Eb. "My grandma used to say, 'You only have luck like that once in a blue moon.' So it's a lucky cake, and who couldn't use a little good luck?" Even Miss Dupree would have to admit that a cake like this might be a good thing, once in a blue moon.

Miss Dupree cut big blue slabs for Eb and me, but only a thin sliver for herself. We carried our plates to the living room and ate in front of the TV.

"Great cake," said Eb, spraying blue crumbs. Using the toe of the opposite foot, he pried off one sneaker, then the other. He slid the arch of his foot down his calf, rolling the sock. When it popped off his toes, he switched legs and rolled down the other sock. He put his horrible, disgusting feet up on the coffee table, right on top of Likely Prospects, pink, and wiggled his toes.

Miss Dupree took a tiny bite of blue cake. "Delicious, Anna." She grabbed one of Eb's ankles and gently lowered his foot to the floor.

In spite of everything, she seemed to want to like us. Why did we have to make it so hard?

Chapter Seven

OUT THERE FLAPPIN'

W here's the knives?" Eb asked, pulling out a drawer. "I want to take him a piece."

"I thought you were scared of him."

"I don't want to *talk* to him. Just sneak up and leave it." A second drawer rattled as he opened it. "I mean, if I was living in the woods, I'd want someone to bring me a piece of cake. Wouldn't you?" He tried a third drawer. "What's she do, hide the knives?" He grabbed a spatula instead.

"Try this drawer," I said, but by then he had already spread his feet wide and raised the spatula.

"Hi-ya!" He whacked off a big piece of cake. "Now all we need's a fork and a plastic container." He opened the door of the bottom cupboard, stepped up on the shelf, and reached for the Tupperware.

"No way, we won't get it back." I wrapped the cake in foil and found a plastic fork. Eb insisted on carrying the cake himself. He stuck the fork in his back pocket and headed toward the door.

"Don't sit down," I said. "You'll stab yourself in the butt."

"Where are you two going?" Miss Dupree called from her office.

"Out," Eb answered.

"Just don't leave the neighborhood, okay?"

"Maybe we should we tell her where we're going," I whispered.

"Nah," he said, opening the front door. "It's okay…as long as we don't get caught."

She never told us where the neighborhood ends, I thought, putting my hat on, *so we aren't breaking any rules—technically.*

Probably leaving the neighborhood—but possibly not—we crossed Roberts and headed into the woods. "Come *on!*" Eb called. He jumped the broken tricycle, which lay in exactly the same spot as before. "I thought you liked adventures. I thought you were an explorer."

"Smart explorers always tell someone where they're going."

"Why? Nothing could happen here."

"Things happen everywhere," I said. Nothing was wrong exactly, I just had a bad feeling about the man in the woods. "Do you want Lisa to see your picture on the side of a milk carton?"

He ran ahead, but I looked back toward the road, fixing in my mind the fastest way out.

After a while we saw the dark-stained dresser and the back of the stuffed armchair through the trees. At first we thought the chair was empty. We were really close before we saw the top of the man's head sticking up. "This is a bad idea," I whispered, but Eb crept forward. A twig cracked. Eb jumped like he'd been shot, then froze. As he breathed through his mouth his lungs squeaked, like when you squeeze the neck of a balloon and let the air escape slowly. Eb was scaring himself into an asthma attack, but he kept on going.

Leaves crunched under our feet. Eb's teakettle whistle got louder and louder, but the head above the back of the chair never moved. It was still as a jack o' lantern on a windowsill. "Maybe we're too late with the cake," I whispered. "It looks like he's dead."

Suddenly, we heard a horrible loud snort, followed by a rumble like a shoe falling down the stairs. My heart pounded. "I have an idea," I whispered. "I count to three and we run."

The snort from the chair repeated, then the rumble, exactly the same. Eb made a face. "He's snoring. I'll just put it on the dresser, then we can run."

With each snore we moved a little closer…a little closer. Eb slid the plastic fork out of his pocket. Closer…

We eased around the chair and stopped. The homeless man's head hung at a weird, broken-neck angle. Spit bubbled in the corners of his mouth. Eb stood no more than two feet away from the lifeless arm that hung over the side of the chair.

Eb leaned slowly toward the dresser, sun gleaming on the foil package. He reached out…. Then suddenly, he let out a yell. The package of cake sailed up and up, right over my head. The fork flipped into the dirt. The hand that had been hanging limp against the side of the chair was clamped to Eb's ankle.

"Run!" Eb yelled, trying to jerk his ankle loose. "Go, Anna! Get the cops!"

The man in the chair flinched, but then he tightened his grip.

"Anna, go!" Eb kicked his trapped leg wildly. "Run, Anna, run!" He fell down and tried to claw his way across the ground, but the man held on. Eb twisted and looked up. "Don't hit me," he whimpered. "Please don't hit me, mister."

I snatched up the plastic fork. "You let go of him, *now!*" I waved the fork around. I didn't want to jab him.

"That's plastic," Eb blubbered. "It'll just make him mad. Get help, Anna!"

"Shoot," said the man, still hanging on. "I'd never hurt a kid." Then he let go.

"You wouldn't?" I said as Eb scrabbled back a few feet, then lay there, panting. "Then why are you going around grabbing kids by the ankle?"

"*Who's* going around?" The man rubbed the back of his neck. "Seems like *you're* the ones going around, sneaking up. About scared the piss outta me."

I retrieved the package. Eb used his inhaler. "He only wanted to do something nice for you," I said, dropping the crumpled foil packet on the arm of his chair. "He wanted to give you this."

The man eyed the package. "What is it?"

"Go ahead," I said. "Open it." I wiped the dirty fork on my T-shirt, then reached out as far as I could and placed it on the arm of the chair.

The man poked the package with a finger. "How'd ya know where to find me?"

"We ran across your spot before," I said. "We were the ones who sort of accidentally spilled coffee in your drawer."

"So, *you* were the ones. I wondered about that." He flipped the silver package over. When nothing happened, he peeled a corner of the foil back. "I'll be, cake. Looks homemade."

"It's blue moon cake," I said. "I made it."

"It was my idea to bring you a piece," Eb cut in. "I remembered the fork."

The man picked the cake up in his fingers and took a bite. Blue crumbs sprinkled his beard. "Go on, sit. There's a blanket in the bottom drawer."

Once when Aunt Eva was stopped at a traffic light, a man holding one of those hungry-will-work-for-food signs came up to the car. She rolled the window down a smidge and slid a dollar out. She didn't look in his eyes when the man said, "God bless you, ma'am." And she looked relieved when the light changed. "You do your act of charity, but you don't get involved," she said. "People who need help stick like glue if you let them."

Eb and I had done our act of charity, but I wasn't ready to leave yet. I'd read about South American tribes in *National Geographic,* but I'd never actually met anyone who lived in the woods before—especially not one who slept in an armchair.

Eb and I spread out the blanket and sat down. It had twigs stuck to it and smelled like mildew.

The man crossed one bony leg over the other, resting his ankle on his knee. There was a hole in the bottom of his shoe that went clear through. He wasn't wearing socks. *Doesn't dirt get in?* I wondered. But maybe that was a personal question. "What's it like living in the woods?" I asked politely. "You must get bitten by bugs and things. And what do you do when it rains?"

Eb rushed in. "What if you have to go? I mean, where do you do it?"

The homeless man sucked the last of the frosting off his fingers. Then, using a wet finger, he picked up the crumbs that had fallen on the front of his shirt. "Well," he said, licking his fingertip, "I got me a big tarp I can throw over the whole mess when it's wet out." Out of all of our questions, the only one he answered was the one about rain. "You have any more of that cake?"

"Not on me," I said. "What's your name?"

The man's eyes glittered like broken glass. "Who wants to know?"

"Just me. By the way, you have crumbs in your beard."

"The name's Sam Miller." He left the crumbs where they were. "You know," he said, wagging a finger at Eb. "You know...that boy looks kinda familiar."

"His name's Eb and I'm Anna. You saw us at Goodwill."

"Not Goodwill. This was a long time ago." Mr. Miller snapped his fingers. "I got it. Cosgrove. With a few more years on him he'd be the spittin' image."

"He would?" Mr. Miller and I stared at Eb. "Who's Cosgrove?" I asked.

"A guy I used to know. The two of us went through basic training together at Fort Jackson."

"Did you like him?" Eb asked.

"Like him? He was the best friend I ever had." He stared at Eb, then nodded. "You sure do look a powerful lot like him."

"The best friend you ever had," Eb repeated.

"Until...you know." Mr. Miller's eyes darted around, then fixed on Eb. "You remember that day, don't you, Cosgrove?" He rubbed his fingers across his lips. "I mean, you were there when it happened." He lowered his voice to a hoarse whisper. "Couldn't've been no closer."

When what happened? A shiver crept up my spine.

Mr. Miller shook his head fast, like he was trying to clear it.

"What am I talking about? You couldn't be him. Sorry. Sometimes I go off funny; I lose hold of things."

"What do you mean?" Eb wrapped his arms around his knees. "What do you lose hold of?"

Mr. Miller ran his fingers through his beard, dislodging a few crumbs. "Time mostly." His voice was quiet. "When this happened... when that happened.... Things get all mixed up. I forget easy, on account of this." He slowly lifted the hair that hung over his forehead. With one yellow fingernail he traced the jagged scar that started at his eyebrow and continued up until it disappeared into his hair.

"Wow!" Eb leaned forward, breathing loudly through his mouth. "What happened to you?"

"Wrong place, wrong time. I should've been at the front of the patrol. I was supposed to have been, but I stopped to take a leak. If I had been up front, I would've been dead meat when the mine went off. If I'd been a little slower I might've got off without a scratch." He shook his head. "But I was in the exact wrong place. I got sprayed with all this metal. My foot, my leg, all up the one side. Worst part was the head." He traced the old scar again, reading it with his fingertips. "See, there's this clock inside your head. Blow your head half off, and that clock can go haywire on you. Mine sure did. Now it can run any which way it wants—slow, fast, backwards, forwards. Sometimes I'm just out there, flappin'."

"That's too bad," I said.

"Just dumb luck." Mr. Miller let the hair fall back over his forehead. "Stuff happens. Yes indeed, stuff happens." He gave Eb a sharp look, then winked. "But you know that already, don't you Cosgrove? I'd say you know better than anyone."

Mr. Miller craned his neck to steal a quick look around each side of the chair. Then he whispered, "I know I can trust you, Cosgrove, but can the girl keep a secret?"

"Of course, I can!" I told him. But Mr. Miller didn't go on until Eb nodded.

"All right then, com'ere." When Eb got up and walked over to him, Mr. Miller grabbed his wrist and mashed Eb's fingers against the scar. "Ya feel it?"

"The scar?" Eb squeaked.

"Not the scar. It's *under* the scar. Ya gotta feel for it; it's not big." Eb's fingers bent back as Mr. Miller pushed harder. "They wouldn't make it big or everyone would catch on. Feel it?"

"Maybe. What is it?"

"Shhhh," he hissed. "A receiver. Might be two-way, I don't know. All I know is I hear all kinds of things on it. Classified reports… marching bands…Russian submarines; you name it." He put a finger to his lips. "Shhhh. Enough said. Just wanted you to know what I'm up against, Cosgrove."

"Amazing!" Eb sat down again. Mr. Miller looked back and forth between us as if now that we knew about the receiver in his head, we were connected.

Holding that secret, we got very quiet. Eb and I would never be able to leave if we didn't get back to something normal. We'd sit there forever, guarding what we knew. "Too bad you don't have family to help you out," I said, louder than I meant to.

"Who says I don't have family?" Mr. Miller snapped. "I have family." He seemed to forget all about the receiver in his head. "I'll show you." He reached back and dug around in a pants pocket, then jerked out an old black wallet and flapped it open. "See?" On top was a photograph of a boy and girl, sitting on a beach towel. "Sam Andrew and Claudette. My kids."

When he passed the wallet to me the leather felt damp. The picture was old, faded. "How long ago was this taken?" I asked.

"I dunno. A while. Couple of years. A lot of years." His gaze wandered. "I forget."

"Thanks for showing us the picture. Your kids look nice," I said, passing the wallet back to him. "Eb and I should go now."

Eb helped me shake the blanket out. When we folded it up it had a few more twigs stuck to it. "See ya," I said, steering clear of the chair, but Eb walked right over and put a hand on Mr. Miller's shoulder.

"Good to see you, Cosgrove." Mr. Miller put a hand over Eb's. "Don't be a stranger now that you know where I am. If I have to break camp and go, I'll leave you the sign. You know the one." His hand slid off Eb's and he leaned forward.

"Oh, no. Here it comes, the weather in India." He looked tired, worn down by the voices inside his head. "Monsoons? Well, that figures." When we left, he was still listening to the weather report from Asia.

"Mr. Miller is suffering from a temporal shift," said Eb as we walked out of the woods. "There's a distortion in his space-time continuum."

"His what?"

"*Star Trek*," he said, walking backward ahead of me. "Don't you know anything? It might be kind of cool, though, to have everything just floating around in your head, coming and going."

"I thought he looked scared. And Eb, does he seem kind of crazy to you?"

"No worse than your friend, Miss Johnette." He turned and stepped off the curb onto Roberts. I had to pull him back.

"Careful, Eb." We watched three cars pass.

"To me he seems all mixed up. And he said himself he can't remember things."

"Maybe he doesn't want to remember," Eb said as we crossed. "Do you want to remember everything? Not me."

"What about the receiver he thinks he has in his head?"

"We agreed to keep that a secret," Eb said. "We shouldn't talk about it."

"Eb, did you actually feel something?"

"Sure. I mean I *think* I did."

"And what about the way he kept calling you Cosgrove?"

"The best friend he ever had," Eb said softly.

≈

When we walked into the living room, Miss Dupree was on the couch with a small, bald man wearing wire-rimmed glasses. The pink photo album was open, one side on each of their laps. "Hello, children," she piped. "I'm with a client right now, but there are Rice Krispie Treats in the kitchen." Her blush was as bright as her magenta blouse.

The man with the twinkly glasses blushed too, and jerked his leg away from Miss Dupree's. "Please eat your snack in the kitchen," she said. The client pretended to look over a page of Likely Prospects.

"Junk food," Eb said, tearing the top off the box. "She's buying our silence. Did you see how close he was to her?"

"They had to sit close to share the book."

Eb made a disgusting kissing sound against the back of his hand, but I was already thinking ahead. *If Miss Dupree gets married, Eb and I will have a set of parents, ready-made.* Maybe I was getting carried away—I do that sometimes—but why jinx it? I would keep Eb in the kitchen for as long as they wanted to sit out there, knees touching.

"Hey, look." A postcard was propped up against the sugar bowl on the kitchen table. When I saw the picture of a restaurant shaped like a shoe, my heart beat faster. "Bet this is from my uncle. Mrs. Riley said she gave him my address." When I flipped it over, there was my uncle's quick, scratchy handwriting on the back. I read it to Eb. "'Hey Kid,'—he always calls me kid. 'How do you like this picture? The specialty of the house is fillet of sole and shoestring potatoes. Funny? Be good. Miss you. Love, Uncle C.'" I checked the postmark. "He's in Omaha, Nebraska."

He used to send me and my cousins postcards from all over, but none of the cards ever told us what we really wanted to know, which was when we would see him again. "The man has itchy feet," Aunt Eva told me. "He doesn't like to be with us. He likes to be somewhere else, missing us. And you're going to be just like him with your maps and your Borneo stories."

Eb pretended that it was no big deal that I had a postcard and he didn't. I didn't want to rub it in. I put the card in my pocket to look at later.

Eb had eaten two packages of treats when we heard the front door open and close. Miss Dupree came into the kitchen. "Guess what? Mr. Perry has invited us all out to eat barbecue." The words rushed out. "He'll pick us up at seven."

"Very professional," Eb mumbled.

He didn't repeat his comment when she asked, "I beg your pardon?" He must have liked the idea of eating barbecue instead of the usual dried-out meat and butter-free vegetables.

It wasn't long, though, before Eb decided that it wasn't worth it. Miss Dupree made him shower and put on a button-up shirt. When he shoved a foot into its usual grungy high-top, she made him go get his dress shoes. And polish them.

"What's the point?" he grumbled, buffing a shoe with a rag. "We're gonna eat barbecue, for cryin' out loud. Drippy, sloppy barbecue."

She stopped in front of the mirror in the entryway and gave her hair a fluff with her fingers. "But we'll be with Mr. Perry. He is tidy, likes order, and prefers an ironed shirt to a knit."

She *had* to be quoting from the "Perfect Match" questionnaire.

"Then why's he taking us out for barbecue?" Eb shoved a foot into a shoe that still looked dull. "Does he want to torture himself?"

"He thought that you kids would like barbecue," Miss Dupree said as she disappeared into her room.

He had thought about us? Maybe I wasn't getting *that* carried away.

Chapter Eight

FIREWORKS

E b and I were ready way ahead of Miss Dupree, who couldn't seem to make up her mind what to wear for barbecue. We sat on the couch while she dashed in and out wearing a different outfit each time. After four changes she joined us on the couch where the three of us waited in silence. We all jumped when Mr. Perry knocked.

"Seven on the dot," Miss Dupree murmured and gave her hair one last pat before opening the door.

Mr. Perry stood one step down, his eyeglasses dazzling with the reflection of the yellow flowers on her dress. "You look lovely, Miss Dupree." His scrubbed ears were as pink as pencil erasers. He wore gray slacks with a crease down the exact center of each leg and a stiff white shirt. When it came to shine, Eb's polished shoes couldn't compete with Mr. Perry's gleaming bald head.

Then there was his car. It was so clean you could've eaten off the upholstery. I was sure no one had ever put a cigarette butt in the ashtray or tossed a beer can into the backseat. It still had that new car smell. It was a privilege to ride in such a car.

Mr. Perry parked in front of Tiny Register's Highway 20 Bar-B-Q. Propped against the window was a wooden cutout of a pig that said Pig In-Pig Out. I guess that meant you could eat it there or get it to go. Mr. Perry was *way* too formal for pig-to-go.

We placed our orders at the counter, then Mr. Perry picked out a table for four with a checked plastic cloth. He pulled out a chair for Miss Dupree. She sat and quickly wiped the table with a paper napkin, even though it already looked clean. He slid out a second chair.

"That's okay," Eb said. He walked over to one of the long tables in the middle of the room and sat down next to a guy in a shirt that said "Marty" on the pocket. Marty's pants were slung so low, he was showing his butt-crack to half the room. I sat across from Eb. I didn't want to be anywhere near that butt-crack.

"You know, it would have been more polite for us to sit with them," I whispered, watching Mr. Perry scoot his chair over. Maybe he wanted to shield Miss Dupree from the Marty-view. Maybe he just wanted to sit closer.

"*I'm* not on a date with Mr. Perry," Eb said. He kicked at the leg of the table until Marty gave him a slow, cut-that-out look.

"Miss Dupree looks happy," I said.

"Bad news for us."

"No, it isn't. It could be good news for us—great even."

"No, it won't. It's like when I get a new video game. I just chuck the old ones in a box."

Miss Dupree laughed. Mr. Perry leaned toward her as if she were a magnet. Their eyeglasses seemed to beam at each other.

"That's what I mean," Eb said, looking over his shoulder. "We're headed for the box."

The woman behind the counter bawled, "Forty-nine. Number forty-nine."

Waving a little slip of paper over his head, Mr. Perry leapt from his chair. "That would be me!" I followed him to help carry. I smiled at him when we picked up the trays, but he turned and looked over me to smile at Miss Dupree, who hadn't taken her eyes off him since he'd left their table. Tray in hand, he floated back to her. I stumped along behind him, carrying Eb's food and mine.

Eb's corn on the cob wallowed in a trough of butter. As soon as he lifted it, butter drooled down the front of his shirt. Next came Tiny Register's secret barbeque sauce. Eb hadn't taken one bite of his sandwich before it started leaking. The man with the low-riders shook out a paper napkin and stuffed it into the front of Eb's shirt. "Like this," he said, bracing himself on his forearms. Leaning over their plates, they each took a big bite. The red juice ran over their fingers and dripped off their chins.

Between their hunched shoulders I could see Miss Dupree and her date picking at their barbecue sandwiches with forks and knives, taking delicate bird-bites. *Now that's a perfect match,* I thought. Not a single drip fell on either one of their clean, freshly ironed outfits.

Leaving the restaurant, Mr. Perry held the door. Miss Dupree said, "Thank you, Dan." She was calling him by his first name. Things were moving along. When he opened the car door for her it was, "Thank you, Dan," again. To me, Dan is a name for a big man, like the one wolfing down ribs with his butt showing. Mr. Perry looked more like a Fred—like Mr. Rogers—the kind of man who would hang his sweater on a hook in the closet and tell you about all the fun you would have that day.

Personally, I would've picked someone more exciting, but maybe for Miss Dupree eating barbecue was enough of an adventure. As I climbed into the car, I decided that I wouldn't mind living with Miss Dupree and Mr. Perry—and Eb. Eb's mother would have come by now if she was going to. Luckily for Eb, Mr. Perry didn't look like the kind of man who would make him go out in the yard and throw a ball around.

The adults in the front seat began talking about the opening shot of *The Sound of Music.* They both liked the way Julie Andrews spun around on the top of the mountain singing, "The hills are alive…with the sound of mew-sick."

Eb slid down in the seat. "Lame-O," he whispered.

"Would you give them a break?" I whispered back, still thinking about the four of us becoming a family.

As Mr. Perry drove into our neighborhood, a bottle rocket zinged over the hood of the car. "Oh, my!" he said. Eb scrambled up on his knees. Bike riders in the road were drawing patterns in the air with sparklers as they pedaled.

"Hey, there's Jemmie." I waved but she didn't see me in the dark car. Besides, she was kind of busy doing cartwheels with a sparkler in her teeth.

Of course, nothing was happening on our street. Mr. Perry pulled into the driveway and turned the motor off. There was an awkward silence in the front seat. Neither of the adults knew what to do. "Why don't you two go inside?" I suggested. "There are still some Rice Krispie Treats. Eb and I'll be at the fireworks."

With my permission, the adults headed for the house. Just before stepping inside, Miss Dupree called to us, "It's getting late. Don't be gone too long."

"We can watch from here," Eb said, even though most of what was going on didn't show above the houses. "They won't want us butting in."

"They won't notice us with all the smoke and noise. Besides, it's almost dark. Let's go." I grabbed his arm and pulled him around the corner. A single streetlight at the end of the block gave everyone fifteen-foot shadows, but the only bright lights came from flickering sparklers and the sudden flair of bottle rockets.

I could barely see the adults who were seated on porches and lawns, hidden in the shadows. Some of them were smoking, some talking quietly. A woman's voice called out, "Cody, you *walk* with that sparkler, now." None of the adults ran in the street. None tossed sparklers or rode bikes. I felt sorry for them, and hoped I wouldn't grow up to be one of them.

But Eb was like an adult in a kid body. "Let's sit here," he said, picking a spot where we would blend right in with the shadow of a hedge. Luckily it was too late to blend. Jemmie was trotting toward us.

"Hey, hey, Eb! Haven't seen you at the track lately." She put a strangle hold around his neck with one skinny arm and knocked on the top of his head with the knuckles of her other hand. "Hel-lo? Is the evil Eb still in there?" She cocked her head like she was listening. "No, I don't hear him. Guess that bad boy checked out." She led him over to a boy who was standing in the middle of the road, a grocery bag between his feet. "Got a sparkler for the Eb-man?"

The boy who reached into the paper sack looked like Ben, but I couldn't tell for sure. "Here ya go." He handed Eb a sparkler, then dug a lighter out of his pocket, spun the little wheel, and flicked the tab. The flame lit. It *was* Ben. His shirt was off. He wore an old pair of jeans with ragged cuffs. The way he handled the lighter, I wondered if maybe he smoked; I hoped he didn't.

Ben held the lighter up to the sparkler in Eb's hand until it hissed and spat silver sparks. The sparks fell on Eb's polished shoes. With a flick of his head, Ben flipped his hair out of his eyes. "How about you?" he called. "You want one too?" He was talking to me.

"Okay." I walked over to him. Ben was even cuter by sparkler light.

Maybe I wasn't holding still enough. He put his fingers against the back of my hand to steady it. After he took them away, I could still feel where they had been.

I raised the sparkler above my head. Sparks fell like a veil all around me.

"Hey," Ben said. "Statue of Liberty."

Jemmie leaned toward me. "You know, it's his birthday."

The sparks crackled. "How old?"

"Thirteen," he said.

"Big thirteen," Jemmie teased. "We're all gonna spank him after a while."

"Oh, grow up." Ben thrust the lighter back into his pocket.

Eb wasn't paying any attention to the sparkler in his hand. He was peering into the paper bag at Ben's feet. "Where'd you get the fireworks?"

"My uncle bought 'em in Alabama. You can get about anything up there." Ben lit another sparkler and handed it to a little boy. "Here you go, Bobby."

The boy ran away, holding the sparkler out in front of him.

"Don't trip, now," Ben called.

Some adult carried over a pot of water and set it in the middle of the road. It hissed as a kid tossed a burnt sparkler wire into it.

"So, what else do you have?" Eb asked.

Ben toed the bag. "Roman candles, one real big one. Fireballs."

"Got any M-80s?"

"Nah, those'll take your hand off. My uncle won't buy 'em."

"They're not that bad."

"How come you know so much about fireworks?" Jemmie asked.

"My mom's boyfriend's into them. One night he climbed up and shot them off the roof of his truck. He set Mrs. Wilson's porch on fire. You should've heard that old lady yell!" He looked into the bag again. "So, when're you gonna do the good stuff?"

"Later," Ben said. "After it gets all the way dark."

A screen door banged, and Cass ran into the street. "Did I miss anything, Ben? Mama made me do dishes."

"Just sparklers so far, and Black Cats…a few bottle rockets."

"Can I have a sparkler?" Cass was as tall as Ben, but she lowered her head and looked up at him.

"Hey, me too." Jemmie slapped his bare arm. The way they circled around him, I knew they thought he was cute too.

As soon as he lit their sparklers, the girls began writing in the air. Maybe they were writing their own names, maybe they were writing BEN, BEN, BEN. The letters turned to smoke and stink before I could read them.

I dropped my sparkler in the pot. I had wasted the whole thing just standing there.

Eb had wasted his too. "I've seen plenty of fireworks before," he said. "Bigger ones. Let's go, Anna."

"I don't want to."

"Let him go," Jemmie said. "It'll leave more of my grandmother's homemade ice cream for the rest of us."

Eb hesitated. "Ice cream?"

"Homemade."

"You can't make ice cream."

"No? An' why not?" Jemmie tossed her dead sparkler in the pot. "Follow me."

Jemmie's was the biggest house on the block, and old. A smallish woman sat alone in a rocker on the wraparound porch. Moths swirled around her, bumping the light over her head. Her dress was hiked up. She was leaning over the bucket she held between her legs, turning a crank. Jemmie hung her arm around the woman's neck. "This is my grandmother, Nana Grace. Nana, this is Anna and Eb."

Nana Grace quit turning the crank and held out a hand. "Pleased to meet you, Anna." As we shook, she gave my hand a squeeze. When she shook Eb's hand she held on. "Your name wouldn't be Ebenezer, would it?"

"It's Eb."

"That's too bad. Ebenezer's a fine old bible name, means 'stone of help.' Someone called Ebenezer is strong as a gladiator, but kind and steady." She looked into his eyes. "Too bad it's not your name."

For a second, skinny Eb squared his shoulders like a gladiator, then he fell back into his usual slouch. "It's just Eb."

"Just-Eb says you can't make ice cream," Jemmie said.

"Well, Just-Eb's about right." Nana Grace fished a tissue out of the front of her blouse and blotted her face with it. "My old arm's so tired it's like to fall off." She slapped the seat of the chair next to hers. "Have a seat, Ebenezer. You don't mind if I call you that, do you? Because I sure could use someone strong about now." As soon as Eb sat, she plopped the bucket down in front of him and put his hand on the crank. "Grab ahold with your knees and turn the handle, Ebenezer. That's all there is to it."

Eb cranked halfheartedly. "This isn't going to work," he said.

"No?" Nana Grace nudged her rocker back and forth with the toes of her slippers. "Be surprised if it didn't." She closed her eyes and began to hum.

Cass and Jemmie and I sat down on the steps. A big orange cat walked up, rubbed against my side and purred, then climbed into my lap. It was a nice heavy cat, like Buck.

"This is a lot of work," Eb grunted. "What flavor is it?"

Nana Grace kept her eyes shut but stopped humming. "That make a difference?"

"Sure. I wouldn't sweat like this for rum raisin."

"What are you talkin' about, rum raisin?" Nana Grace opened one eye. "Wouldn't catch me sweatin' for no rum raisin neither."

"What is it, then?"

A porch board creaked as she rocked. "A surprise."

"If y'all would find a seat," Ben shouted from the street, "the show is about to begin."

"Be careful, Ben," an adult voice warned. "Don't want anybody getting hurt."

Clay and Justin, the two other boys from the Race-A-Rama, shooed the kids back. Most sat on the top step of Jemmie's porch, like a row of birds on a telephone wire. When the step got too crowded, Jemmie climbed up on the railing. In a second Cass was up there too, squatting barefoot on the rail. I would have gone too, but I liked having a cat in my lap.

"Hey!" Ben's younger brother plunked down in the chair next to Eb. "Hey! Remember me? I'm the one who told you about the Race-A-Rama. My name's Cody, remember?" He watched Eb turn the crank. "What'cha doin'?"

"Making ice cream."

"Can I help?"

Eb locked his knees around the churn. "You don't know how."

"Oh." Cody chewed his bottom lip, then smiled. "I know how to whistle."

Eb stopped in mid-crank. "What does that have to do with anything?"

Clay lit the first of the larger fireworks and a geyser of sparks poured down onto the blacktop. Showing off, he pretended to catch the flow in his hands. "Ahhhh…" said everyone on the porch.

"Son…" The warning voice came from across the street. Clay stepped back.

Justin lit one. It hissed and buzzed then burst with a *bang-bang-bang!* Everyone laughed when Justin clutched his chest and fell to the ground.

Inside the house a small child started crying, then a woman's voice called, "Coming Artie. It's okay, baby." In a minute a woman with a little boy in her arms cracked the screen door open with her hip. "What's going on out here?"

Jemmie said, "Nothing, Mom."

Nana Grace waved a hand. "Just Ben and them, acting like fools."

"Lord, I hate this time of year. Kids blowing their fingers off. Hope nobody gets hurt." Jemmie's mother stepped out onto the porch and rested her back against the wall. She hugged the sleeping boy.

Next out of the bag was a pair of miniature tanks. Justin and Ben each took one and paced off, as if they were having a duel. They lit the fuses and turned the tanks loose. The tanks lumbered forward, throwing jets of flame until they ran right into each other. Muzzle to muzzle, the tanks caught fire. Everybody cheered.

"Fire brigade!" Clay yelled and dumped the pot of burnt sparklers and water over both of them. There was a loud hiss and a pall of smoke. We cheered again.

Ben held up his hands for silence. "And now, for the grand finale!" He lifted the last of the fireworks out of the bag. When he set it on the road it stood knee-high, and it was thick.

"This'll be good," Cody said in a hushed voice. "It costed eight dollars."

Clay went to light it, but Justin gave him a shove. "Hey, back off. It's Ben's birthday. He gets to light it." Cass and Jemmie stood on the railing for a better view. Each wrapped an arm around one of the roof columns.

Ben tried, but the fuse of the Roman candle wouldn't light. He fiddled with it and tried again. Justin cupped his hands around the flame. There was a sudden hiss, and the three boys jumped back. Everyone on the porch leaned forward as the flame crawled along the fuse. When it reached the top, it stood straight up like the flame on a birthday candle. Justin, Clay, and Ben covered their ears. Jemmie's mother hugged the little boy tight, covering one of his ears with her hand and pressing the other one against her chest. I did the same with the cat. We all waited for the *ka-bloom!* but nothing happened.

Clay's arms dropped to his sides, then Justin's, then Ben's.

"Well, that wasn't much." Nana Grace went back to rocking and humming.

Ben walked toward the eight-dollar Roman candle. "Watch yourself, now," Nana Grace called.

As Ben leaned over to look at the spot where the flame had disappeared, Jemmie's mother cried, "No, Ben!"

He straightened up, turned around, shrugged. We all laughed. But the laughs were blotted out by a roar like a jet engine, then a blinding flash. Cat claws stabbed my thigh. Cass shrieked, "Ben!" and leapt down from the rail.

"Mercy," screamed Jemmie's mother. She shoved the crying child into Nana Grace's arms and ran down the steps. The smoke was so thick it made my throat hurt. I couldn't see Ben at all.

Then, with a whoop, Ben danced out of the smoke. Seeing that he wasn't hurt, Cass climbed back up on the rail. "Show off." She faced away from him and crossed her arms.

"Singed the hair off your arms," Clay yelled. "About set your pants on fire!"

"Ben Floyd!" Jemmie's mother marched to the middle of the street and stood with her fists on her hips and the smoke all around her. "Ben Floyd, you could have lost your eyesight. You could be blind right this very minute."

Ben stopped dancing around. "Yes, ma'am."

"Fine birthday present that would have been."

As he hung his head, other adults gathered, talking to him low, checking him over.

"Why's she getting on him?" Eb asked. "It wasn't his fault."

"Well, he *could* have been more careful," Cass said.

"Yeah, but she doesn't need to chew him out. She's not his mother."

"My mom's a nurse. When it comes to accidents, she's everybody's mother," Jemmie explained. "She's all the time seeing kids who get shot, or blown up, kids who eat roach poison. She gives them all a real talking-to so it won't happen again."

I could tell by the way he stared at his feet that Ben was getting a real talking-to right then. Mrs. Lewis was giving the lecture, but other adults chimed in with "You listen to her," and "You know that's right. Tell him, Leona."

"Trust me," Jemmie said. "When she's done with him, he won't want to even leave the house until he's twenty-one."

Mrs. Lewis came switching back to the porch. "That should keep him out of trouble a while."

"It should," said Jemmie, squeezing Cass's arm, "but it won't. What do you say, Cass? Is it time?" As the girls walked down the porch steps, Jemmie yelled, "Day of reckoning, Ben Floyd. Bring your sorry butt over here."

"Yeah, right. Like I'm gonna hold still. Jemmie…Cass…" As they walked toward him he backed away. "Sheee-it!" He took off running.

"What was that word just come outta your mouth?" Nana Grace yelled, as the three of them disappeared beyond the streetlight. "That boy's just lucky I can't run fast as my granddaughter. Now, how's that ice cream feel, Ebenezer? Good and stiff?" She reached over and put a hand on Eb's. Together they gave the crank a turn. "This ice cream's as ready as it ever will be."

Since Eb had done most of the work, he got to open the lid and take the first taste. "Hey, chocolate chip," he said. "All right!"

"Told you it wasn't no rum raisin," Nana Grace said.

Nana Grace was spooning ice cream into paper cups when Ben's parents came up the porch steps, each carrying a tray of birthday cupcakes. I helped pass them out, but all the time I was listening and wishing that I had taken off with Cass and Jemmie. I heard them crash through some bushes. Ben shouted, "Can't catch me," from behind the house. But it was only a matter of time. They finally trapped him against the fence between Jemmie and Cass's yards. I heard slap after slap, then Ben complained, "Can't you two even count? Thirteen, that's all you get, plus one to grow on. Ow! What was that?"

"Pinch to grow an inch," Cass said.

Ben's father laughed, then called, "Take it like a man, son."

They walked back to the porch, Ben rubbing his backside. "You two are *so* mature," he said. "That's the last time, I mean it."

"Says who?" Jemmie gave him one last slap and ran up the steps.

Cass was walking behind him. For one second she hooked her finger through the belt loop on his jeans—so quick, he probably didn't even feel it.

Ben ate his ice cream with Clay and Justin. Every now and then one of them let out a loud laugh. Cass huddled with Jemmie, the two of them whispering. I ate out of my Dixie cup with Cody talking in one ear. All the time I kept sliding closer to the girls.

Before I got half close enough, a man walked over from next door. It was Cass's dad. "Let's go, Cass. Bedtime." He pointed at the rest of us with the orange tip of his cigarette. "I hope that's it with the whoopin' and hollerin'. Some of us have to work in the morning. Y'all were lucky no one called the cops."

"Relax, Seth, eat a cupcake," Ben's dad said. "We're celebrating a birthday."

But Cass said, "Night," and slipped down from the porch railing. She and her dad disappeared around the fence. In a few minutes, the rest of us went home.

Chapter Nine

KINGS OF THE RACE-A-RAMA

Everything looks better without them," Miss Dupree sighed. "Soft, like candlelight…romantic."

Eb clanged his spoon against his cereal bowl. "You take your glasses off and Mr. Perry has hair, right?" It was mean, but he still hadn't heard from Lisa, and Miss Dupree had been seeing a lot of Mr. Perry.

Miss Dupree sailed right over his mean comment, as if she couldn't hear him. "Without my glasses, the window over the sink sparkles, and then there are those pretty red flowers."

"They're not flowers," Eb grumbled. "They're letters on the side of a cable truck."

"They're prettier as flowers." She leaned her cheek on her hand and smiled at the cable truck letters. A bouquet of real flowers from Mr. Perry sat in the middle of the breakfast table. Lately, everything in her life seemed to be turning into flowers.

Someone knocked on the front door. "Oh dear." Her hands shot up to her hair, which wasn't combed yet. "But it couldn't be him. He always calls first." She stood up to answer the door.

She put out a hand and drifted into the living room. We heard her run into the couch. Somehow, she made it to the front door. "Yes?" she said. She couldn't tell who anyone was without her glasses.

"I'm sorry to bother you so early, Miss Dupree." It was Jemmie's voice. "Here's your paper. Could I talk to Anna or Eb a minute?"

"I'm not running!" Eb yelled from the table. I dashed to the front room.

Jemmie stuck her head around Miss Dupree, who was trying to decipher the headlines. "We already ran," she called. "While you were in dreamland. Hi, Anna."

Miss Dupree held the paper close, then far. She shook her head and went to find her glasses.

I slid out the door. "Hi, Jemmie." We leaned against the wall of the house. Her sneakers were soaked with dew from the grass.

"Listen. Ben said to tell you, there's a bike race at nine. Do you and Eb wanna go?"

"We don't have bikes."

"Forget the bikes. The guys just want an audience, someone to break their necks for. Cass and me'll stop by and get you, okay?"

"Okay."

She pushed off the wall and jumped over the three steps. I watched her run until she turned the corner. She had come over just to invite us. *Us.*

"What did *she* want?" Eb was mushing his cereal with the back of his spoon.

"She wants us to go to a bike race," I whispered.

"No way, I'm not racing." He hadn't forgotten the mountains and gorges of the Race-A-Rama.

"They just want us to watch."

"Nuh-uh. Remember last time Jemmie said I could watch? Asthma-city."

But he must have changed his mind. He stood up as soon as we heard the slap of sneakers on the walk.

"Gotta hustle," Jemmie called, knocking once on the screen door. "Race starts in five minutes."

Eb checked to be sure he had his inhaler, then grabbed his Game

Boy and stuffed it in his pocket. It only took a second, but when we popped out the door, the girls were already a block away.

"Can't they walk?" Eb grumbled as we followed at a slow trot. "Can't they ever just walk like normal people?"

We cut through the woods, but when we got to the end of the path Justin was blocking the way.

"You got tickets?"

"Tickets?" Cass shook her bangs out of her eyes.

Justin's feet were spread, his silver-taped sneakers planted. "Fifty cents."

"We don't have any money on us," Cass said.

"Get some."

"You're kidding," Jemmie said. "Fifty cents to watch a bunch of boys fall off bikes? I don't think so." She turned her back but she didn't walk away.

"Fine with me," Justin replied. He didn't walk away either.

"Whatever." Eb pulled out his game and sat down on the ground.

Justin gazed over our heads. "I *could* make it a quarter."

Cody trotted up. "We have to pay? I don't have any money."

"Nobody has money." Cass put her arm around Cody's neck and leaned him against her.

I peered around Justin. I spotted five boys and several bikes scattered on the glaring white sand in front of the track. I recognized Clay by his red hair and the electric blue bike leaning against his hip. Ben's bike was flipped onto its seat and handlebars. He dripped a little oil on the chain, then cranked the pedals. "Who are those other three boys?" I asked Jemmie.

She glanced over her shoulder. "The tall black guy is Leroy. The short fat one's his brother, Jahmal. The little peanut of a kid with the rainbow helmet is called the Weeble. I don't know his real name."

"Hey, Ben," Cody yelled. "Can you give us money for tickets?"

Ben spun the pedals. "Let 'em in, Justin."

"But they don't wanna pay," Justin shouted back.

"I said let 'em in."

"And how are we gonna raise money if we let everyone in free?"

"What do we need money for?"

"What do we need money for?" Justin repeated. "What do we need money for?" He turned and shouted, "We're knockin' ourselves out here, Ben! Wouldn't hurt to take in a little cash." He motioned us to follow. "Come on." He led us across the hot sand, then pointed. "Audience over there." Not counting the two dogs that were already there, we were the whole audience.

The dogs were curled up in chairs at the edge of the track. The chairs were real, not the folding kind, but actual furniture, like out of a house. "Where'd you guys get this armchair?" Jemmie asked, nudging the brown dog out of it.

"Somebody dumped it on Tyson Street," Ben said. "We dragged it over."

Jemmie squeezed her fingers between the cushions and felt around. "Hey, Justin, here's your quarter. Catch." She tossed a coin at him. He reached out to catch it but it bounced off his arm. He left it lying on the ground.

Jemmie and Cass shared the armchair, resting their feet on the brown dog. Cass patted the arm of the chair. "Come on up, Cody." Cody swooped down on the quarter, stuck it in his pocket, then climbed up.

The beanbag chair the second dog was lying on had little round burn marks on its plastic leather. Eb climbed in, trying not to disturb the dog. "Whose dogs?" he asked, patting the black dog's head.

"Nobody's. They belong to themselves," said Jemmie.

"No, they don't," said Cass. "They're the Cortezes' dogs, Fran and Blackie. They just *think* they belong to themselves."

The only chair that was left had a big gash in the seat. I got that one.

Ben yelled, "Line up!" The five other racers formed a wavy row: Clay first, then Justin and the two brothers, Leroy and Jahmal. At the far end stood the Weeble, bike between his legs, seat jamming him in the back. He looked as if he had borrowed his dad's bike. Ben's bike was still upside down, wheel turning slowly.

"Final instructions." Ben paced back and forth. "Do your best, but don't get hurt." He stopped and looked at each of the boys. "Remember, if you get hurt, I'll kill you."

"Yeah, yeah," said Clay. "Can we get started already?"

Ben stared him down, then went back to pacing. "Now, we're going to do the track three times. When you get to the tombstones, you don't have to jump. Unless you're *sure* you can make it, you ride around it, understand?"

"We understand," said Clay. "We get hurt, you kill us. Come *on*."

But the other riders gazed at that final jump, mouths open. The tombstones was the widest, and deepest, and meanest hole on the course. I had been to the bottom of it. I knew personally that it went halfway to China. "See the writing?" Ben asked. Someone had written R.I.P. on both of the hole's steep ramps.

"We get it," Clay said. "Rest In Pieces."

Ben looked from rider to rider. "And everybody wears a helmet."

"No fair," Clay protested. "You're infringing on my rights."

"*Everybody* wears a helmet."

Ben waited for Clay to put his helmet on, then flipped his own bike back over and walked it to the end of the line. "Hey, Cody?" He threw a leg over the bike. "You think you could holler ready, set, go?"

Cody stood on the arm of the chair. "Ready!..." He yelled so loud he scared the birds off the wires. "Set!..." He was getting louder. "GO!"

The six bikes wobbled. It was hard to get traction in the loose sand, so the start was slow. But the bikers quickly picked up speed. Cass grabbed the brown dog's collar. "They don't need you in the race, Fran."

The first hurdle was only a foot and a half wide—a little puddle jump. One after another the bikes hopped it, *blip, blip, blip*. Clay was in the lead.

The second jump came after a sharp, leaning turn. Riders had to jerk their bikes up fast and pedal hard to make it. At the last instant the Weeble lost control, missed the jump, and careened off the track. He slid into the tall grass, one leg under the bike. Jemmie sprang out of her chair, yelling, "Weeble down!"

Ben slowed and turned in his seat. "Is he okay?"

Jemmie helped the kid up. "Scraped a little, but not bad." While she dusted the sand off him, Ben caught back up with the pack. Jemmie helped the Weeble stand his bike up. When he was on it, she put one hand on the bike seat and the other on the handlebars and ran alongside him. "You go, Weeb!" And she shoved him back into the race.

The fastest riders had reached the double jump. A racer could barely set his wheels down before he had to jerk the bike up between his knees for the second hop. Clay did it, *thwump, thwump,* then reared his bike up and raised a fist. "Yes!" he shouted. Ben was right behind him.

It was easy to see that Clay and Ben were better than the other boys. Both were fast, both made the jumps. But Clay made a big show out of each jump. He let out a whoop when he landed; he sprayed sand on the turns. Ben was different: quick and quiet. He didn't make his jumps any bigger than he had to. He hit the far side of each hole clean. It didn't seem fair, but he also had to keep an eye on the other riders. "Straighten up, Jahmal, straighten up!" he yelled. "You can do it, Weeb!"

He was watching Leroy when he and Clay made the turn for the tombstones. "Pay attention, Ben!" Cass shouted. He grinned, stood on his pedals and pumped hard. They hit the ramp, Clay first, Ben right behind. They pulled up on their handlebars. Standing on their pedals, the boys sailed across the hole, a band of light beneath their wheels.

Justin came next. He didn't sail as high and his back wheel caught on the lip of the hole when he landed. The bike came to a dead stop. Justin didn't. He ran smack into the handlebars.

"Bet that hurt," Jemmie said.

Leroy, the older of the brothers, made the jump without a hitch, then looked back in surprise. At the last second, Jahmal skirted the left edge of the hole. The Weeble gave it a wide berth on the right. "One lap down," Ben yelled, encouraging the stragglers.

They lapped the course again, but only Ben and Clay attempted all the jumps. Clay hollered as he cleared the tombstones by an even wider margin. "Yes!" He held his arms up over his head.

Cass crossed her legs and ticked a bare foot up and down. "Isn't *he* just in love with himself?"

Ben, who was right behind Clay, made the jump with the bike so low there was no bounce when he landed.

The other riders went around the tombstones without even looking, as if ignoring it meant they hadn't chickened out.

"It's Ben and Clay now," said Jemmie, pulling her feet up into the chair. "And Clay's gonna take it."

"Jemmie!" Cass wailed. "How can you even say that?"

Clay had two bright splotches of pink on his cheeks. Trickles of sweat ran down his neck. His helmet sat on the back of his head as if his springy red hair had pushed it out of the way. "Eat my dust, suckers! One more lap and I'm King of the Race-A-Rama!"

I whispered, "Go, Ben!"

As if Ben had heard me, he hunkered down and pedaled. They hit the first jump at the same second. Clay couldn't hotdog anymore, not if he wanted to beat Ben Floyd. They hopped over that first small ditch, then leaned into the turn so fast their wheels should have skidded out from under them. Both held on. Clay had to put a foot down, but in a second he was pumping like mad to catch Ben.

Cass almost knocked Cody off the arm of the chair as she jumped up and stood on the seat. "Come on, Ben!" But Clay was shaving the distance between them. He lifted into the double jump an instant after Ben. When they landed, they were dead even. There was just a hand's width of light between them as they broke for the tombstones.

"No!" Jemmie jumped up too. "They better get some space between 'em before that jump!"

Both boys were curled down low, eyes barely higher than their handlebars. The muscles in their necks strained. They stood on their pedals, and Clay surged ahead. Ben never took his eyes off the ramp. If Clay was watching anything, it was Ben. When he was half a length ahead, Clay turned and waved at Ben. And that's when he hit the ramp. He must have realized it when his bike angled up. He clamped his legs and tried to lift.

The crash seemed to take forever. Ben flew across the pit. He was looking back over his shoulder when Clay smashed into the second tombstone. With the clank of gears, Clay and the bike disappeared.

We heard a dull thud, then a moan.

We bailed out of our chairs. Ben skidded to a stop and dropped his bike. Running toward the tombstones, we heard a terrible groan from the pit. Ben jumped into the hole. The rest of us threw ourselves down around the edge of the pit just as Ben pulled the bike off Clay.

"Give it here," said Leroy, hanging his arms down to take it. When Leroy dragged the bike out of the pit, its handlebars were twisted sideways. He had to walk it away with just the back tire on the ground.

The sand burned our bare legs as we lay looking into the hole, but no one got up.

"Oh my gosh, blood," Cody whispered.

The front of Clay's white T-shirt was redder than his hair. The sand of the tombstones was sprayed with blood.

As Ben dragged Clay by the armpits, Clay's sneaker heels gouged tracks in the sand. When he had him propped against the wall, Ben reached back and pulled his own T-shirt off. "Where's the cut, Clay? Show me." He wadded up his shirt and swiped at the spots of blood, trying to figure out where it was coming from. But each time he pulled the shirt back, there was just skin, no cut. "Talk to me, Clay."

Cass twisted a loose strand of hair around her finger. "Want us to run for help, Ben?"

"No," Clay blubbered. "They'll see the track."

Ben asked, "Where are you hurt, then?"

"His nose," Cody said.

"What?"

"The blood's coming all out his nose."

Ben blotted Clay's nose with his shirt, then pulled the shirt away. In a second, fresh blood ran down Clay's upper lip.

"See what I mean?" Cody said. "It's a gusher."

Clay opened his eyes and grinned. "Really had you going, didn't I?"

"You mean all you have's a bloody nose?" Ben made a fist like he was going to give Clay something worse. Blood dribbled off Clay's chin. "Here," Ben tossed him the shirt. "Pinch the end of your nose with this."

"This shirt stinks like BO," said Clay, but he pinched his nose with it anyway. Holding his nose he sounded funny. "I hid by dose on de handlebars," he mumbled.

"You're sure you didn't break anything?"

"I don' tink so."

"Better check." Ben put a hand under Clay's arm and lifted. "Now walk around."

But when Clay saw all the blood on the ground, he sat down again. "I'm bweeding to det!"

"That's it," Ben said. "We're coming out here with shovels tomorrow, fill the whole thing in. It's too dangerous."

"Doe way!" said Clay. "It took us a ho' week to dig it."

Ben scuffed sand over some blood. "We'll have to fill it in anyway when you tell your folks."

Clay whipped the shirt off his face. "Telling? Who's telling? I won't. How about you guys?" He looked up at each of us around the edge of the hole. "Cody?"

"Not me," Cody said.

We all shook our heads no.

"Would you hold your nose? You're leaking again," Ben said. "So, if you weren't racing, how'd you get the bloody nose?"

Clay pinched his nose again. "Basketbaw in de face?"

Ben pulled Clay to his feet. "Could work." He laced his fingers together and gave Clay a boost. We grabbed his arms and dragged him up. More wall crumbled as Clay crawled over the edge. "You guys see that he gets home," Ben said. "I'll fix the bike and cover the blood."

Walking home, Clay talked about making the tombstones bigger, deeper.

"Sounds like he injured his one working brain cell," Eb mumbled.

Chapter Ten

LISTENING

When we got back from the track, Miss Dupree was putting new pictures in the blue Likely Prospects books. Photos with note cards clipped to them were lined up on the kitchen table.

Eb picked one up and read, "Matt, forty-eight, likes dancing, Chinese food, and romantic nights in front of the fire." He staggered, then grabbed the edge of the table. "I think I'm gonna hurl."

"Eb?" Miss Dupree looked at him until he met her eyes. "Your mother called."

"She did?" He dropped Mr. Likes-to-Dance on the floor. "Can I call her? Is Eddie's phone hooked up?"

"She's in a new place, with a new number. She'll call you."

Eb stood stock still. "A new place," he whispered. "A new number!" He began to do a jerky dance. "New number, new place. She finally did it! She dumped Eddie. I'm going home."

"Don't get your hopes up," Miss Dupree called as he dashed off to his room. "I'm afraid she didn't say anything about coming to get you."

"Oh, like she'd tell *you*." His bedroom door slammed.

Eb was so sure about the new place that he packed his bag and dragged it to the front door. After that he wouldn't leave the house for anything. We drew pictures and watched TV all afternoon and listened for the phone.

It rang. Eb answered. It was someone collecting money for the fire department.

It rang again. Eb answered. It was Mrs. Riley inviting us to a foster picnic. "No thanks," Eb told her. "I won't be foster by then." He hung up. "'What do you mean by that, Eb?'" he said, imitating her voice. "'This is the first I've heard about it.'"

The afternoon passed without a call from Eb's mother. We ate supper, did dishes. Still no call. Miss Dupree let us stay up for *Star Trek: Voyager.*

"I love this one," Eb said as *Voyager* began. "Tuvoc gets melded with Neelix to form Tuvix and everyone likes the half-and-half guy better." But he wasn't paying attention to *Voyager.* He was listening for the phone.

He got up once, as if he was going to the bathroom, but when I turned around and looked in the kitchen he had the phone up to his ear. As soon as he knew it was working, he slammed it back down. He didn't want his mom to get a busy signal.

He was back on the couch when the phone rang. "Got it!" he yelled, sprinting for the kitchen. It only got out half a ring before Eb snatched it off its cradle. "Hello?" As he listened his face fell. "For you, Anna." He held the phone out. "Hurry up."

"Hello?"

"Hey, kid."

"Uncle Charles!"

"Who else? Listen, I was just sitting here, wondering how you're doing, so I thought I'd check."

"I'm fine. Where are you, home? I mean your new home? Are you back from Omaha?"

"Omaha was what, last week? I forget. I'm in Phoenix now. There's a palm tree outside my motel window. They feeding you okay?"

"They're feeding me fine." I turned, wrapping the cord around myself. I didn't want to watch Eb run his finger across his throat, signaling me to cut it short. "How are Mark and Macy? Have you talked to them?"

"Talked to them last night. Your cousins are good. Macy lost a front tooth."

"It was getting loose."

In his motel room in Phoenix, my uncle sighed.

"She kept making me wiggle it." There was a pause while we both imagined Macy with a gap in her grin. "And how's Aunt Eva?"

"Nothing but a stake through the heart would hurt that woman."

"Should you say that to me?" I was thinking about Mark and Macy. If he said it to me, he might say it to them too.

My uncle sighed again. "Probably not, kid."

I could hear Eb begging Miss Dupree to make me get off the phone. But I knew we wouldn't talk long. Uncle Charles is a doer, not a talker. If I was with him we'd play a game of Clue or something.

"Just thought I'd check on you," he said, with that about-to-hang-up sound in his voice. "Nice talking to you, kid."

"Nice talking to you too. Wait, give me your number at the new apartment." I wrote his number down on a paper napkin and stuffed it in my pocket. "Say hi to Mark and Macy when you see them, okay? Say hi to Aunt Eva." I hung up.

"About time," Eb said.

We all went back to watching *Voyager* and listening for the phone. The show was almost over. Tuvoc and Neelix got unmelded. The eleven o'clock news came on. It was time for bed. Miss Dupree gave Eb a hug. He didn't hug back, but he didn't fight it. "She didn't call," he said, leaning against her.

"Maybe she got busy." Miss Dupree stroked his back.

Eb's back stiffened. "How hard is it to pick up a phone and make a call?" He pulled away.

Dragging his suitcase back to his room, Eb looked smaller than usual. When the door closed behind him, Miss Dupree and I hugged each other. "That poor boy."

"I can't stand his mother," I said into the front of her shirt.

She held me at arms' length. "You shouldn't say that. Maybe if you—"

"I still wouldn't like her." His stupid mother—the one who couldn't bother to give him more than a two letter name, the one who wouldn't waste a ten-minute call on him—how could Eb miss her?

I missed my family too—Mark and Macy and my shouting aunt and uncle—but there was a difference. I *knew* that my family was broken and that it would never be put back together.

Chapter Eleven

"EARTH TO SAM MILLER"

When Eb didn't come to breakfast the next morning, we thought he was just sleeping late. "Let him," Miss Dupree said. "He's probably all worn out." After I finished my cereal, I listened outside his door, but I didn't hear a thing.

He still hadn't come out when the first client arrived at ten. After Miss Dupree and the woman sat on the sofa for the preliminary interview, Miss Dupree walked the new client into the office. "And now we'll make your video." The office door closed behind them.

I went into the pink room to get Eb up. All I found was a crumple of sheets, no Eb. Also missing were his high-tops and Game Boy, and my explorer's notebook. I looked for a note, but Eb was not a note leaver.

I sat on the edge of the bed and shook. *I should tell Miss Dupree,* I thought. *And then?* And then she would call Mrs. Riley and Mrs. Riley would call the police. Then everything would crumble.

I walked to the office door.

"Just relax," I heard Miss Dupree say. "Your hair looks fine."

I touched the door with my knuckles, then stopped. How far could Eb go? He hated to walk and he had no money. I left a note. *Gone out. Anna.* It was the truth, but I felt like a liar. If something happened to Eb, it would be my fault for not telling Miss Dupree. I skinned out the front door, closing it quietly.

It was only ten-thirty and it was already a temperature that would make Eb yearn for air-conditioned comfort. *Good,* I thought. *Eb won't go far on a hot day. Eb hates hot.*

I walked slowly, wondering where a kid with no money, one who didn't like to walk, would go on a hot day.

Maybe he felt like talking. But who would he talk to? Eb didn't know anybody, didn't trust anybody. But there was one person, someone like him.... I walked faster.

Fran and Blackie trotted up. They walked with me, one on either side. I felt better with them along, but they turned back as soon as we reached Roberts Avenue. Even the dogs knew that Roberts was the edge of the neighborhood.

I watched them trot away, Blackie's brush tail waving. Then I crossed the street and stepped into the woods.

The tricycle lay on its other side, as if someone had tried it out, then tipped it over again. As I got closer to Mr. Miller's spot, I became less sure that Eb was there. I could see the chair, but it seemed to be empty. No top of the head showed over the back. No one was talking.

Then I heard a rattly wheeze coming from the chair. It was nothing like the clatter of Mr. Miller's snore. It was the sound of a boy with asthma.

I tiptoed up to the chair and looked around the side. Eb was slumped over, his face scrunched against the ratty upholstery. The dirty cheek facing me had a tear track down it. His legs and arms were covered with mosquito bites. I whispered, "You're a sorry sight, Eb Gramlich." My grandmother would have said that if she had seen him.

The only good part was that, asleep, he wasn't feeling bad about Lisa. The bad feeling would be waiting for him when he woke up. It would jump right on him, but for now it couldn't touch him.

I slid out the bottom drawer of the dresser, retrieved the blanket, and spread it on the ground. I carefully slipped my explorer's notebook out of his lap and sat down. The book fell open to the first page that we'd done together. There was Eb's sea serpent. THIS WAY BE MONSTERS, he had written. I looked over at him, hoping he was dreaming a good dream. One without monsters.

A train whistled in the distance, but Eb didn't stir. The rumble got louder and louder. I could feel the vibration of the passing train right through the ground, but Eb kept on sleeping. When it seemed like it couldn't get any louder, the pitch of the train's whistle started to go down, and I knew it had passed.

"That boy could sleep through mortar fire," said a raspy voice. I whipped around. Mr. Miller stood behind me, leaves in his beard, one bootlace dragging. He lowered himself down to the blanket with a grimace, then stared at me. "Do I know you?" He smelled like cigarettes and old vegetables.

"Yes, Mr. Miller. We brought you cake. I'm Anna, that's Eb."

"Funny name, Eb. What's it short for?"

"His name's just Eb."

He eyed me suspiciously. "You don't have any of that once-in-a-blue-moon cake with you, do you?"

"No, sir." If he didn't remember us, he remembered the cake.

"That's too bad."

I was scared sitting so close to him. Any little noise from the woods made him jump and jerk around to see what was coming. "So, that's Eb," he said, staring at him. "What's he doing in my chair?"

I told him about Eb's mom, and about the fact that she didn't call.

"A real shame," he said. "Out of everything, a kid should be able to count on his mother. But that don't explain why he's here."

"I think he figured that if his mom doesn't want him he could go off and live on his own the way you do."

"Is he nuts?" He spat a milky glob on the ground. "You gotta have skills if you want to bivouac. I was trained by the U.S. Army. I know how to live rough. Just look at him, sleeping like a baby. You have to keep one eye open. Else-wise Charlie can sneak up on you."

"Who's Charlie?" I asked, and I began looking around too. Were there other people living in the woods?

"You know…Charlie." He lowered his voice. "Viet Cong. Charlie sneaks up on you, and you wake up dead."

The clock in his head was running backward today. Back to the Vietnam War where they called the enemy Charlie. My uncle had a cousin who got killed there. Uncle Charles was only a little boy, but after he heard about his cousin getting killed by Charlie, he wouldn't let anyone call him Charlie anymore. I whispered, "Charlie won't get you here, Mr. Miller. That was a long time ago."

He rubbed the back of his neck. "I know that," he said, like his brain hadn't stuttered on him. "But there's other things, like taking a nap in a crazy old man's chair. Now does that sound smart to you?"

"I'll wake him up."

"Nah, that's okay." Eb's eyelids fluttered. He twitched and sighed. Mr. Miller shook his head. "Looks like a dog dreaming about chasing rabbits, don't he?"

Eb was about to wake up, but he was fighting it. Wherever he was, it was a better place than where he would be when he woke up. When he woke up, he'd be back in his own life. He gave one last long wheeze and opened his eyes. "What're you two staring at?"

"I don't know about her," Mr. Miller said, "but I got my eye on a kid who stole my chair."

"Sorry," Eb mumbled, and he climbed out of the chair. The cheek that had been smashed into the upholstery was pink. His hair was all crushed and shiny on that side. As Eb stumbled around trying to get his legs to work, Mr. Miller fell into the chair.

I started to stand so the two of us could go, but Eb flopped down on the blanket.

"So, you think you can live in the woods?" Mr. Miller said. Eb opened his mouth to answer but Mr. Miller cut him off. "You got a soft bed, a roof, hot meals. Don't blow it. You live out here, you gotta be tough. There's wind and bugs, not to mention rain."

"But you have a tarp—"

"Son, you ever sit under a sheet of plastic? You know how sweaty you can get under a sheet of plastic, or how cold if it's wintertime? Freeze your tail off."

"Isn't there a homeless shelter?" I asked.

"Shelter," Mr. Miller snorted. "Sure there's a shelter, but it's way-the-heck-and-gone down Tennessee Street. Like to see *you* walk it. And first thing in the morning, they put you back out, no matter what the weather is. No sir, living rough is no walk in the park."

Eb leaned toward him. "Why do you do it then?"

"I can't stand people. Have as little to do with them as I can."

"Sorry if we're bothering you," Eb said, pulling back.

Mr. Miller rubbed at a stain on the arm of his chair. "Oh, you're not too bad."

And Eb leaned forward again. "We're not?"

"I've seen worse. Can't stand the sight of most people. Hate the way they run their mouths like they can't breathe without talking. It's bad enough I have this thing in my head, talking, talking, talking all the time." He whacked himself in the temple, then muttered, "Earth to Sam Miller. Very funny."

"Are they talking to you right now?" Eb asked.

"Oh, they talk all the time, Cosgrove. You can't imagine. Bet it's pretty peaceful where you are. Real peaceful."

I wondered where he thought Cosgrove was. Cosgrove-Eb wasn't more than three feet away from him.

"Between the voices and the static, quiet means a lot to me," he said. "Best I can do is stay away from people. Lucky thing there are places nobody cares about, throwaway places like this one." He cleared his throat and spat over the arm of the chair. "In general, people like to stay on roads, walk on sidewalks, follow signs. They're not over-curious."

"You're right," I blurted out. "Most people walk around with their eyes shut."

"No sense of adventure!" he agreed. "They clump together like a bunch of herd animals." Dust rose when he brought a fist down on the chair arm. Suddenly he cocked his head as if he was listening. He hummed a few notes. "Darn, I hate it when they play music."

"The government's playing music in your head?" Eb asked.

"A marching band. Marches, that's all they ever play." Mr. Miller beat time on the chair arm. "Lord, look out, here come the drums." He covered his ears and winced, trying to muffle a noise that came from inside his own head.

"Come on, Eb," I said softly. "Let's go home. I'll fix you something to eat."

For a second I thought he was going to say that he wanted to stay. But he couldn't. This throwaway place belonged to Mr. Miller.

"Sorry about using your chair," Eb said.

"Oh, that's okay. Watch your back, Cosgrove. But maybe you don't have to do that anymore. I mean, what else could happen to you, right?"

"There's still a few things," Eb said.

As we walked away we could hear Mr. Miller talking back to the voice in his head. "No need to tell me twice. I got it the first time."

Miss Dupree was reading a magazine on the couch when we walked inside. "Eb!" I was afraid she was going to swoop down and plant a display of affection on him, or say how sorry she was that his mother hadn't called—something that would send him out looking for a throwaway place of his own. But she restrained herself. "Did you two have a nice walk?"

Eb shrugged.

"I was wondering, would you like to go to the mall?"

"The mall?" Eb sat down next to her. "You mean like, the mall?"

"I mean exactly like the mall. I don't have anyone scheduled for the rest of the day. We could have some fun, eat lunch, maybe see a movie."

"Could we stop at a store with video games?" he asked. "Just to look, I mean?"

"I don't see why not. We have the whole afternoon." She touched him, very lightly, on the shoulder. He stiffened, but he didn't pull away.

Chapter Twelve

THE MOST DANGEROUS
THING IN THE WOODS

The next morning Eb wanted to go back to the mall, but Miss Dupree had to work. "You could drop us off," he said. "Lisa used to do that sometimes."

"It's not safe," Miss Dupree replied, then disappeared into her office.

Eb snapped his fingers. "Listen, Anna. I just had a great idea, brilliant—foster parents who work at the mall! We'd get into movies free, get free stuff at the food court. And there are trees in the mall, so we'd never have to go out in the heat again."

"Those are indoor trees, Eb. Some of them are fake."

"Who cares? How about if our foster dad was a security guard? Then we could stay when they closed for the night. We'd cruise around, with the place all to ourselves. When we got tired we could crawl into a couple of the beds at Sears."

"Great plan, Eb."

But Eb was stuck with a long, boring day in the real world. And after a while we went out into the usual heat. We found Miss Johnette in front of our house walking Gregor. "Greg's about had it," she said. "You two want to come home with me for some lemonade?"

"It's too hot to live," Eb said. "And you don't air-condition." But he followed her. I knew Eb would never turn down the possibility of junk food—there had to be some to go with the lemonade—and I would never turn down a chance to look at her specimens.

I said hi to Charlotte, then ducked under her web.

It wasn't that hot in the house. Miss Johnette had fans going. Gregor had one all to himself. Eb sat on the kitchen floor with him and they shared the breeze.

I tried to sit, but all the chairs at the table were full. Miss Johnette wrapped her arms around the open carton that sat on the nearest chair. It was heavy, even for Miss Johnette. All she did was lower it to the floor. I sat down and peered into the box. "What are those?"

"Fossils," she said, clearing a chair for herself. "And a lot of things that look like fossils but probably aren't. I haven't had a chance to sort them yet."

"Can I give it a try?" I was itching to touch the things in the box.

"Help yourself," she said, going to the cupboard. "What do you think? Is it too early for peanut butter cups?"

"Never," said Eb, and she dropped a package in his lap.

I put two knobby things from the box side by side on the table. "Where'd you get these?"

"I picked them up hiking, or when I was out in the canoe."

I reached into the fossil box and picked up a flat rectangle with a raised tab in the middle. "What's this?"

"An alligator scute." She took a bite of candy.

"What's a scute?"

"It's a plate from the gator's back—one of the bumps. Gators haven't changed much since day one. The plates on their backs are still pretty much the same, only this one's fossilized." She picked it up and knocked it against another fossil. It clinked like glass.

The next fossil I pulled out covered my whole hand. "What's this? It looks like icicles."

"So that's where that got off to," she said. "Boy, am I glad to see that one. That's a mastodon tooth. I did a dance when I found it, didn't I, Greg?" Greg opened one eye, then let the lid slide shut again. She took the fossil and blew the dust off. "The parts that look like icicles are the roots." She passed the fossil to Eb. He weighed it in his hand, then tried to show it to the dog, but Greg was asleep.

For a while I ate candy and sorted, making piles of things that looked alike. The biggest pile was a bunch of lumpy rocks. "What are these?"

"Nothing, probably. One or two of them could be coprolites." She picked one up and rolled it over in her fingers. "This one looks promising."

She tossed it to Eb, who rolled it in his fingers too. "A coprolite, huh? What's a coprolite?"

"Fossilized poop."

"Jeez!" He threw it back at her and wiped his hands on his shorts. "It should be called a *poop*rolite."

Miss Johnette laughed. "Nothing to worry about, Eb, it's a rock now."

"Yeah, but it didn't used to be." He stood and pointed at another lump, being careful not to touch it. "What's that one? Dinosaur snot?" He slid the explorer's notebook out of the waist of his shorts and put it on the table. "It was cutting into my stomach," he said, helping himself to another pack of candy before sitting back down on the floor.

"'Explorer's Notebook,'" Miss Johnette read. "Mind if I take a look?"

Eb and I both said, "Go ahead."

The first page showed the area around Aunt Betsy and Uncle Harry's, the first place I lived after my grandmother died. The way I made maps—which was the right way—took forever. I paced everything off. That map had every house on it—even the doghouses.

"Anna, I sure could use you on field trips," Miss Johnette said. "I always get lost."

"I'm available any time before August twenty-eighth. That's when school starts."

"I'm available until then too," she said turning the pages slowly. "What are these maps of?"

"Places I've lived in the last four years."

"You've lived a lot of places, Anna. The maps get better as they go along."

"In each place I was older."

Even the not-so-good maps had taken me a long time to do. In my mind, I could still walk around those neighborhoods I'd never see again. The only place I never drew a map of was my grandmother's. I didn't think I'd need to remember it. I thought I'd never leave.

Miss Johnette whistled between her teeth. "Would you look at this." She had come to page one of Eb's map.

"That one's Eb's," I said. "It's of here," I added, in case she couldn't tell.

With one elbow on either side of the notebook she rested her chin in her hands. Eb's map was like a spill that had spread over six pages. Roads and houses had been drawn any way they would fit. Nothing connected. Eb covered mistakes with made-up trees. The only way to correct Eb's map would have been to start over. I could have taught him the right way, but you couldn't tell Eb how to do anything.

Still, in its own way, Eb's map was better. You couldn't use it to get anywhere, but you sure could look at it for a long time.

"Hey," Miss Johnette said. "Aren't these the Cortezes' dogs, Fran and Blackie?" The dogs were trotting down the street. "And there's that track Ben and the boys dug."

Eb and I glanced at each other. How did she know about the Race-A-Rama? In Eb's drawing it was race day, the dramatic finish. Clay was at the bottom of the pit.

Miss Johnette laughed. "Thanks for putting me on the map, Eb." She had just seen herself picking up trash.

Eb stood beside her chair. "Remember the night Ben tried to burn his butt off with the Roman candle?"

"I must've missed that one."

He turned the page, and there was Magnolia Way. Ben's fireworks display was going full tilt. Cass and Jemmie were there, holding sparklers. (They were also watching the race and running at the track.) Mr. Miller sat in his chair in the woods, a cloud of notes around his head. All the things we had seen or done since coming to Miss Dupree's were on Eb's map, everything happening all at once.

"You're an artist, Eb," said Miss Johnette. "Maybe you'll be a professional someday."

"Like, get paid to draw?"

"Like, sure. Why not?"

"I'll blow it—lose my hands in an accident or something."

"Then you'll hold the pencil in your teeth. The talent is in your head, not your hands."

"See up here?" He put his finger on a spot in the notebook where there were no dogs or kids or trees. "We haven't been over there yet."

I tried to figure out where "over there" was in the real world, but too many things were crammed in, falling all over each other, getting in the wrong places.

But Miss Johnette knew right where it was. "That's the other side of Rankin," she said. "What's missing is my woods. You want to see them? It isn't far."

Eb had been yearning for an air-conditioned mall; instead he was being offered a walk in the heat to see another woods, one that probably didn't even have a guy living in them. "Yeah, I guess," he said without much enthusiasm.

"Great!" Miss Johnette separated the wrapper and the little piece of cardboard from her peanut butter cups. The wrapper went into the trash and the cardboard into the recycle box. When Eb threw both parts of his package in the trash, she made him fish the cardboard out.

He stared at that little piece of cardboard, turned it over, then held it out. "You're worried about *this?*"

Miss Johnette grabbed a canteen off a hook on the wall. "Just do it, Eb." She held the canteen under the tap. "Do it so your kids won't to be up to their butts in your trash, okay?"

He put the scrap of cardboard on the recycle pile. "Are you happy now?"

"Thanks, Eb. You're a hero." She screwed the cap on the canteen and dropped the strap over his shoulder. "Come on campers, let's hit the trail." She clicked her tongue. "Hey, Greg. Stir your old bones."

Gregor raised one eyebrow, then the other. He let out a shuddery sigh, and closed his eyes again. She knelt and put a hand on his head. Miss Johnette's hands were rough and strong looking—if you had a jar you couldn't open, you'd hand it to her—but she patted Gregor gently and in a moment he was asleep. "I guess one walk's all he's got in him these days."

~

A truck passed us as we stood on Rankin Avenue, looking into the woods. The hot wind blew my hair across my face. "It's a miracle this is still here," Miss Johnette said. "A woods within the city limits. At one edge there's even a swamp."

"Oh, goody," Eb said. "Snakes and mosquitoes."

"You'll like it, Eb, come on."

"I don't know about this nature stuff," he complained, following her in.

The air was cooler in the woods, better smelling. I took a deep breath.

Miss Johnette picked up a stick and swept some vines out of the way. "There are miles and miles of woods around Tallahassee." She pushed back brambles with her stick. "Flying into the city you see nothing but trees below. But in a lot of places it's like you're looking at corduroy. The pines are planted in big long rows."

"Somebody plants pine trees?" Eb asked.

"The paper companies. The trees are a crop, like cotton or corn. When they're big enough, the companies chop them all down and start again." She looked around. "A forest is so much more than rows of trees. Now *this* is the real deal." She plucked a shiny leaf and turned it over to show us the velvet on the underside. "Magnolia," she said. Eb ran a finger over the velvety side. When she wasn't looking, he put the leaf in his pocket.

"Is that poison ivy?" I asked, pointing out a vine that was growing up a tree.

"That's right." She kept on walking.

Eb cringed. "Man, oh man, am I allergic. Get me out of here."

"Just follow the rule, 'leaves of three, don't touch me.' You'll be fine."

"Yeah, but—"

"Come on, Eb." She held a branch back for us. "Every living thing has a little something extra to help it survive. Poison ivy makes its enemies itch. You, oh human kid, have a brain and eyes. Use them."

He scuffed along after her. "Isn't there some chemical that can wipe out poison ivy?"

"Oh, probably." She jumped over a stump. "But poison ivy feeds the birds. You ever notice the way the leaves turn bright red in the fall? The plant is just advertising that its berries are ripe. It's telling the birds to come and get it."

"So, everything's good for something, according to you? Like if a tiger came running along right now and grabbed you by the throat that would be okay with you?"

"Tigers aren't exactly native to north Florida, Eb."

"But if they were—"

"If they were, I'd learn their habits and stay out of their way. The most dangerous thing in this woods right now is us."

"Us?"

"Sure. Humans turn forests into parking lots. Walk this way," she said.

Eb scratched his knee. "What's over there? More trees?"

"Wait around for twenty years and there will be." She led us to a clearing where the sun beat down on a huge fallen tree. "A few weeks ago this big old oak just gave up the ghost and fell. But nature doesn't waste any time." Miss Johnette knelt and brushed her hand across the tops of the seedlings that had sprung up around the fallen tree. "There's a race going on here. When it's all over, there'll be a new big tree where the old one was. Right now a couple of hundred trees are competing for the spot."

Eb and I sat down on the log.

"I'll bet on that one." Eb pointed to one that was a little taller than the others.

"We'll come back in a week or two, take another look," she said.

"Great." Eb opened the notebook on his knees. First he drew Rankin with the heat waves rising off it. Then he drew some trees, and the fallen oak with us sitting on it. Where the seedlings were growing he wrote The World's Slowest Race.

When Miss Johnette cut back into the woods, Eb stood up. Giving the world's slowest race one last look, he held up his hand and separated his third and fourth fingers. "Live long and prosper," he said.

"What was that about?" I asked.

"The Vulcan salute? *Star Trek?* Jeez, you really *don't* know anything."

We followed Miss Johnette to the top of a small rise covered mostly by pines. "The ground's just a little drier here," she said, kicking at the sand with the toe of her boot. "Pines like it. In nature everything has a certain place where it can thrive, some place that it just naturally calls home."

Eb picked at a scab on his arm. "Can we go now?"

She laughed. "What's the matter, Eb, enough nature for one day?"

"Enough for the whole year."

We tramped back through the woods, Eb in front. "Back to civilization!" he yelled, crashing through the underbrush.

"Watch out for those leaves of three, Nature Boy," Miss Johnette warned. But Eb was in such a hurry to get away from nature he seemed to forget all about poison ivy.

Chapter Thirteen

THE BIG ITCH

Jemmie tapped the toe of her sneaker. "You keep this up, it's gonna be next week before we get there, Eb-man." Eb was sitting on the sidewalk at her feet, scratching. "You'll scrape the skin right offa that ankle."

"Well, it itches." He looked up at Jemmie, then Cass. "You two swear you won't make me run?"

"On a stack of bibles," said Cass. "Quit stalling."

One final scratch, and Eb stood up. He walked three steps, then stopped again.

"Come *on!*" Jemmie ran in place. "We said you don't have to run."

"Eb has allergies," I said. "And lots of things bite him."

"I'm about to bite him myself," Jemmie said. "Let's go, Eb! It'll be noon before we get to the track."

Eb switched ankles. "Meet ya there."

We had already run a lap when Eb arrived. The whole rest of the time we ran, he sat on the sidelines and scratched his ankles raw.

We were walking back—with scratch breaks every few steps—when Cass invited us to her house for lunch. I called Miss Dupree to let her know where we were. "I'm glad you two are making friends," she said. *Friends?* I looked over. Cass was flipping grilled cheese sandwiches, listening to Jemmie. You could tell the two of them were best friends. When school started, Eb would probably find some boys to hang around with. Maybe I could hang out with Cass and Jemmie. *Can three people be best friends?*

Cass's sandwiches were good, but Eb didn't seem to notice. He'd take a bite, then scratch an ankle. Bite. Scratch. Bite. Scratch.

Jemmie grabbed his wrist. "I don't know what you have, Eb-man, but you're making it worse."

After lunch we watched TV in Cass's living room. Her pretty older sister, Lou Anne, brushed my hair. "She's going to study cosmetology as soon as she graduates," said Cass. "Anyone who comes in our house gets a beauty consultation whether they want it or not."

"Thin," said Lou Anne, gathering my hair in one hand. "A perm would do wonders." She stopped brushing my thin hair to point the brush at Eb. "What's the matter with that boy? Does he have fleas?"

Eb was scratching his knees by then and one wrist. The itch was creeping up.

"Cass, show Anna and Eb your medals," Jemmie suggested. Cass ran out of the room and came back with a bunch of ribbons hanging over her arm.

As she announced what each medal was for, Cass hung the ribbon around Eb's neck. "This silver's for the 200 meter. I won it at Regionals. Jemmie got the gold. This gold's for the 4 x 400 relay. Jemmie's got one just like it; we're on the same relay team. And this one's from State." Before dropping the blue ribbon over Eb's head, she shined the medal on her shirt. "I won this in the 1500 meter."

"I stay out of that race," Jemmie said. "It goes on and on. Cass doesn't mind. Once this girl starts, nobody can find the off-switch."

"Jemmie has a gold from State in the 100," Cass bragged. "She is *so* fast!"

By then Eb was scratching so hard Cass's medals clinked like tags on a dog collar.

"I know, let's go next door and look at Jemmie's," Cass said, retrieving her medals from around Eb's neck.

Next door, Nana Grace was mixing a batch of cookies. We forgot the medals and got into cookie baking. But we were at least twice as much help as Jemmie's grandmother needed. "I'll just let y'all finish up," she said. "I'll set on the porch a while." Eb went with her, saying that the heat in the kitchen made the itch worse.

By the time we brought the cookies out to the porch, Eb was lumpy all over. "That rash looks kinda weepy," Nana Grace said. "If I didn't know no better, I'd say this boy has poison ivy."

Eb stared at his arms. "Oh, great! Miss Johnette gave me poison ivy."

"She did not," I said. "Anyway, you didn't touch any poison ivy."

"*I* didn't touch it. It touched *me*. Nature's sneaky, Anna. That's why normal people go to malls."

We chewed our cookies in silence. Eb chewed and scratched.

Jemmie's mother came home from her job at the hospital. She had barely set her purse down before Jemmie made her look at Eb. "Oh, Lord," Mrs. Lewis said. "That is *definitely* poison ivy. Now, listen to me, Eb. You're hot and sweaty and your scratching is spreading that rash all over the place. I'm going to give you a special soap and some lotion to stop the itch. Tonight, wear socks over your hands so you don't scratch."

Then she walked us home to give Miss Dupree the same instructions. Walking beside Mrs. Lewis, Eb didn't dare scratch, but not scratching made his fingers twitch.

Clay pedaled by, as if he didn't see us. Suddenly, he squealed to a stop. "What happened to you?"

"Poison ivy." Eb kept his head down.

"Awesome," said Clay. "You look like you have maggots or something under your skin, trying to break out."

"And what happened to you?" Mrs. Lewis asked.

Clay had two black eyes from the wreck at the Race-A-Rama. "I got hit in the face with a basketball." He pedaled the bike slowly around Eb, looking. "Impressive case."

"Thanks," Eb said.

"I mean it. And I should know. I've had it bad myself. *Real* bad. One time I went to camp and I didn't know what poison ivy looked like. I went to the bathroom in the woods. Guess what I used for toilet paper?"

"You're kidding," Eb said.

Clay held up a hand. "Scout's honor."

Clay escorted us the whole way to Miss Dupree's, circling slowly. When we got there he said, "Awesome display," before pedaling away.

Mrs. Lewis and Miss Dupree consulted. When she heard about Eb's asthma, Jemmie's mother agreed that they should take him to a nearby clinic.

They were back in forty-five minutes. Mrs. Lewis gave Eb instructions for using the medicated soap. "The child will be fine," she assured Miss Dupree. "Just fine."

When Eb turned the shower off, Mrs. Lewis said, "Excuse me." We heard her knock once on the bathroom door. "You have your drawers on?" She gave him about half a second before walking in. Eb let out one sharp yelp, and then there was silence.

He came out of the bathroom looking stunned. Smothered in pink lotion from head to toe, he tottered toward the all-white couch. Miss Dupree grabbed the back of his shorts. "Anna, quick!" she yelled. "Get a lawn chair."

"Let go," he whined. "You're giving me a super-wedge!"

When he was safely seated in a plastic chair, Mrs. Lewis said, "You think you can stay out of trouble for a while, Eb?"

Eb smiled, cracking the crusty pink lotion. "I guess."

Not long after she left we heard a knock at the front door. "Hey, Eb," Clay called from the steps. "Mind if I show Cody your poison ivy?"

Eb turned his arm so the really bad side showed. "Come on in."

"Wow," Cody breathed. Then louder, "Wow! Can I touch it?"

"Duh!" Clay slapped the back of the boy's head. "You touch it, you catch it. You want that?"

It almost seemed like he did.

Cody had to go home, but Clay stayed. "You should see the lumps on his back," he prompted when Cass and Jemmie came over. It was show-and-tell time.

Jemmie leaned in close to study the bumpy geography of Eb. "Eb-man," said Jemmie, "You are first-class ugly now."

His chest swelled. Eb seemed proud to be first-class anything, even ugly.

Cass held her hair back with one hand and examined an arm. "Seems a little better to me."

"No it isn't," said Eb. "You should see my stomach." He was lifting his shirt to show her when we heard another knock.

I got the door. Ben and Justin stood under the porch light.

"Are you two here to view the rash?" They nodded. I let Ben in, but stopped Justin. "Hold it. That'll be fifty cents." I held out my hand.

Justin's face turned red.

Ben hooted. "She's got you, man."

"I'll let it go this one time," I said, stepping aside.

Justin brushed by. "Your face looks terrible," he told the main attraction.

"That's nothing," said Clay. "Get a load of his stomach, but hands off or you'll catch it."

"You can't catch poison ivy," Justin said. "Clay, you're as dumb as a pile of rocks."

For a while we had a houseful of company, everyone admiring Eb's rash, but you can only look at bumps for so long. The kids seemed ready to go home, but they stayed when Miss Dupree offered us snacks. We listened to her rattle around in the kitchen. No one had much to say.

"Want to see me touch my nose with my tongue?" Eb asked. When no one paid attention, he nudged Clay with the toe of his sneaker and whispered, "Hey, Clay, check out those Likely Prospects books."

"What are they?" Clay picked the pink one up and opened it.

"Stop it, Eb," I hissed, "we can't show those to people." I looked back toward the kitchen. "We'll get in trouble."

Ben must've seen how scared I looked. "Close the book, Clay."

"But Eb said—"

"Yeah, well, Eb's delirious."

But Clay didn't close the album. Instead he tapped each photo with his finger. "Fat. Fat. Ugly. Old. Really ugly. Fat *and* ugly." He flipped a page and started again. "Not bad. Gross. Whoa!" He closed his eyes and pulled back. "This one here's the mother of all ugly." He turned the page before looking again. "Here's a woman who collects china cats. She wants to meet a man with a similar interest."

Justin flopped down next to him. "A similar interest—like what, porcelain dogs?" He looked at the woman. "She looks like Wide-Load Simms."

"The math teacher?" Jemmie leaned over the book, then gasped. "Get over here, Cass. Miss Simms is in this book."

"Couldn't be," said Cass. "Oh my gosh—it *is* her. I recognize that blouse. Why's she in this book?"

I couldn't believe what was happening. "Close the book, please."

"Close it," said Ben. "Anna's having a heart attack."

"That's the big book of losers," Eb said. "People who can't get themselves a date. The one with the blue cover is guys."

"Guys?" Cass and Jemmie sat down on the floor and opened the blue Likely Prospects book.

"Stop it," I begged. "Miss Dupree will be out here any second." I went over to get the kids to put the books down.

But Jemmie said, "Check out number thirteen, Anna."

I didn't mean to look. What I meant to do was close the book, but Jemmie was acting friendly, telling me, "Look at this." I was checking out number thirteen when Miss Dupree came out of the kitchen.

"Here are your drinks, children." She stopped. The color drained out of her face. "What are you doing?"

"Not much...just looking," said Clay. "Our math teacher's in here."

Her face got even paler. "Who is your math teacher?"

"Wide-Load—I mean, Miss Simms." Clay closed the cover. "Hey, they told us to look. It wasn't our idea."

One by one, the kids slid out the door. Ben was last. "Sorry, Miss Dupree," he said. "It kind of got out of hand." He pulled the door closed behind him.

Miss Dupree set the tray down without spilling a drop, then sank to the couch and began to weep.

Ten minutes before, Eb had been a king on his lawn chair throne, now he was just a pasty pink blob with wide eyes. "Sorry. I always mess up."

Miss Dupree rocked back and forth, hugging Likely Prospects, pink. "Eb, Anna, these people trusted me. And I trusted you."

"It's not such a big deal...," said Eb.

"I suppose I should have put them away, but I *told* you. I said these books were private. Tomorrow I'll have to call Eileen Simms and tell her that her records have been compromised...by kids in her class." Tears ran down her cheeks in two straight lines.

"Do you really have to tell her?" I asked. "We didn't mean anything."

"Of course I have to tell her." She put her head down on her arms. Eb left the room.

I walked over to her, stretched my hand out, then pulled it back. "Miss Dupree?"

"I expected more of you two," she said softly. "Especially *you*, Anna."

"I'm so sorry, Miss Dupree." I sat on the sofa, near her, but not touching.

Her whole life was wrecked, and we were the ones who'd wrecked it—me especially. I climbed the stairs to my attic room. I crawled under the covers, shoes and all, then reached out for my family picture. I hugged my photo the way she was hugging her book and closed my eyes.

Chapter Fourteen

MORE HOMELESS THAN EVER

"A nna?"

I lurched up in bed.

"Anna, are you awake?" Eb sounded far away and scared.

"I'm awake." The attic room was dark except for a little weak light from a streetlamp. In my arms was something hard and flat. Suddenly, everything that had happened rushed back—the kids, the albums, Miss Dupree crying. My stomach ached.

For a moment, faint lightning made the room a little brighter. I saw boxes and the twisted shadow of the tree, but no Eb. "Where are you, Eb?"

"Downstairs. I can't sleep." Thunder rumbled. "My poison ivy's itching me to death."

"Come on up." No answer. "Eb?" I didn't want to shout or turn on a light and wake up Miss Dupree. I crept down the stairs.

Another flash of lightning, and there was Eb in his summer pajamas, trailing his sheet like a super-hero cape. Behind him was the TV, the coffee table, and the empty white couch. I looked for the Likely Prospects books, as thick and terrible as bibles, pulsing out a judgment in the flickering light, but they were gone too—hidden because she couldn't trust us.

"I was having a nightmare," I said, talking to the spot where Eb had been when the lightning faded. "I was at some school. I didn't know which room to go to. I was in this hall, all by myself. Do you ever dream that you don't know where to go?"

Silence. "Sharks," he finally answered. "I dream about sharks. Tidal waves too, but mostly sharks." As my eyes got used to the dark, I could vaguely see Eb and his white sheet. He was still standing in the same spot.

"Come on up to my room, Eb."

"Let's sit down here."

Thunder rumbled.

"No, we'll wake up Miss Dupree. We can talk if we go upstairs."

"There's all that haunted, dead-lady stuff up there." But I saw the light shape of Eb's sheet move toward the foot of the stairs.

"That's it, Eb. We can watch the storm from my window."

It wasn't raining yet, but a storm was coming. A good hard rain would cool things off. In the morning I'd surprise Miss Dupree with French toast. I make good French toast.

Eb went up the stairs first. I accidentally stepped on his sheet-cape, ripping it off his shoulders. He let out a yelp. We held our breaths, waiting to hear Miss Dupree's door open. But a thick silence wrapped us like cotton. I felt for Eb's sheet on the steps and hung it back over his shoulders. So I wouldn't step on it again, we went up the stairs with me holding the end like a king's robe.

"Let's get up on the bed. We'll watch from there."

So we sat together, legs hanging over the side. "How come you have your shoes on?" he asked.

"I never took them off."

"You should try it some time. It's more comfortable."

Lightning flashed. The rocks on the windowsill seemed to stir. I picked up the edge of his sheet and wrapped it around my shoulders too.

Eb grabbed my pillow and hugged it to his stomach. "I remember one time Lisa and me were in the trailer when this really big storm hit. We lay on the floor for hours," he whispered. "I had to pee so bad. The next morning the trailer park was all torn up. Mrs.

Jacob's trailer had rolled over. A tree had squashed old man Murphy's place like a soda can."

"Did anyone get hurt?"

"Mrs. Jacob's cat got a broken leg. The sofa fell on it. Hey," he said, reaching toward the table by the bed. "Is this a picture of your family?"

"Uh-huh."

He took a good look when the lightning flashed again. "You have a lot of family."

"It just looks like a lot."

"You have more than two. That's it in my family, just Lisa and me."

"What about your dad?"

"He doesn't count. He moves around just so he won't have to pay child support."

"Don't you have any grandparents or cousins or anything?" I pulled my feet up and crossed my legs. "What about that aunt Mrs. Riley mentioned?"

"Aunt Terry? She's Lisa's older sister. She kind of raised my mom so she thinks she's still in charge. She never lets Lisa get away with anything." Eb yawned, then set my picture book on the table. "They wanted to put me with her instead of making me foster, but Lisa said no. They don't get along so great."

"Do you ever see her?"

"Only when we have to. All she does is get on us. She tells Lisa to take the GED test. She bugs her to take me to church and the dentist. When we visit she makes me eat weird stuff, like broccoli. She thinks she can boss us, but no one tells us what to do."

"What's your mother like?"

"Lisa's fun." He scratched his arm and thought it over. "Like one time she was driving me to school? We got right up to the front of the building and she said, 'You want to go to the beach instead?' She stopped at the first pay phone and called in sick to work. We had a blast. And in the summer? When the trailer gets hot? We sneak into the Howard Johnson's pool. We just ignore the Guests Only sign."

"Don't you ever get caught?"

"One time the pool guy asked if we were staying. Lisa made up a room number. He said there wasn't any such room, but he let us stay. She gets away with stuff; she's pretty."

Lisa sounded more like a friend than a mother—the kind of friend who might get you in trouble.

"It gets kind of scary sometimes, but I can handle it."

"Scary, how?"

I felt the sheet tug. "Lisa changes when she has a boyfriend. She calls me the man of the house; then she turns on the TV, and she's out of there. The last time, she didn't come back for three days. The only food in the trailer was a jumbo bag of barbecue chips. Those things can really make your lips hurt if you eat a whole bag."

"What did you do?"

"Something dumb. When I woke up the second morning and she still wasn't there, I got scared, so I called Aunt Terry. I was her project for two whole days. She made me get a haircut and bought me sneakers—some no-brand pair that looked like a girl's." He punched my pillow. "She was trying to set up an emergency visit with her dentist when Lisa and Eddie drove up. Eddie honked, Lisa opened the door, and I dove in. We screeched out of there like we'd just robbed a bank."

"You didn't tell your aunt good-bye?"

"She knew I left. When she heard the horn, she came running out of the house. She chased the car like I was being abducted by aliens." There was a long pause. "I felt kinda sorry for her, but Lisa said Aunt Terry would just bring her down about Eddie…and she would've."

"How'd you end up with Mrs. Riley?"

"Aunt Terry again. She had to be the one who called in and said Eddie was beating me up. She has this friend two trailers down from Eddie's who spies for her."

"Was he really beating you up?"

"I could take it. Lisa would've dumped him after a while. Her boyfriends don't last. Most of the time it's just her and me. That's the way we like it."

Suddenly, the branches of the oak clawed the window. Twigs and leaves pelted the glass. Rain roared across the roof. The light of the next lightning bolt bounced off the walls. An instant later I felt the thunderclap deep inside my chest.

"Mr. Miller!" Eb grabbed my arm. "Mr. Miller's out in this!"

"He's got his tarp." But I could just see that sheet of plastic, whipping and snapping in the wind.

"But there's lightning! What if he gets hit?" As he said it, a fork of lightning stabbed the sky, and we saw that the rain and leaves and all the things snatched by the storm were blowing sideways. Eb rushed to the window. "His tarp'll blow off for sure." It'd tumble away like some old plastic bag, leaving Mr. Miller and his velvet chair out in the rain.

It had been hot all day. The rain would cool him off. But before long there wouldn't be a speck of dry on him anywhere. He'd go from sticky-hot to freezing. I knew what it felt like. Just before my aunt and uncle broke up, my cousins and I went outside in a thunderstorm to get away from the fight they were having. At first the rain felt good shivering down our arms. Mark and I stomped puddles. Macy picked flowers and put them into the stream of water flowing along the curb. She waved to each one until it got sucked down the storm drain.

After a while, though, we got really cold. We sat down on the curb and hugged ourselves. The water that rushed toward the storm drain was warm from the hot road. It swirled over our feet. Macy sat right down in it.

"Maybe we'll get struck by lightning," Mark shouted over the rain. "Then they'll be sorry." We sat, teeth chattering, half-hoping we would get struck, when a car came around the corner. It almost hit Macy. She wailed and climbed up into my lap. Through the picture window we could see Aunt Eva, who does half her talking with her hands, waving her arms around. Uncle Charles was turned away from her. Neither of them heard Macy crying and crying.

I carried her inside. We stood there dripping. "Look at that, just look at that!" Aunt Eva yelled, like our puddles were my uncle's fault. Then she went back to chewing him out in Spanish. She could call him anything she wanted because none of us understood. And in Spanish she could curse him out twice as fast.

We all got colds. Nobody cared. We ran out of tissues and nobody picked up more. By then my aunt and uncle were saying "Trial Separation" like it was a vacation they couldn't wait to go on.

"Poor Mr. Miller," Eb groaned. "He's soaked by now. And his chair's all soggy."

~

Even though it was barely light, Eb was stuffing food in a paper bag. "We have to check on him."

"We're in enough trouble already."

He yanked the roll of paper towels out of the holder. "I'm going."

"Wait, I'll go with you." We let ourselves out of the house.

Branches were down all over the neighborhood. Early as it was, Jemmie's grandmother, Nana Grace, was out sweeping leaves and twigs off her porch. "How's that poison ivy, Ebenezer?"

"It's fine." We smiled and tried to walk by fast, like it was normal for us to be going somewhere when the sun was barely up.

"Where you two going so early?" she called, resting the broom against her shoulder.

"Out," said Eb.

"Out, huh?" We could hear the quiet scratch of the broom as she began to sweep again. "You just make sure 'out' don't go past the edge of this neighborhood."

Roberts Avenue was black and shiny as we trotted across. Mr. Miller's woods dripped. The ground, buried under fallen leaves, smelled like wet newspaper. Eb was going so fast he almost tripped over the tricycle. "Come on!" he called back to me.

We hadn't gotten to Mr. Miller's chair yet when we came across a plastic sheet that had blown up against some trees. Pockets of water and leaves and dirt had collected in the folds.

"I knew it!" Eb rushed ahead.

By the time I got to Mr. Miller's spot, Eb was standing there, staring at the empty armchair. "Do you see?" A pair of branches, exactly the same in length, lay crossed on the cushion to form an *X*. "It's the sign," Eb whispered. "The one he said he'd leave for me."

"What does it mean?"

"Only Cosgrove knows," he wailed. "And I'm not really him. What if it means he needs help?"

"Maybe there are some other clues." We tried to open a dresser drawer, but the rain had swelled it shut.

"All his stuff is ruined," Eb said. "Mr. Miller's more homeless than ever." He left the bag of food and the paper towels on top of the dresser, even though I told him we'd get in trouble over the towels.

The only good thing was that we got back before Miss Dupree woke up. I had time to put up another roll of paper towels, make French toast, coffee too. She ate, but she was very quiet. All she said was, "I am so disappointed."

"Disappointed?" Eb whispered when she was out of the room. "Big deal." To him, people who were really mad beat you up.

"We let her down, Eb, and now she can't trust us. She doesn't like us anymore."

"So?"

~

We spent the day looking for Mr. Miller. Eb led. I followed. Eb did the searching. I worried about Miss Dupree.

We looked everywhere we could walk to, including Goodwill, which was so far outside the neighborhood that if we had gotten caught, Miss Dupree would've phoned Mrs. Riley to come and take us back right there on the spot.

"Is Mr. Miller working today?" Eb asked the man at the counter.

"What happened to you, son? You fall in a bucket of paint?"

Eb's pink lotion was all cracked and flaking. "Poison ivy. Is he here?"

The clerk studied a piece of paper taped to the counter. "Afraid he's not due in 'til the end of the week, if he shows up then. He has a little trouble keeping track of time."

"USA Store next," said Eb when we were back outside. "He has to buy food, doesn't he? Mr. G.'s is the closest place."

"Eb and Anna!" Mr. G. exclaimed as if we were the very people he wanted to see. When Eb asked him about Mr. Miller he said, "Yes, yes. I know the man well. He always gives me the weather in India."

"He's missing," Eb said. "Do you remember when you saw him last?"

"I must think." He put his fingertips together, then rested them against his lips. "The day before yesterday. He bought batteries and a loaf of bread. 'Been a lot of rain in Bangalore lately,' he said. I thanked him for the information, and rang up his purchases. I have not seen him since. Does this help?"

"Not really." Eb pushed the door open.

I smiled. "Thanks anyway."

When we had run out of places to look, we went to Miss Johnette's. She was the only one we could tell.

"I have a friend who works at the homeless shelter," she said, not wasting any time being shocked that we knew a man who lived in the woods. She picked up the phone. She explained the situation to her friend, then put her hand over the receiver. "Does Sam Miller have a bad leg and a radio in his head?"

"That's him!" Eb rushed over to her. "Is he there?"

Miss Johnette shook her head. She talked to her friend a little longer, then hung up. "Micky knows who he is, but he hasn't used the shelter since the weather got warm. She drummed her fingers on the table. "Wait. Is this the same guy we saw at Goodwill?"

We both nodded.

"And you checked there?"

We nodded again.

"Don't get discouraged, Eb, I know a couple of other places we can try."

She called Miss Dupree and introduced herself as the biology teacher who keeps the neighborhood clean. "Do you mind if I take the kids to the library?" Miss Dupree didn't object. I guess she was too disappointed in us to care where we went.

Miss Johnette drove past the university and the fast food places on Tennessee Street. "There are a few corners in the library where homeless people go to sleep," she said. We parked in front of the library and went in. He wasn't there.

We tried the bus station next. It was a block away from the homeless shelter. "Lots of folks sit in the terminal until the shelter opens," said Miss Johnette as she held the glass door for Eb and me. She asked a few of the men sprawled in the waiting room chairs if they had seen Mr. Miller. The only answer she got was, "You have a cigarette on you, lady?"

"How about the grocery store?" I asked as we got back in the car. "Publix might have free coffee."

At Publix we split up and checked all the aisles.

Eb insisted that we walk around back to the dumpsters. "Maybe he's out there looking for old bread and stuff. Homeless people do that sometimes."

But Mr. Miller wasn't back there either.

The last place we stopped was the police station. We asked if there had been any reports of a homeless man caught in the storm. When they said no, we described Mr. Miller. "Oh, you mean Sam." The officer behind the counter tipped back in his chair. "Haven't seen him lately, but we'll keep an eye out."

"He's dead," said Eb as we rode back home.

"He is not dead," I insisted. "If he was, we would've found him drowned in his chair or struck by lightning."

Eb picked at a crusty patch of poison ivy. "He is too dead." Eb always expected the worst.

"He is not. He left the message, didn't he?"

Eb cheered up for a whole second. "Fat lot of good that is. We don't even know what it means!"

Chapter Fifteen

MAYBE RABIES

It's a rematch," Jemmie whispered through Miss Dupree's screen door. "Clay says he's gonna whip Ben's butt once and for all."

Behind Jemmie I could see Ben, sitting on his bike, foot up on the curb, talking to Cass. Cody was drawing on the road with a piece of chalk. The Weeble and his tall bike were missing, but Clay and Justin, Jahmal and Leroy were there, circling their bikes in the road. "And where's the Eb-man?" Jemmie tried to peer past me. "Bring him too."

Eb didn't want to go. It was day two of Mr. Miller's disappearance. He wanted to go back to the camp in the woods. Maybe this time the drawers would open. Maybe he'd find more clues. Maybe Mr. Miller would be there.

"Come on, Eb," I said. "After the race we'll spend the rest of the day looking, I promise."

Since the storm, it had gotten hot again. There wasn't any breeze.

We went down the street in a bunch, Eb coated in a fresh layer of pink lotion. "Hey, candy-boy!" Clay rode his bike around us. "Can we look at those books again sometime?"

"I don't think so, raccoon-eyes."

"Raccoon-eyes? Oooh, heavy-duty insult." Clay's chain clanked as he shifted. "I can't wait to ask Simms about her china cat collection. Then I'll say, 'And while we're on the subject, Miss Simms, how's your love life?'"

I trotted beside his bike. "Don't do it, please. We're in enough trouble already."

"I have to." Clay turned the front wheel one way, then the other, dipping the bike. "Simms flunked me last year. I hate her guts."

"Please, Clay."

"Sorry." He was pedaling just a little faster than I could run. "No can do."

"It took us all yesterday morning to get the track back up," Ben was telling Cass. "The rain washed some of the walls down. The little jumps about filled up."

We were coming to the fringe of trees that hid the power line cut. "Dibs on the armchair!" Cody shouted, running hard to get there first. Guess he'd forgotten that since the storm, the chairs would be soaked. He barreled down the narrow path through the trees, then stopped and put his hands on his hips. "Hey, you!" he called out. "Whaddya think you're doing?" He turned and yelled, "Hey, Ben, there's some guy sitting on our racetrack."

"Whaddya mean, some guy?" Ben asked.

We hurried down the path, piling up at the edge of the clearing.

"It's that weird guy who goes around talking to himself," Jahmal said.

But Eb and I broke away from the rest and dashed toward him. "Mr. Miller!" Eb shouted.

He was sitting on top of one of the tombstones, legs dangling into the pit. "What happened to you?" Eb yelled. "We looked everywhere." Mr. Miller's hair was matted. He'd lost a boot. There wasn't any white in his eyes at all, just a streaky pink. The lids were all crusty. "Mr. Miller?" He didn't seem to know us; he didn't seem to know anything.

Eb poked himself in the chest. "It's me, Eb. Remember?"

Mr. Miller stared.

"It really is Eb," I said. "The pink stuff's poison ivy medicine."

Eb grabbed my arm. "And this is Anna. She made the blue-moon cake. You remember us, don't you? Eb and Anna?"

When Eb and I sat down, one on either side of him, Mr. Miller cringed as if we were going to hit him. He smelled like a dead possum.

"Eb?" he mumbled, staring into the pit. "I met a kid one time, called himself Eb. Couldn't trust him. Never would tell me his real name."

"It's short for Ebenezer," Eb blurted out. "That's my real name, Ebenezer."

"Ebenezer?" Clay had reached other side of the hole. "Like Ebenezer Scrooge?"

"No!" Eb shouted. "Like Ebenezer Gramlich, my great grandfather."

I touched Mr. Miller's knee. "Are you all right, Mr. Miller? Did you get caught out in that rain night before last?"

"Get away," Mr. Miller whimpered. "I don't know you two."

"Yes, you do. You know me." Eb lowered his voice. "Cosgrove, remember?"

"Cosgrove?" Mr. Miller searched Eb's face.

"Better not get too close, Ebenezer," Clay warned. "I think the man has rabies."

"Shut up, Clay," Eb said. "Leave him alone."

"Ooh, you're scaring me, Ebeneeeeeezer."

"What's so great about your name, *Clay?*" I snapped. "It means mud."

Mr. Miller hadn't taken his eyes off Eb.

"You remember me now, don't you?" Eb whispered.

"That really you, Cosgrove?" Mr. Miller answered slowly. "I didn't recognize you under all the camouflage."

The kids now stood in a half circle on the far side of the hole. Cody tugged at his brother's arm. "What about the race, Ben? I thought we were going to have a race."

"Later, Cody." Ben called across to Mr. Miller. "Are you okay, mister? Are you sick?"

"He has rabies," said Clay.

"No, idiot." Justin spat into the hole. "Rabies makes you froth."

"Whatever." Clay spat too. "Are we going to race or not?"

No one answered. Everyone was watching Mr. Miller and Eb. Eb's bare leg touched the leg of Mr. Miller's dirty overalls.

"Shoot, I wouldn't be sitting right next to him like that," Leroy said. "No way. What if he decides to barf?"

"This is real exciting." Clay put a foot up on a pedal. "May as well get out of here if we aren't going to race. Come on, you guys."

"But he's sick," said Cass. "We can't just leave him here."

"No? Just watch me." He stood on the pedals and pumped toward the gap in the trees. He slowed, then stopped when he realized no one was following him. "So, what are we going to do?" he shouted.

"Get help!" Cass shouted back.

Clay pedaled back over. "Let's think about this a minute. We get help and that blows the whistle on the track."

"But what if he's really sick?" Cass said. "Maybe we should take him somewhere."

"Yeah? Like where?"

"Not Miss Dupree's," I said quickly.

"Not our house," Cody said. "He'd make stains."

Clay looked at each of us. "Does anybody want to take this guy home?" We all stared at the ground. "I rest my case."

Then I had an idea. "Miss Johnette might help us."

"Yeah," Eb agreed. "We can take him there. Her house is a mess already."

But Mr. Miller couldn't, or wouldn't, stand up. "Look out for yourself, Cosgrove," he said. "It's too late for me." He shoved me away when I tried to help him up.

"Hey," said Ben. "I know you feel sick, mister, but don't go pushing girls around. I'll take over your side, Anna." As Ben got closer he smelled the homeless man's dead possum stench. He didn't sit down. "Mr. Miller, sir, I'm Ben Floyd. Eb and me are going to boost you up on three, okay?" He put a hand under Mr. Miller's arm. Eb did the same. They counted, "One...two...three."

But Mr. Miller was a bag of rocks. "Leave me alone. I feel lousy. A man has the right to die in peace."

"You can't die!" Eb tried to drag him to his feet, then stopped. "I'm going for help. Don't go anywhere." He lit out running. "I'll be back!"

"Wait up, Eb!" Cass yelled. "We'll go with you."

"That's right, Eb-man," called Jemmie. "Don't give yourself an asthma attack." Eb and the girls dashed across the dry grass and into the trees.

I sat back down in Eb's place next to Mr. Miller. Ben sat too, breathing shallow. Tired of standing around, the kids on the other side of the hole sprawled on the ground. Justin picked up a stick and drew a tic-tac-toe grid. He put an *X* in the middle and handed the stick to Leroy. Cody ran around the racecourse, twisting a pretend motorcycle handle. "*Vroom, vroom.*"

It seemed as if we sat there forever before Miss Johnette came down the path with Cass and Jemmie running ahead and a wheezing Eb straggling behind.

"How're you doing, Mr. Miller? You had us worried." Miss Johnette looked at Ben and me. "I think you two better get back. He looks pretty sick." Ben and I slid away. She walked over, put her hands on her knees, and leaned down, bringing her face close to his. "Mr. Miller? Mr. Miller, we need to get you back to my place so you can lie down. Do you think you can walk a little?"

"I'm staying right here!" he shouted. "You can't push me around."

Still wheezing, Eb knelt and put a hand on the man's knee. "We can't stay here, Sam. Charlie's going to get us."

"Charlie?" There was a new sharpness in his eyes. "Look out for yourself, Cosgrove. Go, go!" He tried to shoo Eb away.

"No. You'd never leave *me,* would you?"

Mr. Miller pulled a filthy handkerchief out of his pocket and blotted his eyes. He blew his nose loudly. "Never meant to."

Miss Johnette and Eb lifted him to his feet. Together they half-carried him across the power line cut, through the trees, and out to the street. The boys walked their bicycles. When we reached the road, Leroy, Jahmal, and Clay jumped on their bikes and raced off.

"Later, you guys," Clay said. "We're going to Mr. G.'s." Cody ran home, but the rest of us trailed along to Miss Johnette's.

Mr. Miller wouldn't duck under the spiderweb. He snapped a few threads, sending Charlotte scurrying.

Miss Johnette and Eb lowered him onto the couch, where he went limp. "Should we take his one boot off?" Eb wondered. But it was too hard to get the knot untied. They did their best to arrange his arms and legs in a comfortable position, then stepped back.

"What do we do now?" Eb asked.

"Beats me." Miss Johnette stuffed her hands in her pockets. "Guess I could call the shelter."

"Not the shelter. Maybe he's just thirsty." Eb ran to the kitchen and came back with a glass of water, but Mr. Miller wouldn't drink. He wouldn't even open his eyes.

"You ever seen a dead person?" Justin whispered, when we were all seated on the floor at what Miss Johnette thought was a safe distance. "No? Well, I have. My grandfather. He looked just like that. Only cleaner."

"Mr. Miller?" Eb called. "Mr. Miller?" But Mr. Miller didn't stir. Suddenly, his arm dropped. Everyone gasped. The arm hung limp against the side of the couch.

"That's it," Miss Johnette said. "I'm calling the hospital."

"No, don't," Eb pleaded. "He'd hate that."

From out in the kitchen, we heard the flap of Gregor's ears. The dog shuffled into the living room. Greg sniffed the lifeless hand, then gave the palm a lick. Slowly, Mr. Miller's fingers opened. They ran along Gregor's side. The man's whisper was dry, like the rustle of leaves. "Good boy, Scout. Good old boy." Gregor lay down, as close to the sofa as he could get. As the hand stroked him, he heaved a deep sigh and closed his eyes.

"I have an idea," Jemmie whispered. "My mom's on the night shift this week, so she's home right now, sleeping. I'll go get her." The screen door slammed behind her.

A few minutes later, Mrs. Lewis came in, fussing at Jemmie for waking her up. Then she saw Mr. Miller. "Well, look at you." She set her medical bag down. "Aren't you a sight?"

The dead Mr. Miller opened his eyes and grinned.

"Clay thinks he has rabies," Justin said.

"Rabies?" She looked at us, all huddled against the wall. "I seriously doubt that."

"I told Clay he was full of it," Justin said.

Jemmie's mother stood over the couch. "Now, Mr. Miller, can I get you to stick your tongue out for me?" We were all surprised when he obeyed her. In fact, he did everything she asked. He let her take his temperature and look down his throat. He took deep breaths so she could listen to his chest. He held out his wrist so she could take his pulse. "Still beating?" he asked.

"Still beating," she said. "Can someone fetch me a wet washcloth? Warm water, please." When I brought it, she washed the crust off his eyelids. Then she crooked a finger at Miss Johnette. "Come with me, Johnette. We need to talk."

They closed the kitchen door, but we could still hear.

"I don't think the man's sick, but he's definitely suffering from exposure. He needs fluids and rest and food. Lord knows he needs a shower. What I want to know is what you plan to do about it. You don't know this man from Adam, Johnette. He could be a drunk or some kind of a criminal."

Eb's jaw clenched.

"You aren't going to let him stay here now, are you?" Mrs. Lewis asked.

"I doubt if he has anyplace else to go."

"Nonsense, Johnette. I know your heart's as soft as a Georgia peach—and maybe your head too—but that man out there is *not* your problem. There are programs for people like him. And he must have family somewhere."

"The picture," I whispered. Eb and I raced for the kitchen.

"He has family," Eb said. "Two kids, a boy and a girl."

"Sam Junior and Claudette. There's a picture of them in his wallet," I added.

"Well, happy day!" Mrs. Lewis threw up her hands. "There you go, Johnette. Mr. Miller," she called, walking back into the living room. "Sam?" He was dozing again so she put her hand on his shoulder and gave him a brisk shake. "I'd like to hear about those kids of yours. You have a boy and a girl? I do too. Jemmie and Arthur. What are your kids' names?"

Mr. Miller blinked up at the ceiling.

"You showed us their picture." Eb knelt beside the couch. "Remember? It's in your wallet."

"Wallet's gone."

"Now, don't you be telling me that." Mrs. Lewis checked for herself.

"Try his back pocket," I said, and she shoved her hand under him.

"Look at that. She's frisking him," said Justin. "Just like on a cop show."

"Nah," said Ben. "On the shows they have to spread their legs and put their hands on the hood of a car."

Mrs. Lewis dug the wallet out of his back pocket and flopped it open. She turned the see-through sleeves. "Well, now, this must be them." She held the photo up so Mr. Miller could see it. "Are these good-looking children yours, Mr. Miller? The boy favors you a little."

"Yeah, they're mine. Both of them. The girl looks more like her mother."

"Do you know where they are now?"

"No, I don't," he bellowed. "And they don't know where I am either, and we're all pleased as pie."

She shook a finger at him. "I hope you don't think this nice woman is going to let you live on her couch. Now tell us how to reach your kids."

He clamped his mouth shut and went back to acting dead.

"All right, we'll talk about that later," said Mrs. Lewis. "After we get you showered."

That brought him right back to life. "I don't want no shower."

"But you'll take one anyway. And if you don't come out as clean as a newborn baby and smelling like Ivory soap, I'll walk you right back in and do the job myself."

"Believe me, she'll do it," said Eb.

Wrestling Mr. Miller into taking a shower, Mrs. Lewis and Miss Johnette forgot the search for his kids. But I didn't. I knew someone who could help us find them—if I could talk her into it. I slipped out of the house.

~

Miss Dupree looked up from the recipe she was reading. "Hi, Anna." I tried to decide if it was a friendly "Hi, Anna" or a mad "Hi, Anna." It seemed kind of neutral.

"Are you cooking something?"

"Dan, I mean Mr. Perry, is coming for supper. Southern fried chicken is his favorite, but I don't usually cook fried things."

"I can do it. Aunt Eva taught me how." Finding Mr. Miller's kids could wait a minute. I had a chance to get back on Miss Dupree's good side. "My aunt's Puerto Rican, but Southern fried chicken's her specialty. She says she's 'way Southern.'"

I caught Miss Dupree smiling. "Could you help me make it for tonight?"

"Sure. I'll make it every night all week if you want." Then I remembered Mr. Miller. Instead of trading a batch of Aunt Eva's world's-best Southern fried chicken for getting back on her good side, I was going to have to trade it for help finding Mr. Miller's family. And when I told her about Mr. Miller, she'd be disappointed again. Even though she had never exactly told us where the boundaries were, we knew we had left the neighborhood. I didn't want to tell her, but I knew this was important to Eb. Crucial. "Miss Dupree? There's something I sort of need to tell you."

As I told her about Mr. Miller and his camp in the woods, the color drained from her lips and cheeks. Her whole face turned paste white, an exact repeat of the Wide-Load Simms disaster. "You've been meeting a homeless man in the woods? He could have hurt you, he could have... Oh, Anna!" She covered her mouth with her hands.

"I'm sorry, I'm sorry! We shouldn't have gone. But don't blame Eb. I'm the one who's always making him go places. He'd rather stay in the house his whole life." I expected her to turn away, too disappointed to care.

Instead, she reached out and grabbed me. "Thank God, you're all right," she whispered. She hugged me until my ribs hurt. "Thank God." Then she pushed me out to arm's length and just looked at me. "I never spelled the rules out, did I? In foster-parenting class they stressed that. 'Make the rules clear,' they said. But once I actually became a foster parent I just wanted you two to like me."

"You did?"

"Of course I did. But that's no excuse. I should have given you rules. That's part of the job of being a parent." And she hugged me again.

As I leaned against her I smelled the rose and mint scents of deodorant and soap and powder. It was a made-up smell, nothing like the open-window smells at Miss Johnette's, but I could get to like it. I had a tiny sliver of hope now, as small as a fingernail moon. She had called herself a parent.

I talked into her shoulder. "This isn't the best time for me to ask for a favor, is it?"

"A favor?" She pulled back. "I think I'm supposed to be disciplining you two."

"Maybe you could discipline us after the favor. It's a good favor, really. And you'd be helping Mr. Miller, not us." She didn't answer so I rushed ahead. "We need you to find Mr. Miller's kids on the computer."

She frowned. "Find his family?..."

"Please... Pretend you're searching for one of your client's high school sweethearts."

"Who are we looking for, exactly?"

"His son, Sam Miller."

"Sam Miller?" She groaned. "There must be a million Sam Millers out there. Anna, if you're going to lose someone, be sure they have a distinctive name."

"His daughter's name is Claudette."

"Better," she said, "but not great. If he fought in Vietnam his children are probably married. She may not even be a Miller anymore, but I suppose it's worth a look."

~

I counted the list of names that came out of the printer. "Only fourteen Claudette Millers."

"That's good," she said. "But even if she hasn't changed her name, she still may not be one of them. Many women don't list their first name, just initials so they won't get hassled," she said.

We looked at the map. The Claudette Millers were scattered all over the place, from big cities like Detroit to a tiny dot of a town called Antler. Antler was so close to Canada that the Claudette Miller who lived there could probably throw a stone across the border.

"Let's try to narrow the list down," Miss Dupree suggested. The only way to do that was to talk to Mr. Miller.

Before we walked over to ask Mr. Miller which Claudette to call, I put the chicken parts in a bowl of salty water to soak—Aunt Eva's secret.

We had just closed the door behind us when we heard the phone faintly ringing inside the house. "Could we let the answering machine pick it up this one time?" I asked.

She took a quick glance at her watch. "Dan will be in his aerobics class until six," she said. If there had been a remote chance that the caller was Mr. Perry, she would have whipped back into the house; anyone else could leave a message.

"If we hurry, Mr. Miller could be back with his kids by the weekend, living in a house, eating regular meals," I said as we rushed over to Miss Johnette's.

Miss Dupree put a hand on my arm and we stopped. "Don't get your hopes up too high, Anna. Not everyone I track down is looking for a reunion. Some people prefer to stay lost."

~

When we got to Miss Johnette's, Jemmie let us in. Mr. Miller was dozing, but Eb was talking to him anyway. "She'll come get me on my birthday," he was saying. "Lisa likes to pull surprises. The whole problem is Eddie. Oh, hi, Anna." He looked at Miss Dupree, then slid down in his chair. "Oooh, busted."

"She'll bust us later," I said. "She's here to help Mr. Miller now."

Mr. Miller twitched, and threw a wild punch at the back of the sofa. Then he began to snore.

Miss Johnette came out of the kitchen with a glass of juice for the patient. "He's kind of in and out," she said as she shook Miss Dupree's hand. "We'll catch him the next time he wakes up."

While we waited, I showed Miss Dupree Miss Johnette's collections. "Want to see the wasps nests next?" She kept her arms close to her sides as I led her around.

But even a bug and dust hater like Miss Dupree couldn't look at all the things on Miss Johnette's shelves and not get interested. It was the nests that got Miss Dupree. She liked the small tidy ones best. The cobweb hummingbird nest, no bigger than a tablespoon, was her favorite. She had just picked it up for a closer look when Mr. Miller sat bolt upright and jerked his head around, "What in the Sam Hill?..." Then he blinked and rubbed the back of his neck. "Where am I?"

"You're at Miss Johnette's," Eb said. "Don't mind all the bones and stuff, you're okay."

Miss Dupree set the nest down. "Mr. Miller?" She smiled her most professional smile. "Mr. Miller, I'm Anita Dupree." She perched on the edge of the chair that faced the couch. "We'd like to help you find your family."

Mr. Miller flopped back down and squinched his eyes. "No!"

"Don't you want to see your children? Don't you want to go home?"

"No and double-no!"

If he hadn't been so sick, I bet he would've staggered back to his waterlogged chair in the woods, maybe even found himself a new forgotten spot that Eb and I didn't know about.

"Is your daughter on the East Coast?" she fished. "New England perhaps?"

Mr. Miller rolled on his side and faced the back of the couch. "Leave me alone."

We left with the same list of Claudette Millers. He hadn't eliminated a single one.

Chapter Sixteen

LONG DISTANCE

We were walking home in silence when Eb blurted out, "Are you still mad?" When Miss Dupree didn't answer, he added, "It's not like we meant to do it. How could we know their math teacher would be in the book?"

"You mean Wide-Load Simms?"

Eb winced.

"I called her today."

"How'd it go?" he asked.

"Badly."

We didn't talk the rest of the way home.

As soon as we got in the house, Eb held out the list of possible daughters. "You are going to call these people, aren't you? I know we don't deserve it, but Mr. Miller needs help."

"Not now, Eb. Mr. Perry's coming for supper. There is chicken to fry, and I have to do something about my hair. Tomorrow."

Eb drew a deep breath. "I'll call. I'm his friend. I mean, if it's okay with you." He stared at the list. "I guess they're all long distance."

"That's all right, Eb. Go ahead."

He sat in the chair by the phone with his hands in his lap, afraid to pick up the receiver. The light on the answering machine was blinking. "Look, there's a message."

"I'll check it later. Go ahead and make your calls, Eb. Don't put it off." When he hesitated she made a face at him. "I don't like calling strangers either."

"I thought that was your job."

"I don't like everything about my job. Go on, Eb, give it a try."

He put a hand on the receiver. "It would be better if you did it. I mean, who wants to talk to a kid?"

"Be brave, Eb. You can do it."

I went over to the kitchen counter to fry chicken, Aunt-Eva style. I was pouring flour into a bowl when Eb made his first call. "Hello?" His voice was soft. "My name is Eb Gramlich." There was a pause, then he shouted, "Eb Gramlich. Is your father missing?" Another pause. "She hung up."

As I dredged the chicken in flour Miss Dupree coached him. "You started out just fine by identifying yourself," she said. "After that you might say something like, 'I'm trying to locate a Claudette Miller, Sam Miller's daughter.'"

The person who answered Eb's next call wasn't Mr. Miller's daughter either, but at least she didn't hang up on Eb. "Better," said Miss Dupree, then she came over to help me with the chicken.

Once I'd showed her how to dredge the chicken, she took over that part. I poured oil in a pan and turned on the burner. As we worked we listened to Eb.

"My name is Eb Gramlich. I'm trying to locate…"

I showed Miss Dupree how to tell if the oil was hot enough. "You sprinkle a drop of water on it. When it crackles and spits back, it's ready."

"Thank you anyway," Eb said. "Not her," he reported.

Most of Eb's calls were quick. "Hey, I got a machine. Should I leave a message?"

"Leave a brief one. These calls are long distance."

The next person he got wasn't Sam Miller's long lost daughter either, but she talked and talked and talked. "Weird," said Eb, hanging up and rubbing his ear. "That lady said her father's name was Frank Miller, but she had a dog named Sam. She told me all about him."

"She's probably lonely, Eb," Miss Dupree said. "A lot of people have no one to talk to."

I helped Miss Dupree ease the first batch of chicken parts into the pan. She jumped back when the oil popped. "The oil has to be spitting hot or the crust comes out soggy," I told her.

It sounded as if one of the lonelies was telling Eb about someone missing in her own family. Eb finally cut in. "Listen, I have to go," he said. "This is long distance."

Miss Dupree nudged the chicken with a fork. "Good work, Eb. I sometimes get stuck for hours."

The chicken was getting brown on one side, so we turned all the pieces over.

"No ma'am, that's Sam Miller," Eb said. "S-A-M." He listened a while longer, then said, "I'm really sorry. But if his name is Slim and he's dead besides, he couldn't be the guy I'm calling about, now could he?" He hung up. "This is hopeless."

Miss Dupree moved the chiken parts with a fork to make sure they weren't sticking. "One time I made fifty calls to find someone's old girlfriend, and after all that she told me she didn't want to see my client."

"Now, that's encouraging." But he kept going, working his way down the list, listening to people who didn't know Mr. Miller but wanted to talk about him anyway.

When the chicken was brown on both sides, I had Miss Dupree poke the biggest piece with a fork. "If the juice runs clear, it's done," I told her. "If it's pink, it's still bloody inside." I covered a platter with paper towels while she tested the chicken.

"Clear," she said, and we began taking the fried chicken out.

"Last one," Eb said. "Antler, North Dakota." He dialed the number. "Hello. My name is Eb Gramlich. I'm trying to locate Claudette

Miller, Sam Miller's daughter." There was a long silence. "Florida… Yeah, he's okay. I mean, he's homeless and sick, but he's okay. Do you think you could come get him?"

"He got a hit," Miss Dupree whispered.

"Tallahassee." Eb wrapped the phone cord around his hand, unwrapped it, wrapped it again. "Well, no, he didn't ask me to call. But he didn't say not to. So, when can you come?" He scratched a patch of poison ivy on his arm and listened, then he covered the phone with his hand. "She says she can't get off work right now." He uncovered the phone. "What about his other kid, Sam? Could he come?… In Germany? Why's he in Germany?"

Miss Dupree dried her hands on a towel. "Let me see what I can do." She took the phone. "Hello? Miss Miller, my name is Anita Dupree. I know this call must be a shock… Of course I understand you can't just drop everything… Yes, it is difficult when someone just pops up after such a long time, but we're in an awkward situation here." She explained that Mr. Miller was sick and lying on Miss Johnette's couch. "She's just being a good Samaritan…"

Eb wandered over to the counter. "His daughter doesn't want him."

"Let me give you the number here." Miss Dupree recited our number and hung up. She had her back to us and she paused, as if she was trying to think of what to say to Eb. When she turned around she wore a big smile. "Good job, Eb. I'm so proud of you!"

"She isn't coming, is she?"

"Not right away."

"Not now, not ever. She doesn't want him."

"You have to understand, Eb, he walked out on her family when she was twelve years old. He came back a few times, but never stayed for long. She's hurt. Give her some time to think about it. She might come around."

"So, what's she going to do, leave him on Miss Johnette's couch?"

"She'll call the Veteran's Administration first thing in the morning, then she'll get back to us." The winking light on the answering machine caught her eye. I think she punched the button so she wouldn't have to go on making excuses to Eb.

Suddenly there was a new voice in the room. "Hello? This is Lisa Gramlich, Eb's mother?" Eb rushed to the phone. "This is for my boy. Eb, honey? Now don't freak, but Eddie and I are on our way to California. Eddie's brother's a stuntman out there. He says he can fix Eddie up with a job. We'd love for you to come along, but you know the court won't let me have you back until I can prove there's some kind of stable situation." I heard the sounds of a busy road. I could imagine Eb's mother standing at the pay phone with the wind of passing cars and trucks blowing her hair into her eyes. "But before you know it," the voice said, "you'll be out there with us, rubbing elbows with movie stars. You'd like that, wouldn't you?"

Lisa was quiet a moment. The line crackled.

"Listen, Baby? I talked to Aunt Terry." Eb's shoulders pinched in tight. "She's gonna come see you. I know she's a drag, but she's family and she loves you." A horn honked. "Gotta go, Eb. I'll send you a ticket soon as I can. Be good, okay? Remember, you're still my best guy and—" The message cut off.

The machine beeped three times.

Eb just stood there. He looked as if he would break if he tried to move. Miss Dupree only put a hand on his back, but he pulled away. "Leave me alone!" He stumbled out of the kitchen, and I followed him.

He yanked the front door open and almost knocked Miss Dupree's date off the steps. As Eb ran past, he stomped on one of Mr. Perry's shiny loafers.

Mr. Perry was so surprised he dropped his bouquet. I picked it up and handed it to him. "Here, Mr. Perry." I ran down the steps. "Nice to see you."

"Anna, where is Eb going?" Miss Dupree called from the door. "Will he be all right?"

"Don't worry, I'll stick with him." Mr. Perry was still standing on the step holding his upside-down bouquet. "You two enjoy your dinner!" I ran after Eb.

It wasn't hard to catch up to him. He was crying, so he couldn't see where he was going. Running and stumbling, he was headed for Miss Johnette's. But when we got there, he sat on the stone wall in front of her house and put his head down on his knees. Every now and then he turned and tore a handful of leaves off one of Miss Johnette's plants, then threw it as hard as he could toward the street. I didn't touch him or talk to him or anything—not even about the plants. Eb would've torn up the world if he could've. In a while he stopped, pulled the front of his T-shirt up and wiped his face.

"Come on," he said. "I want to see Mr. Miller."

Chapter Seventeen

NURSING MR. MILLER

Mr. Miller's daughter called back in the morning. She had made her father an appointment at the VA hospital in Gainesville, but they couldn't see him until the end of the week. "What are we supposed to do with him until then?" Miss Dupree asked. "And who's going to take him to Gainesville?"

As soon as she hung up, the three of us walked over to Miss Johnette's to pass on the news. Eb went right in to see Mr. Miller, but I stayed outside on the front walk where Miss Dupree was whispering to Miss Johnette. "She made the appointment and she's sending some money. She said it was the best that she could do at the moment." Miss Dupree shook her head slowly. "Maybe if he called her…"

"I already suggested that he give his kids a call," Miss Johnette whispered back. "He won't do it. I think he's ashamed of walking out on his family. Would she call him?"

"I don't think so. She wants an apology." They both sighed. "Meanwhile," said Miss Dupree, "there are five days before his appointment in Gainesville. We'll have to find some agency that can take him."

"He's okay here," said Miss Johnette. "He's not a lot of trouble."

"And who's going to drive him to Gainesville?"

"Me, I guess."

For those five days Eb and Mr. Miller were inseparable. Mr. Miller was so exhausted from wandering around after the storm that he spent most of the first day sleeping. That didn't keep Eb from talking to him. Once when Mr. Miller woke up, he called Eb Cosgrove. I could tell Eb liked it. As Mr. Miller got more rested, he went back and forth: sometimes Eb was Cosgrove, sometimes Eb was Eb.

On the second morning, Mr. Miller opened his eyes and sat up. "Now that was a nice little nap," he said. "About time I was going." But he didn't budge an inch. "You know…" He rapped his knuckles against his head. "It's been awful quiet. No CIA reports, no marching bands." He turned his head as if he was trying to catch the signal. "You think the battery finally wore down?" He sat for a long minute listening to the silence in his head.

But after a while it began to bother him. "This quiet sure seems loud. Anna, hand Eb that paper. The boy's gonna read me something."

Eb gawked at him. "You mean you can't read?"

"Well, of course I can read. But I need glasses," he said. "I lost the pair I had. Question is, can you read?"

I handed Eb the paper. "What do you want first?" he asked. "Sports?"

"Nothing but a lot of running back and forth for no good reason." Mr. Miller stuck his feet up on the coffee table. I noticed he was wearing a pair of Miss Johnette's purple socks. "Start with the weather." After the weather, he asked, "Any murders, robberies, swindles?" Mr. Miller liked bad news best. "Didn't I tell you kids?" he said, after Eb had read him about a scam to take old people's money. "People are no good."

"Totally no good," Eb agreed, propping his feet up too.

They both looked at me, so I slammed my feet up there too. "Totally no good. Really."

Eb read the paper until Mr. Miller announced, "Too much news, I'm all wore out. Think I'll look at the inside of my eyelids a while."

Eb moved to the nearest chair and read the comics while Mr. Miller napped.

After the first day Mr. Miller felt good enough to sit up for longer stretches. "There wouldn't happen to be a deck of cards in this museum, would there?" he asked. Miss Johnette rummaged around and found a pack in a drawer. Mr. Miller was surprised when Eb said he didn't know how to play gin rummy. "Come on, Cosgrove, you and me played all the time. You always had a deck in your pocket."

Uncle Charles and I used to play gin rummy too. I signaled to Eb. "Come in here, Cosgrove. And bring the cards." I gave the fake Cosgrove a quick lesson on the kitchen table.

When they began to play I sat behind Eb, making a little throat-clearing sound if he reached for the wrong card. But Eb didn't like being corrected, so I had to let him lose. It wasn't long before he caught on, though.

After that they played by the hour, betting pennies out of the penny jar Mr. Miller had spotted on a shelf.

"Can I play too?" I asked. But they ignored me.

"It's a guy thing," said Miss Johnette. "Look, even Greg's in on it." Gregor lay curled up against their legs, chin resting on Mr. Miller's foot. After Mr. Miller played a card, he sometimes reached down and gave the dog a pat, calling him a "good old boy." Pretty soon Eb was doing it too: play a card, pat Greg, say "Good old boy."

"Come on, Anna," Miss Johnette said. "We need a break from these good old boys. Let's see if we can rustle up a pair of shoes for Mr. Miller." He couldn't walk into the VA hospital in Miss Johnette's socks, and all he had of his own was half a pair of boots. We took that one boot with us to Goodwill. We put Mr. Miller's boot sole-to-sole with shoe after shoe. The only ones that seemed to be the right size were some turquoise sneakers with white stars on the ankles.

We didn't think Mr. Miller would like them, but he put them right on. "Now, aren't these jim-dandy," he said, lacing them up. I was afraid he'd walk off in his new shoes, but Mr. Miller went only as far as the backyard. He went straight to the bench sitting in the shade of the live oak Miss Johnette called the Old Senator, a tree so big it shaded the whole backyard. Once they'd found the bench, Mr. Miller and Eb spent quite a bit of time out there, with Gregor resting against their legs.

While they occupied the bench, Miss Johnette and I sat with our backs against the Old Senator's trunk. We watched the birds at the feeder that hung from a limb. "Cardinal," she said, "and that's a chickadee. Listen, it says its own name." She identified each bird that came winging in. We relaxed against the tree trunk until Eb or Mr. Miller asked for iced tea or something to eat. We complained that they were running us ragged, but we were having a great time.

Sometimes we took breaks from our jobs as fake nurses. Miss Johnette got out her microscope and we looked at things: one of my hairs, one of her hairs, a shred of onion skin, a leaf.

People visited. Jemmie brought a bunch of her grandmother's roses. Cass baked cookies. Even Miss Dupree came. "Oh, Anna," she said. "I forgot to tell you how much Mr. Perry liked your chicken."

"You told him I made it?"

"You deserved the credit, Anna."

"I wouldn't've minded."

"But what if he asks me to cook it sometime when you're not around?"

"You could do it." I didn't let it show, but I couldn't help wondering about the words "not around." *What does she mean, sometime when I'm away from the house? Sometime when I don't live with her anymore? Where would I be if I wasn't around?* I wished that Eb and I could hide out at Miss Johnette's forever. It seemed like the only safe place.

Jemmie's mother stopped in every day to check on her patient. "Feeling any better, Mr. Miller?" she asked each visit. When he finally answered, "Sort of," she said, "That's good, because today we're going to do something about that hair of yours." She pulled a comb and a pair of scissors out of her skirt pocket.

"You some kind of a barber?" he asked.

"I'm a nurse," she said, starting to comb through his coarse, wild beard. "That means I can do just about anything."

"Ow!"

"Hold still. You won't feel a thing."

She trimmed his beard.

"How's it look?" he asked Eb.

"Not bad. You don't look half as homeless."

Next came the haircut, short with a side part. Gray hair fell on the ground all around the bench.

Mr. Miller looked at Eb. "Well?"

"You look like you have a regular job," Eb answered.

"Like what?" snorted Mr. Miller. "Bagging groceries at the Publix?"

The last thing Mrs. Lewis did was clip the wild hairs that sprouted from his eyebrows. "There. Do you have a mirror, Johnette?"

Miss Johnette hunted around, but all she could find was a broken-off wing mirror from a car. "I don't know why I hung onto this. It was lying in the road one day when I was picking up trash." She handed it to Mr. Miller. "Well? What do you think, Sam?"

"That's not me." He turned the mirror slowly. "That's some old man."

"A nice old man," said Mrs. Lewis. "It's a big improvement over your Wild Man look." She dusted hair off the back of his shirt. "Done."

After she left, we went inside. Mr. Miller took his place on the sofa and shook his head. "An old man.... Seems like yesterday I was a kid. I was just twenty years old when I went to Nam—G.I. Joe, right out of the box. Nothing could hurt me. I was immortal," he said. "I remember one time, standing in the middle of this clearing taking pictures of incoming enemy fire. Ground blowing up all around me. It was like I had no nerves at all."

"It was just like that when Eddie used to hit me," Eb said softly. "I'd go into my movie mode. I knew he was hitting me, but I pretended I was watching the whole thing, like it was some Stallone or Schwarzenegger movie."

"Shock," said Mr. Miller nodding. "Like the day the mine went off. We were just tramping along, Cosgrove up front, me next."

Eb went stiff. "Wait, Cosgrove was in front of you when the mine went off?"

"That's right, Cosgrove was first, then me, then Taylor. One second I was looking at the back of Cosgrove's scrawny neck; next thing I know I'm lying flat, looking up at some clouds. Someone was shouting at me, just shouting and shouting. I could've cared less. I felt like I could slide right out of my body and float. I wasn't worried. I wasn't scared. Like you said, it was like I was watching the whole thing from the outside." He picked up the deck of cards. "Whose turn is it to deal?"

Eb gripped the sofa cushion. "But what about Cosgrove? What happened to him?"

Mr. Miller just shook his head.

"What?" said Eb. His voice sounded funny.

"Blown to kingdom come. Cosgrove never even knew what hit him. He was the best friend I ever had." He put a hand on Eb's knee. "Say, did I ever mention you look quite a bit like him? Because you do."

∾

After that Eb didn't want to be called Cosgrove anymore. He insisted on Eb. Most of the time Mr. Miller remembered. I guess Eb didn't want to play gin rummy either. I saw him hide the cards. When no one could find them, Miss Johnette brought out some old board games.

"Checkers." Mr. Miller slapped his knees. "Now there's a sport!"

Eb resisted. "Checkers? That's the cheesiest game of all time. There's no sound, no light, no batteries."

"What is it, son?" asked Mr. Miller. "Afraid you'll lose?"

"Bring it on," said Eb.

They played game after game of what Eb called go-for-the-jugular checkers.

They were straddling the bench with the checkerboard between them when Miss Johnette casually told Mr. Miller she was taking him to Gainesville in the morning.

"To the VA?" Mr. Miller looked up, holding the black checker over the board.

"Your daughter made the appointment."

"My daughter?" he shouted. "Why'd you have to go and get her into it?"

Miss Johnette stayed calm. "You *do* need a physical."

"And a psychiatric examination too, I'll bet." He slammed the checker, *whomp, whomp, whomp,* and swept up three of Eb's checkers.

"Hey, you sure that was legal?" Eb whined.

"Your move." Mr. Miller crossed his arms. He glanced at Miss Johnette, then looked away. "I'm not going to some army head-shrinker."

"But you need to—"

"Mind if I make a call?" He stood up so fast that he nearly flipped the board.

We all jumped.

"A call?"

"You know, a phone call. Can I make one?" When Miss Johnette nodded, he swung his stiff leg over the bench. He lurched toward the house, almost skipping. We followed him to the house with our eyes.

He was gone for half an hour. When he came back the first thing he did was survey the checkerboard and take his next turn. "It's all set," he said, picking up another red checker. "I'm going down to Johnny's. I'll be off your hands."

Miss Johnette's lawn chair creaked as she leaned forward. "Who's Johnny?"

"My kid brother. He's got a marina in Key West. Haven't seen him for years, but I knew he'd still be there. He says he can use another mechanic. Half the folks down there are crazy, so I'll fit right in."

"You're a mechanic?" Eb asked.

"Son, do you think I've spent all my life listening to voices in my head, living rough? Yes, I'm a mechanic. A darned good one."

"Let me take you for that checkup first, then you can head south."

He reached over and gave Miss Johnette's hand a squeeze. "Don't put yourself out, darlin'. They got a VA in Miami too."

When we told Miss Dupree she said, "You're just going to let him go? He needs medical help."

Miss Johnette said he had the right to make up his own mind. She mentioned the Veteran's Administration in Miami.

"But what about his daughter?" Miss Dupree pressed.

In the end, though, Mr. Miller and Miss Johnette won. The next morning we put him on a Greyhound bus headed for Key West. "Riding the dog," he called it. Mr. Miller didn't bring much with him to the station, just a couple of changes of clothes neighbors had given him plus three pairs of Miss Johnette's purple socks. Everything he owned fit in two plastic grocery store bags.

Miss Johnette was at the ticket counter when Mr. Miller spotted someone he knew in the terminal. "Hey, Melvin," he said to a greasy looking man in a plaid shirt who sat with a backpack between his feet. "This is Melvin, kids. How ya been, buddy?" But Melvin didn't seem to know who he was. "It's me," Mr. Miller said, leaning down right in the man's face. "Sam Miller. Don't let the clothes and the haircut fool ya." When Melvin finally recognised him, he looked uneasy, like there was something suspicious about the cleaned-up Mr. Miller.

Miss Johnette came back with the ticket.

"I'll pay you back soon's I get my first paycheck," Mr. Miller said. He tapped his fingers on the legs of his pants, as if he was listening to music. I had noticed that when he was nervous the radio in his head seemed to come back.

We went out to where the bus was waiting, door open. It was all happening so fast. Mr. Miller had his hand on the rail and a foot on the first step, but he stopped. "Wait!" he said. "Where's your manners, Sam Miller?" He turned around and looked back and forth between Miss Johnette and me. "Ladies, I thank you both for nursing me through. And Eb?"

When Eb stuck out his hand to shake, he stood so far back he looked as if he was pushing Mr. Miller away. But Mr. Miller wrapped his skinny arms around Eb, the two plastic bags of clothes slapping Eb on the back. "Eb," he said, talking to the top of Eb's bristly head. "You are one good kid."

"You won't even remember me," Eb mumbled into Mr. Miller's shirt. "You'll stick me in some back corner of your head, and I'll fall off the shelf."

"Maybe sometimes, but you'll come back around. All the important ones do. Hey, I'll tell stories about you to my nieces and nephews. You'll be like a legend."

"A legend?" Eb stepped back and snuffed hard. "Yeah, okay, that'd be cool." He rubbed his nose with the back of his hand, then rubbed his hand on his shorts. "I'll come see you sometime, maybe. When I'm older, I mean."

"I'll have the checkerboard set up."

"Sir?" The bus driver had his hand on the handle that would close the door.

"Be with you in a second," Mr. Miller said. He shook our hands, Eb's last. "Son," he said, hanging on. "Life's rough, and it stinks ninety-nine point nine percent of the time, but once in a blue moon, something good happens. Listen, Eb, when some good thing wants to happen to you, you let it, understand?"

"On or off?" the bus driver said. "I don't have all day."

Mr. Miller climbed the steps, plastic bags swinging. He took a seat on our side of the bus. The door closed with a huff. As the bus backed up, Mr. Miller pressed a hand against the window.

Eb raised his own hand in the Vulcan salute.

"Live long and prosper." I said the words for Eb. He couldn't.

Chapter Eighteen

THE EINSTEIN OF THE DOG WORLD

Mr. Miller hadn't been gone a day when Eb got sick—and he'd barely gotten over the poison ivy. "I have the worst luck," he told Jemmie's mother when she came to see him.

"Hush now, and keep this under your tongue." She stuck a thermometer in his mouth. "You know, there's an old song that goes, 'If it wasn't for bad luck, wouldn't have no luck at all.'"

In a little while Mrs. Lewis checked her watch, then pulled the thermometer out. She rolled it in her fingers until she could see the black line. "One hundred point one." She shook it back down. "I think you'll live."

She closed the bedroom door behind her. "It's nothing serious," she told Miss Dupree. "I'd be more worried about his mood than this little bug he has. Anna, you're getting to be an experienced nurse. Keep an eye on him, and try to cheer him up, okay?"

Soon after she left, the phone rang. "Hello, Mrs. Riley," said Miss Dupree. "His aunt?... I'm glad you were able to arrange it. I take it you finally heard from his mother.... Well, he's a little under the weather right now, but if she doesn't mind, he might like a visit."

I tried to signal her that a visit from his aunt would be the worst possible thing. "He doesn't even like her," I whispered.

"When should we expect her?" she asked, turning so she couldn't see me. "One-thirty will be fine."

At one fifteen a woman clutching a bag of orange popcorn stood at our door. "I'm Eb's aunt." Aunt Terry was a heavy woman, soft as a stuffed chair. She juggled the bag to shake my hand and Miss Dupree's hand. "I hope he's not too sick for cheese popcorn. I always buy it for him when he comes to my house. It's his favorite." Eb must've exaggerated about the constant broccoli.

Miss Dupree offered her a glass of sweet tea. We sat down at the kitchen table so we could chat about Eb before she actually saw him. Aunt Terry told us so many fun things she and Eb had done when he visited her that I began to wonder if this was a different Aunt Terry.

When it was our turn, Miss Dupree and I told her everything that had happened to him lately. Miss Dupree told her how hard he had taken his mother's call. I told her about Mr. Miller. Her eyes welled up. "Poor boy. May I please see him?"

Miss Dupree had me walk Aunt Terry to Eb's room. I don't think she wanted to watch him give this nice woman a hard time.

"Eb," I called. "Someone to see you."

Aunt Terry followed me into the room. Eb's eyes were closed, but I could tell he was faking. I guess she could too. She leaned across the bed and put her palm on his forehead, then brushed her hand over his bristly hair. "My favorite boy feels a little feverish." She sat down on the chair by the bed and picked up the hand that lay on top of the sheet. A tear squeezed out of the corners of each of Eb's closed eyes. "Everything is going to be fine," she murmured, "just fine." When I backed out of the room she was sitting there quietly holding his hand.

≈

She came to see him every day while he was sick; so did Mrs. Lewis. By day three, Mrs. Lewis told Aunt Terry, "Not a thing in the world's wrong with that boy. He had a little bug but he's over it now. He just wants attention."

"And I'm going to give it to him," Aunt Terry said.

On day four Mrs. Riley came with her and arranged for Eb to visit his aunt for the weekend. Mrs. Riley gushed, "Hopefully this will be the first of many happy visits."

Eb was all in favor of it until he spent his first weekend. "Forget it," he said when he came back. "She gets on me about everything—like it really matters if you pick up food with your fingers. And she made me empty the dishwasher and help my uncle wash the car. She's a slave driver."

It took him until Wednesday to mention that his aunt and uncle had taken him to Wild Adventure. That was when I stopped feeling sorry for him.

He kept whining about the housework until Miss Dupree heard him. "You know," she said, "that's something I've been meaning to do here too. From now on, Anna will continue to help with the cooking. Each of you will do your own laundry. And Eb, you will vacuum and help me with the dishes." To show she meant it, she dragged the vacuum cleaner out of the closet.

Eb trotted the vacuum cleaner around for about two seconds before turning it off.

Miss Dupree pointed. "You missed some specks." She turned the vacuum back on for him and went into the kitchen. "Come, Anna. Time to start supper."

"Adults are all slave drivers," Eb yelled over the roar of the vacuum. "Except Lisa. She never makes me do housework." We heard him bang the vacuum into a wall. "She doesn't care if I eat with my fingers." Something crashed, probably a bulldozed chair falling over. He nosed the vacuum into the kitchen so he was sure Miss Dupree would hear. "Just wait," he shouted. "Lisa'll send my ticket and I'll be out of here. Gone."

Having threatened to go to California, he turned back around and nearly ran over Mr. Perry. "Whoa, there, fella!" Mr. Perry had to yell over the roar of the vacuum. "Easy with that vacuum! Leave the socks on my feet." Mr. Perry screamed an apology to Miss Dupree for letting himself in the front door. "I guess you didn't hear my knock!"

Miss Dupree waved her arms. "Turn it off, Eb!"

Eb flicked the switch. The silence was deafening.

"We're always happy to see you," Miss Dupree fluttered. "Aren't we, Anna?"

"Yes," I said. "Very." But if you asked me, Mr. Perry was getting a little carried away. At first he had called her three times before each date, once to make the date, once to confirm it, then a third time to make sure she really liked his plan for the evening—because if she didn't he'd be happy to change it.

But it wasn't long before he had started showing up with no warning. Early in the morning, in the middle of the day, nine at night. Once he came when Miss Dupree was with a client. He excused himself fast and left, beet red. He controlled himself a little better after that, but he still came around a lot. Each time he arrived, he stuttered an apology, came inside, sat down, and became the immovable object.

〜

After a week of laundry and pushing the vacuum cleaner, Eb seemed to have a new perspective on Aunt Terry. It was Saturday morning and Eb was waiting for his aunt to pick him up for his second weekend visit. We were eating waffles when Mr. Perry showed up, this time at the back door.

"He's an addict," Eb whispered. "He's addicted to Miss Dupree." He made a gagging sound. "It's disgusting."

"More like embarrassing," I whispered back.

"I didn't want to disturb you..." Mr. Perry had a box in his arms. "I only thought...." He stood in the doorway, half in, half out, and stretched his ostrich neck to give Miss Dupree a dry little peck on the cheek.

"That's just because we're here," Eb whispered. "If we weren't, they'd be trading spit right now."

Mr. Perry held out the box. "I thought you might like these."

"Donuts!" Eb yelled. "Let the man in." Eb had to eat fast, though, because he only had ten minutes before his aunt was supposed to pick him up. This time he was staying until Monday night. They were taking him to Panama City for a long weekend.

He had been grumbling about it since his aunt set it up. "The shore.... What's so great about sand and water?" I could just see him at the beach. He was still crusty with poison ivy scabs, and his skinny chest was whiter than his T-shirt. And then there were the trunks Aunt Terry had bought him. He wouldn't even take them out of the bag until I promised not to laugh. "Are these lame, or what?" The trunks he held up had little ducks and anchors all over them.

He had a mouthful of chocolate donut when we heard a car out front. "See ya," he sprayed. He grabbed the duffel bag that held his Game Boy and his duck-and-anchor trunks and ran.

"Hey wait, I'll walk you." As soon as we were outside I said, "Thought you didn't want to go to the beach."

"Yeah, well, it beats watching those two drool all over each other. I bet they're locking lips right now."

"No, they're not." I gave Aunt Terry a wave. "They're eating waffles. Quit being gross."

Eb put his lips on the back of his hand and slobbered a kiss. "Have fun," he said. And he climbed into his aunt's car.

When I went back in, the adults sprang apart. "Anna!" Mr. Perry put his hand down on his plate, right in a puddle of syrup. Miss Dupree's fork clattered to the floor.

I backed out of the kitchen. "I just wanted to tell you I'm going outside now."

"But you haven't finished breakfast," said Miss Dupree, quickly smoothing her hair.

"Yes, I have. I'm full." I wished I could make myself small, or invisible. I was completely in the way.

I snatched my hat off the rack and jammed it down to my eyebrows. For once no kids were in the street. No dogs. The world seemed empty and I had absolutely nowhere to go.

I just started walking. Maybe Cass and Jemmie would run by and say, "Hey, Anna, come run with us, okay?" I might see Ben. If I had had my explorer's notebook, I could've started a new map, an accurate one, but it was in Eb's room, or in his bag and on its way to Panama City. I had kind of lost track. The way things were going, I might have to leave without a stone or a map to help me remember.

Not that I would forget Miss Dupree, Eb and Mr. Miller, Miss Johnette and Gregor, Cass and Jemmie and all the neighborhood kids… or even Charlotte the giant spider. I'd remember, and I'd miss them.

It was only after I'd been walking a while that I realized I was headed for Miss Johnette's. Maybe we could label fossils, or sit and talk. As I walked up her garden path, flowers brushed my arms, bees buzzed. I stopped to watch a hummingbird hover, dipping its beak into some red flowers.

Miss Johnette's wasn't like anyplace else. Everyone was welcome, even creatures that stung or made webs or ate leaves. According to her, things that stung were only protecting themselves, and the web-makers were only hunting for food. She even liked the caterpillars that ate holes in her milkweed leaves. "If you want butterflies, you have to feed caterpillars," she said. Miss Johnette was loyal. She gave every living thing the benefit of the doubt.

I stood, surrounded by leaves and flowers. I took a deep breath and held it. This had to be the most peaceful place in the world. Then I heard a sound. Someone close by was crying.

I listened at the window, but the crying seemed to be coming from behind the house. I slipped around to the backyard.

Miss Johnette was on her knees. In front of her, on his blanket, was Gregor. She let out a sob. A shovel leaned against the Old Senator.

I kept hoping Greg would move, even though I knew he wouldn't.

I had never seen his blanket outside of the kitchen, and besides, there was the shovel. "Miss Johnette, is Gregor dead?"

She bit her lip and nodded. "He went to sleep and never woke up. Oh, Anna, I've had him forever. I got him when I was in college. Someone in the dorm moved out and left him. I kept him hidden in my room. He never barked once. Greg was the Einstein of the dog world, a canine genius." She stroked his fur. "A good dog, such a good dog."

I knelt on the edge of his blanket and put my hand on his side. He felt the same as always. "He was pretty old, wasn't he?"

"Fifteen." Her breath seemed to catch. "Old for a big dog like Greg."

"And he wasn't feeling so great either."

"Oh, he had all kinds of problems—bad eyes, bad hips, his hearing was going." She swiped at her eyes. "At least he died easy."

"Before my grandmother died," I said, "they took her to the hospital. They wouldn't let me visit. I felt bad about it. I wanted to talk to her one more time."

She snuffed. "What did you want to say?"

"I don't know... I wanted to tell her she was the best, and let her know that I loved her. I guess I wanted to say good-bye."

She blew her nose and took a deep breath. "That's the hard part, isn't it? Saying good-bye." She put a hand on the dog's shoulder. "Gregor, old partner, you are the greatest dog ever, the best creature to walk on four paws." She talked to Greg a while, reminding him of all the things they had done together. Once, she even laughed. As I listened, my throat felt thick, my eyes stung. Then she gave him one last pat. "I guess that's all Greg. I guess this is good-bye." She folded her hands in her lap.

As we knelt there, silent, a bird called, *chickadee-dee-dee-dee.*

"Shouldn't we bury him?"

Tears dripped off her chin when she nodded.

We buried him at the far edge of the shade of the Old Senator, her favorite dog and her favorite tree, guarding each other. We took turns digging. The soil smelled good, kind of sweet.

When the hole was deep enough, we each took a side of the blanket and lowered him down. "Wait," said Miss Johnette. She ran inside and came back with her prized mastodon tooth. She put it near his front paws. We covered him with the blanket and tucked it in. Using our hands, we pushed the dirt over him and patted it down.

"We could make a marker," I suggested, but we were tired and soaked with sweat.

"We'll do that later." She reached out a hand to pull me to my feet. "We need to think about something else for a while." She dusted off the knees of our pants—mine, then hers—and we walked into the house.

Chapter Nineteen

NINETY-NINE POINT
NINE PERCENT

The next morning Cass and Jemmie came by to ask me to run. After running, we went over to Jemmie's house and drank iced tea with our feet up on the porch rail. "Look at those hairy legs!" Jemmie teased. "You two are a couple of gorillas."

"We are not!" we said. Cass and I both had blond leg hair and so many freckles you could hardly see the hair at all.

Jemmie slid her smooth, shiny leg over next to mine. "Baby oil. That's the secret. And shaving, of course. Ask Miss Dupree to let you." Jemmie's legs *did* look good—in fact, everything about Jemmie looked good. She was way ahead of Cass and me.

She went in the house, came out with a bottle of pink nail polish, and started doing her toenails.

"What happened to your Flo-Jo fingernails?" I asked.

"Took 'em off. I couldn't do a thing with 'em on." Cass and I watched her stroke polish on the nail of her big toe. "And check this out." She dug in the pocket of her shorts, pulled out a tube of lipstick, and passed it to Cass.

Cass took the cap off. "Pretty color."

"Read the name on the bottom," Jemmie said.

"Kiss of Passion," Cass read, then we both giggled. Cass slapped the tube back into her friend's hand. "Jemmie, if you keep this up you'll have to quit running."

Jemmie paused with the brush over her second toe. "What're you talkin' about?"

"You'll be like my sister." Cass grinned. "Too made-up to sweat."

"You wish," Jemmie said.

All three of us did our toenails. We sat with our feet on the rail while the polish dried. "See," said Jemmie, wiggling her toes, "it doesn't hurt to fix yourself up a little." Just then Ben walked by. "Ben Floyd," Jemmie yelled. "Get up here, boy." She stood the three of us up side by side and made him look at our toenails.

"Big deal, you painted your nails." He ducked his head, embarrassed. Cass and I were embarrassed too, but Jemmie stretched out her shiny, shaved leg and tapped the top of Ben's bare foot with her own. Nothing embarrassed Jemmie.

I watched the toes of my sandals as I walked home. My pink nails were like Jemmie's pink nails and Cass's pink nails. I decided to ask Miss Dupree about shaving. But when I got to the house, Mr. Perry's car was in the driveway. I kept right on walking until I got to Miss Johnette's.

When she opened the door I could tell that she had been crying again. "I'm glad to see you, Anna." She blew her nose hard. "Come on in."

$\sim$

Monday was pretty much the same. I ran with the girls. We were just leaving the school track when Ben, Justin, and Clay came to the basketball court to shoot hoops. Cody was tagging along. "Hey!" Jemmie walked over to them. "How about a game? Cass, Anna, and me against the four of you."

"Who wants to play with girls?" Clay asked.

"Yeah," Cody said. "Who wants to play with girls?"

"*Against* girls, you mean," Jemmie said. "Ya scared? We'll spot you ten points."

"No, we'll spot you ten," Clay said.

Clay and Jemmie argued a while. In the end no one spotted anyone anything. Jemmie grabbed the ball and we just started to play.

Everyone was good except for Cody and me. We mostly got in the way. Ben knocked me down trying to get to the ball. "Sorry, Anna!" He grabbed both my hands to pull me up.

Girls won. We beat them by twelve points. I even scored a basket, by accident. All the way home Jemmie razzed Clay, "Y'all are one sorry excuse for a team."

"We gave you that game," Clay said. "I mean it."

I went home for lunch. Miss Dupree made sandwiches, but she hardly touched hers. She kept shifting the salt and pepper shakers around as if they belonged in a certain spot that she couldn't quite find. "Anna," she finally asked, "how long do you think people should know each other before they make a serious commitment?"

"You mean like, get married?"

"Well…engaged."

I wasn't exactly an expert. "My grandmother told me that my parents dated in high school. They got engaged when they were juniors in college, so I guess they knew each other for at least six years."

"Six years!" She switched the salt and pepper again, then sighed. "Longer is better, I guess."

After lunch I went to Miss Johnette's. We spent a couple of hours at the kitchen table, messing with the microscope. But there was a hole in the room where Gregor should've been, and a hole where Eb should've been too. After a while she stopped trying to focus the scope and tipped back in her chair. "I called home last night. My mother said that Gregor was just a dog and that what I need is a man in my life."

"Talk to Miss Dupree."

She laughed. "No, if there's a man out there for me, I'd rather just trip over him." She looked into the microscope for a moment, then up at me. "We need to do something, Anna. We need to go somewhere. I've been in the house for two days, and it's not bringing Gregor back."

I didn't want to go far—Eb was coming home soon. "Let's go check on the world's slowest race," I suggested. So we headed for the woods where the poison ivy had attacked Eb.

We were sweaty by the time we reached Rankin, but in a second we forgot all about being hot. "Hey," she said. "What's going on here?" Standing in front of the place where we had cut into the woods was a metal post, shiny and new and at least eight feet high.

I pointed. "Look, there's another one. And another." A whole line of posts had been planted along the edge of the road.

"Someone's putting up a fence."

"Maybe they're going to turn it into a park," I said.

"Maybe." She didn't sound convinced.

We walked along the road until we came to the last post. But looking back into the woods, we could see that someone had cut down trees in a wide strip. More fence posts ran along the edge of the cut.

"Butchers," Miss Johnette said. "Come on." As we walked along the new muddy road we could see impressions of huge tires, like the footprints of giants in the sandy soil. "They don't even cut them down anymore." She pointed out the twisted roots of an oak. "With a bulldozer they can push over even the biggest tree in seconds."

We walked a long way before we hit the back corner of the second line of posts, then the post line turned again, following another fresh gash through the woods. "They're fencing it in," she said. "But why?"

"Maybe they don't want us walking around on it."

"They don't even know about us. Maybe they're going to build houses... No, there would've been a permit up by the road."

We reached the next corner and turned. Before we got back to Rankin we walked between the posts and into the woods. Everything was the same as before. I tried to forget the pushed-over trees and the bare soil.

"You can tell summer's coming to an end," Miss Johnette said. "See how tired the dogwood leaves look?" They were a spotty, dull green. We walked toward the fallen oak where Eb had made his drawing. "This is the real calendar," she said. "When you get to know nature, you see that life is a big circle. Things die, but they come back." She sat down on the oak. "How's the world's slowest race coming along?"

"The contestants have grown at least an inch."

A black butterfly with gold stripes flitted by. "Zebra longwing," she said. "The state butterfly of Florida." But she sounded distracted. "Anna, let's go back. I've got to find out what's going on." I didn't mind. Eb would be home any time. Maybe he was there already.

"See ya," I called as she turned up the path to her house. I began to jog. I rounded the corner of our street and knew instantly that something was wrong. There were too many cars at Miss Dupree's. Besides her car and Mr. Perry's, I saw Aunt Terry's van and Mrs. Riley's car. My stomach felt funny.

"Hey, Anna." Eb was sitting on the curb by himself. I hadn't even noticed him behind the cars.

"Hey, Eb." I sat down too. I could see us reflected on one of the hubcaps on his aunt's van. Our reflections bent around the edges. "Everything okay?"

His reflection shrugged. "I guess."

"What's going on?"

He picked up a pebble and started drawing pale lines on the road. "They're having a consultation."

"What about?"

"My placement. Aunt Terry wants custody."

"Of you?"

"Yes, me. Who else?"

"But what about your mother?"

He pitched the rock at his aunt's gleaming hubcap. "It was Lisa's idea."

"Her idea! Why?"

"She's having trouble out there. She had a job and lost it. And Eddie's brother flat lied about getting him a job. There's some union he has to join…I don't know."

"Couldn't you just stay here until she gets things worked out?"

"This is a temporary placement, remember? I'm a hot potato. No one wants to hold onto me for long."

"Do you want to go with your aunt?"

"It's not like I have much choice, is it?"

"I know you don't," I said, watching his skinny reflection twist along the edge of the hubcap. "But if you did have a choice, where would you want to go?"

He answered quietly. "With Aunt Terry. For a while anyhow."

"Why?"

"Things with Lisa are just too weird right now. There's Eddie. There's California. At least Aunt Terry's regular. She does what she says."

"But what about the fun?"

"Sometimes the most fun is eating supper or having notebook paper or not getting punched out by some guy who's not even your dad." He put his elbows on his knees, as if he was holding himself up. "Anyway, Lisa's not exactly rushing to come get me."

"I'm going to miss you, Eb."

"Yeah, well." He turned away and gazed down the street. "I tried to get them to take you too."

"Your aunt and uncle?"

He threw his hands up. "Who else? But they wouldn't do it."

"That's okay. I'll stay here." I stared at my knees.

"Hel-lo…" Eb rapped his knuckles on the top of my head. "Anybody home in there? Check out Miss Dupree's finger. She has one hand dragging on the floor. She's wearing a rock."

"No, she isn't! She wasn't wearing one at lunch. At lunch she asked me how long people should know each other before getting engaged. I said six years."

"Six years? Get real, Anna. They're old. They're running out of time to have kids."

"Then they're lucky," I said. "Here I am. Instant kid."

"They're not *that* old. They can still make a couple of their own to shape into little clones of themselves. No offense, Anna, but you're a used kid."

"Oh." I had been hoping so hard they would get together. It never occurred to me that if they did they might not want either of us around. It wasn't fair. Except for one eat-in barbecue dinner, Eb and I hadn't done a single thing with Mr. Perry. We never had a chance to grow on him.

I slid a little closer to Eb. "Are you going right now, today?"

"There's a bunch of paperwork Lisa has to sign. And my aunt and uncle and Mrs. Riley and me all have to go to court and talk to the judge."

"I'm really going to miss you, Eb."

"Yeah…well…I guess I'll miss you too." He tossed a pebble up and tried to catch it. "Anything happen while I was gone?"

"Gregor died. Miss Johnette and I buried him out back under the big tree."

I saw his reflection shrug. "He was old."

"I thought you liked Greg."

"He's dead, Anna. Stuff happens."

"Yeah. Bad stuff ninety-nine point nine percent of the time."

The adults spilled out of the house, all smiles. Mrs. Riley gave Miss Dupree a hug. She started her car, and with a wave, she pulled away. Eb's aunt gave him a quick kiss, which he pretended not to notice. His uncle called him "champ." Then they got in their van and left too.

"Anna?" Miss Dupree held out her hand. "I'm afraid I couldn't follow your advice." The diamond wasn't big like Eb had said. It was kind of small, but pretty.

"Congratulations," I said. I was happy for her, really.

Her face flushed as she smiled. "This is the best thing that's ever happened to me," she whispered. Then, in her regular voice she said, "You had good news today too, didn't you, Eb?" And she hugged Eb right there in the road.

"Quit it," Eb wheezed. "You're smothering me!"

But she went right on smothering. She was happy for Eb and happy for herself. I was happy for them too. But what would happen to me?

Mr. Perry came out of the house. "Anita, darling?" His voice squeaked a little on the "darling," like he needed practice saying it.

"Come on, Eb," I said. "Let's go tell Miss Johnette."

Chapter Twenty

THE SAND BELOW

W e were just starting up the walk when Miss Johnette flung the door open. "I called all over, Anna. No one knew what I was talking about. Then I got the county's environmental planner, a Mr. Jonah Webster. He knew."

"Knew what?" Eb asked.

"About the woods. He said the city owns it. They're going to clear that piece of land!"

"You mean *our* woods?" said Eb. "The one with the killer poison ivy? The one with the world's slowest race?"

"Clear it?" I stopped dead on the path. "But, why?"

"Sand! The utility department uses sand to bed pipes. Mr. Webster told me we have the best grade of sand here. When I reminded him there's sand from here to St. Marks—all of it about the same—he admitted that the real problem is cost. Sand is cheap but hauling sand is expensive. By mining it in town, they won't have to pay to truck it."

"But what about the trees?"

"What about the world's slowest race?" Eb was louder this time.

"Nobody seems to care. I asked the man if he had ever seen the site and he admitted he hadn't. I told him that he owed the woods at least that much." She went back in and came out with a long-sleeved shirt. "He said he would come take a look, but he won't. He just said it to get a crazy woman from the south side off the phone."

"Hey," said Eb, as she stuffed his arm in a sleeve. "What's with the shirt?"

"Poison ivy protection." She stuffed his other arm in.

"Why do I need poison ivy protection?"

She began buttoning him up. "I called everyone I could think of—county commissioners, the paper, a couple of land conservancies—but no one would help." She buttoned Eb's collar. "Let's go."

"To the woods? Why?" asked Eb. "To torture yourself?"

"I don't know what else to do. I just want to look."

We had to trot to keep up. "Hey, by the way, I'm going to live with my aunt," Eb panted.

"Is that good news?" she called back over her shoulder.

"Who knows?"

The woods had never been prettier. We saw three zebra longwing butterflies. Woodpeckers drummed in different trees, tapping out a conversation. "Look." Miss Johnette held up a branch with clusters of berries on the stem. "The beautyberries are just starting to turn." The berries were going from green to lavender. "They should be ripe by the end of August."

There won't be any end of August for the woods, I thought.

She put a hand on the trunk of each of the trees she passed. I began to do the same.

Eb shoved his hands in his pockets. "You two are nuts. Are you *trying* to get poison ivy?"

I looked at the woods harder than I had before, seeing it tree by tree. One had grown around an old fence. Bits of rusted wire poked out through the bark. A jagged black scar ran down the trunk of a tall pine. "Struck by lightning," Miss Johnette said. "And still standing."

"They're just trees, you guys." Eb trudged after us. "There are trees all over."

"We like *these* trees," I told him.

The longer we were there, the harder it was to look at anything. We knew what was going to happen, but none of the birds or the trees, none of the contestants in the world's slowest race knew.

Miss Johnette turned in place. "These trees have survived it all—good seasons and bad, storms and drought. Now a bulldozer will push them over in seconds." She sat down on the ground and bowed her head to her knees.

Eb and I huddled on either side of her. Eb patted her back. "You're not crying, are you? I mean, you're a teacher. Teachers don't cry." I snuffed, and felt my shoulders shake. "Come on, Anna, it's just a few trees." He reached around and patted me, "You two are a total mess."

Neither of us noticed the man who walked up until Eb pounded our backs. "Company, you guys. Zip it."

The first thing I saw were his boots, which were huge, then his legs, the buckle of his belt, his chest, a black beard. From my spot on the ground he looked as big as a redwood. He cleared his throat. "Excuse me. Are you Johnette Walker?"

Miss Johnette didn't lift her face.

He squatted. "Miss Walker? I'm Jonah Webster, you called my office this afternoon about the project here..."

She jerked her head up. "Are you going to stop it?"

Normally, Miss Johnette looked really big to me. Mr. Webster was even bigger, but it didn't matter. She gave him a look so forceful that he sat down as if he'd been shoved. "Try...try and understand," he stuttered.

"You're an environmental planner," she said. "Isn't it your job to protect the environment? Well, *this* is the environment. Protect it."

"I can't," he said quietly. "The county holds land like this for municipal needs, like mining sand."

I grabbed a handful of sand and dry leaves. "But this sand is doing something more important. This sand is holding up a forest."

"Yes, miss, I see that. It's unfortunate."

"If you didn't come to help us," said Miss Johnette, "why did you come?"

He looked uncomfortable. "I came because I said I would. But there's nothing I can do. There don't seem to be any endangered species here. This is all second growth. None of these trees are old or irreplaceable."

"Not yet," she said. "But wait." She pointed out a tree that was no more than a foot high. "Take this dogwood. It's not much, right? Not rare, not irreplaceable. But let it grow up, and it'll provide berries for birds in the winter. The birds will spread the seeds, and there will be more dogwoods for more birds."

"I know the way it works. I'm a biologist." He looked miserable. "But there's not a thing I can do."

Then this will all be gone, I thought. *Every tree, every fern.* No matter how much Miss Johnette or I cared, we couldn't stop what was about to happen.

I crawled over to the tiny dogwood and touched a leaf. "I'm going to dig this tree up," I said. "I'm going to plant it someplace where it can grow up."

"It's the wrong time for transplanting trees," said Mr. Webster. "There's less shock if you move them when the weather is cool."

"But the tree will be gone by then. I'm going to try. I want this tree to live."

"One dogwood, out of all this forest," said Mr. Webster. "It seems like so little."

"Not to the dogwood," I said.

"What about this little tree here?" Eb asked. "Don't you want it to live too?" I knew he was trying to make me feel stupid for saving one tree out of so many.

Miss Johnette leaned over and felt the prickly needles on Eb's tree. "Nice little cedar. It wouldn't be hard to dig up."

Hope rose like a bubble in my chest. "We could dig up other things too. I bet Cass and Jemmie would help," I said. "Maybe some of the boys."

"You do know this is city property…" Mr. Webster cautioned.

"Come, on," said Miss Johnette. "You aren't going to stop us, are you?"

"How could I?" he said. "I don't know a thing about it." He stood up. "But whatever you're going to do that I don't know about, it's got to be this weekend. The fence goes up on Monday." He strode away, disappearing into a stand of pines.

A few minutes later, we heard the sound of an engine starting out on the road.

When Miss Johnette stood up, she seemed different. There was something to do. She had a purpose. "I have a few big pots."

"This is so lame," Eb said. "You're going to get all sweaty and bug-bit for a couple of lousy trees."

"That's right, Eb." Miss Johnette walked briskly. "That's exactly what we're going to do. And you're going to help us."

"Can't," he said with a grin. "I'm spending the weekend with my aunt."

~

When we got back to Miss Dupree's, Eb said he was going inside for a snack. I went looking for the kids.

"They lit out of here, headed that way," said Nana Grace, pointing in the general direction of the Race-A-Rama.

"Thanks." As I ran down the street I worried. I was still an outsider. How could I ask them to sweat and get poison ivy? Then I thought of the trees. The kids might say no and they might laugh, but I had to ask.

I ran all the way to the power line cut, then stopped. I didn't see anyone. What I noticed first was that all the ditches and jumps had been filled in. Even the monumental tombstones had been stomped flat. The place where the Race-A-Rama had been was nothing but sneaker prints in the sand.

"Fore!" I heard the shout from further down the cut and turned just in time to see Ben swing. Cass, Jemmie, Justin, and Cody, who stood behind him, all turned their heads to watch the ball fly. Nothing flew but sand. When I trotted up, Ben was resting the golf club on his shoulder, staring down at the ball.

"Nice swing, Tiger," Jemmie said, "but aren't you supposed to hit the ball?" She held out a hand. "Give it here."

Ben handed the club to Jemmie. "Be my guest."

"What happened to the Race-A-Rama?" I whispered to Cody.

"Clay went and broke his arm jumping the tombstones. Ben made us fill it in."

"Now, this is how it's done," Jemmie said. "First, you take your stance." She planted her feet, then wiggled her butt. "Then you get a grip." Finger by finger she wrapped both hands around the club. "Then you check it out." Arms straight, she took a small practice swing that just tapped the ball. "And then..." She swung the club up as high as she could. "...you hit the sucker. Fore!" She brought the club down so fast it whistled. Sand flew. Jemmie didn't just hit the ball, she clobbered it. It sailed up through the wires, turning brilliant white as it caught the light.

"Keep an eye on it," Ben warned. "It's the only ball I got." It was just a speck when it flew over the place that used to be the Race-A-Rama. The ball landed hard and bounced another couple hundred feet. Ben shaded his eyes but the ball was too far away to see. "Not bad," he said. "Go get it, Cody."

"Why me?"

"Get it quick and you can take the next swing."

Cody trotted off to fetch the ball.

Everybody stood around waiting for him to come back with it. This was my chance. "Listen," I blurted out, "I need your help."

With his sneaker, Ben smoothed over the hole his club had dug in the ground. "What kind of help?"

"You know the woods along Rankin Avenue?"

"Sure. Miss Johnette took us there one time for a nature walk," Justin said. "She told us about this tree, and that tree, and this tree, and that tree."

"That's the place," I said. "They're going to bulldoze it. Before it's all gone I want to move some of the smaller trees—you know, the saplings."

Jemmie spread her feet and swung the club. "It's awful hot to move trees."

"You got that right," said Justin.

Cass pushed her hair off her face with the back of her hand. "I'll help."

"You will?"

"My dad has a couple of shovels we can use."

"I never said I wouldn't help." Jemmie handed the golf club back to Ben. "All I said was that it was going to be hot. How about you boys? You afraid to sweat?"

"We can do anything you can do," Justin said.

Cody stood there panting, holding the ball. "Can I can come too? I'll bring my wagon."

Ben stuck the ball in his pocket. "Better get organized." He led the way home with the club over his shoulder. "First thing we have to do is see how many pots and buckets we can get together. And we'll collect shovels. Mr. Barnett has a wheelbarrow he might loan us. We should ask around to see who wants trees."

Cass's face lit up. "I know, we could offer to plant them."

"For a price," Justin said. Ben gave him a look. "Just a suggestion."

～

I ran into the kitchen. "Eb, guess what?"

He kept spooning Frosted Flakes into his mouth.

"Everyone's going to help. Are you sure you have to go to your aunt's?"

He tipped the bowl up, slurped the milk out of the bottom, and wiped his mouth on his wrist. "Aunt Terry's taking me to the mall and the movies."

"But Eb, this is important."

"To *you* it's important."

"Can you at least help now? We need to gather pots and shovels."

"Yeah, I guess."

Ben designated his family's backyard as the place to drop things off. Since his dad had two and a half cars behind the house with their guts hanging out, a little more mess didn't matter. "What's with the junkers?" Eb asked.

Ben leaned against the door of a white Impala. "Man, these aren't junkers. They're project cars."

Cass and Jemmie hopped up onto the Impala's trunk and sat. Cass patted the spot next to her and I jumped up too.

"My dad teaches auto mechanics," Ben said. "He has some guys from last semester working on these."

"Does he get paid extra?" Eb made a face at himself in a wing mirror.

"Nah, he just likes to mess around with cars. I help him sometimes."

"Ben's getting his own project car soon," Cody bragged. "So he'll be ready when he turns sixteen."

"You have to build your own car?" Eb asked.

"Yeah." Ben ran a hand along the side of the Impala. "It'll be totally customized."

He probably would've gone on all day about dual exhausts and lowered suspensions, but Jemmie hopped down off the Impala. "Customize later, Benjamin. We got trees to move. I'm gonna ask Nana Grace for some pots. She has a whole bunch from all the rose bushes she's planted."

Cass gave my T-shirt a tug. "You want to come with me, Anna? We'll ask Mr. Barnett about his wheelbarrow." We walked together, matching strides. "He's home on disability," she explained as we walked up to his door. We could hear a TV. She cupped her hands over her eyes and looked through the screen. "Mr. Barnett?" Two blurs raced across the kitchen, *yip, yip, yip,* and slid into the door. Down by our ankles two tiny dogs pressed their noses to the screen and growled.

"Be right there. Don't let the attack dogs get you." It took a minute for Mr. Barnett to shuffle to the door. He stuck his head out and the attack dogs skittered back. "Hello, Cass, why don't you two come inside?"

We followed him into the living room. Cass and I sat down on the couch. In an instant the dogs leapt up beside us, forgetting all about wanting to gnaw our legs off.

Mr. Barnett hit the mute button on the remote. "What can I do for you ladies?"

We told him about the woods.

"So, they're going to mine sand, are they?" he fumed. "They've already got one ugly pit over on Tyson. They always put the bad stuff on our side of town. I'd like to see them try something like that on the north side. Everyone up there's a lawyer. They'd sue the pants off 'em." When we asked to borrow his wheelbarrow he said, "Help yourselves. I'm afraid the tire's kind of flat, though."

We thumped back to the Floyd's yard, pushing Mr. Barnett's rusty, flat-tire wheelbarrow. Ben patched the tire and pumped it up again.

"I guess all that messing around with cars is good for something," Jemmie said, dropping a pile of plastic pots.

Justin paced between the project cars. "You know what we need? Publicity. If everybody knew about it, they might keep the city from knocking the woods down, or they might at least come help us dig."

"Yeah, right," said Eb. "People will be lining up to sweat over a few lousy trees."

Cass stopped counting pots. "*Some* people care about trees."

After supper, when Eb's aunt had picked him up, Cass and Jemmie and I sat at the table in Jemmie's dining room making posters. SAVE THE TREES! we wrote. The streetlights came on while we were sticking them on telephone poles. We put the last one up on a pole by Miss Dupree's house. "See ya tomorrow, Anna," Jemmie said, and she and Cass jogged away into the darkness.

Chapter Twenty-One

TO MOVE A FOREST

The project cars looked like dead whales in the dim light when we gathered in the Floyds' backyard the next morning. Miss Johnette sat on the hood of the Impala drinking coffee.

The only one missing was Eb, who was off for a weekend of movies and malls.

Justin rapped a knuckle on Clay's new cast. "Fat lot of help you'll be."

"Hey, I'll be the boss," Clay said.

"I don't even get up this early for school," Justin grumbled.

"This is more important than school," Cass said.

"All right," Ben called. "Line up." He sprayed each of us with bug repellent, then said who would carry what.

Cody insisted on pulling the wagonful of pots. "It's my wagon!"

Justin and Ben, each with a shovel on his shoulder, went ahead on their bikes. The rest of us followed, the wagonload of plastic pots rattling. We hadn't gone far before Jemmie was towing the wagon with Cody in it, a tall stack of pots in his arms.

As we walked into the shadowy woods everyone got quiet. The birds were just waking up. Some sounded hoarse, as cranky as Eb first thing in the morning. Others were singing. We stood with our shovels, not sure where to start, or what to do.

"Pick a small tree like this," Miss Johnette said, forcing the blade of her shovel into the ground. Each time she stepped on the shovel, she'd lean back on the handle, loosening the dirt. The leaves of the small redbud tree she was moving trembled. "Get as much soil as you can with the roots."

I picked a little cedar and stepped on the shovel. Because the soil was mostly sand, the blade sank into the ground pretty easily. I rocked the handle the way Miss Johnette had done, then moved the shovel and stepped on it again. This time I hit something, maybe a root from one of the bigger trees. I wiggled the shovel until it slid past.

I kicked the shovel under the root ball and tried to lift. It wouldn't come out, so I knelt and slid my hands under the lump of roots. Needles pricked me through my shirt. I hung on and leaned back. When the last few roots let go I fell over, sending up a spray of sand.

Clay laughed.

"I need a pot," I said. Since he had only one good arm, it was his job to give out the plastic pots. He threw one at me.

Nana Grace's rosebush pot was too small for my cedar. I shook a bunch of the soil out, then squeezed the roots in. I glanced over at Cody just as he jerked a fern out of the ground. "That's how you pull a weed, Cody, not a plant you want to keep."

"It wouldn't come loose." Sand sprinkled down the front of his shirt. "And it still isn't all the way out."

I crawled over. Long runners still attached his fern to the ground. I tugged at one gently and found that it continued, just under the layer of fallen leaves. The runner was attached to another fern, and another. Cody and I dug up each of the ferns in the chain. When we were done we had eight, all hooked together.

"Pot?" said Clay. Cody and I looked at him. There was no way to put our chain of ferns in a pot.

Jemmie walked by with a potted magnolia in her arms. "What're you going to do with those ferns?"

"Don't know," Cody said.

"My grandmother would like to have them, I bet."

Cody and I put them right in the wagon and tossed a little dirt over all the roots. Jemmie grabbed the wagon handle and trotted back toward the neighborhood, ferns bumping along behind her.

When she came back, she had a pitcher of grape Koolaid in the wagon and a stack of paper cups. "All right!" Clay pumped his one good arm. Now that the sun was getting high, it was hot.

"Everybody take a break," Ben said. Miss Johnette kept digging, but the rest of us sat together on a log, turning our lips purple.

Clay slid a stick into his cast to scratch an itch. "It's too hot."

"It's not that bad," Cass said.

"Yeah, it is. Even the trees think so." We had put our potted plants in the shade, but half of them were already drooping. They looked the way we felt. We drank slowly.

Cody tugged his brother's arm. "I gotta pee."

"Go behind a tree." Ben divided up the last of the Koolaid.

"No, I gotta go *home* to pee."

Leaves rustled, branches snapped. Someone was coming toward us. "Well, there y'all are." Nana Grace had a bandanna tied over her hair. The fingers of a pair of work gloves stuck out of the pocket of her housedress. "My, my." She marched right up to our little trees and shook her head. "Better do something about these before they up and die. You," she said, crooking a finger at Justin. "Grab a shovel and come with me." They loaded all the trees they could on the wagon and left. Cody tagged along.

I tried to dig up a magnolia but couldn't. As I knelt there looking at it, Miss Johnette walked up and leaned against her shovel. "Problem, Anna?"

"I can't get this one out of the ground."

"Let's see what we can do." Together we disentangled the roots and forced it into a pot. "Saved," she said, and we slapped hands.

I dug up the little dogwood that had gotten the whole thing started. When Nana Grace and Justin came rattling back with the empty wagon, I pointed to my dogwood. "Could you plant that one in Miss Johnette's yard, please?"

Nana Grace put it in the wagon and went over to get more trees.

"She's going around knocking on doors," Justin complained, "asking people if they'd like a nice tree. If they say 'yes' she points at me and says, 'My boy here'll be glad to plant it for you.'"

Nana Grace and Cody rolled by with another load of plants. "You coming, Justin?"

By ten we were all sweaty and tired, except for Miss Johnette. She was whistling. "We're doing great!" she said. By eleven we were running out of pots. That was fine by most of the kids. But Cass and I kept seeing more things we wanted to save. "We've just got to get more pots," she said.

"Only four left," Clay announced.

I was up to my elbows in dirt trying to lift a stubborn little oak, when I heard a clatter. Ben stood and peered toward the road. "Somebody just pulled up with a truckload of pots." I heard a few groans.

Miss Johnette stopped with one foot on her shovel and shaded her eyes. "Well, knock me over with a feather. Anna, look who it is."

I pulled my gritty arms out of the hole and knelt up. The environmental planner was back.

"Are you here to trespass with us, Mr. Webster?" Miss Johnette called out.

He had a stack of pots under one arm and a shovel over his shoulder. "I'm here to help." He dropped the pots then strode off to find something to save.

We all went back to work with more energy. Seeing the way Miss Johnette and Mr. Webster worked made us begin to believe that maybe we *could* move the forest.

Late in the morning, Mr. Barnett came over. He kicked the tire on his wheelbarrow, checking Ben's repair job. "You selling these trees or giving them away?"

"Giving," Cass assured him. "You want some, Mr. Barnett?"

He picked out a couple we had sitting in pots. Ben tucked a pot under each arm and the two of them went off.

When he got back Ben said, "Those dogs of his lifted a leg on both trees as soon as I got 'em in the ground."

Clay grinned. "That's one way to water a tree."

A few people from the neighborhood saw our signs and came. Cass's sister dragged over a second wagon, looked at a shovel, looked at her nails and asked, "Is anybody getting hungry?"

At noon Nana Grace brought more Koolaid, orange this time, and a tray of sandwiches made by Cass's sister and mother. She shook out a blanket for all of us to sit on. "Now help yourselves," she said.

I had a peanut butter and jelly. The jelly was still cold from the refrigerator.

When we ran out of Koolaid, Mr. Webster passed his canteen around. Cody fell asleep on the blanket.

The afternoon was long and hot. Our hair stuck to our faces. Cass and I had dirt freckles to go with our freckle freckles. Even Clay, who had done basically nothing, was flushed and sweaty. Mr. Webster seemed to have an endless supply of pots. Miss Johnette and I were helping him get some more out of his truck when a car pulled up.

The car's electric window rolled down.

Mr. Webster flinched. "What brings you out here, Al?"

"Just checking to make sure the posts were up for Monday. How about you?"

"Digging up a few small trees with some of the neighborhood kids."

"Digging up trees?"

"Yeah, you know, trees, the lungs of the planet."

"Trees, right." The window rolled back up, the car drove away.

"Who was that charmer?" asked Miss Johnette.

"Al Malone. My boss."

"Hope he doesn't put your butt in a sling over this."

Mr. Webster slammed the tailgate of his truck. "Wouldn't be the first time."

As it got later our repellent wore off. The mosquitoes got bad.

"Time to call it quits," said Mr. Webster. "Meet you all back here tomorrow."

Walking home, Clay told Justin, "Man, you stink out loud."

~

When we gathered the next morning there were fewer of us. Clay and Justin hadn't bothered to show up. Cass and Jemmie were there, but discouraged.

"Jemmie and me already went around and watered everything we planted yesterday," Cass said. "Some of those trees looked really bad."

"We sure could use a good rain." Miss Johnette looked up. The sky was just getting light. "Not one cloud. All I see is Venus."

Cody wished for rain on it, even though Miss Johnette said it wasn't a star.

We headed back to the woods. Cody didn't even offer to pull the wagon; he just climbed in. Halfway there, Justin caught up. "Where's Clay?" He took a bite out of the Pop-Tart in his hand.

Ben shrugged.

"Who needs him anyway?" Justin said.

We hadn't been there ten minutes when Mr. Webster's truck rolled up.

"Did you hear anything from Al?" Miss Johnette asked.

"I got a phone call."

"Are you in trouble? Is he going to shut us down?"

"He said he'd look the other way, but the fence is definitely going up Monday."

A second truck pulled in. "Hey, glad you could make it, John." Mr. Webster clasped the hand of the man who climbed out. "John owns a nursery that specializes in native plants. He's pretty good with a shovel."

Miss Johnette had called some of her biology students. "Hey, Miss J.," they said as they joined us in the woods. "Want us to move these woods for you?"

Miss Dupree and Mr. Perry came. They dug up one little maple, then had a long, soulful discussion about whether to plant it at her house or his. "Here's another one." Cass whomped down another potted maple at their feet. "Now you have one for each place. Would you like a couple of cedars to go with them?"

In the middle of the morning I heard another car door slam. Someone else the adults had called, I figured. I was working my fingers under the roots of a woods fern when a pair of red high-tops, so new I could smell the rubber, stopped, one on either side of the fern. I knew those bitey shins. I knew those doorknob knees. "Eb!"

The legs of his shorts stood out stiff. "That's right." He crossed his arms over a new shirt. "Eb Gramlich returns to the Forest of Doom."

Jemmie came up. "Eb-man!" She walked around him trailing a finger across his chest, then his back. "Ooh, new threads. Don't you look fine?" She dusted a hand across the top of his head. "Got your hair buzzed too. I swear, you're so sharp it hurts to look at you."

Eb didn't get to do much, because his aunt kept fussing about poison ivy and new clothes. But she pitched in herself, digging and potting and hauling. We loaded her van with plants.

It was twilight when we finally set our shovels down and looked around. "The forest looks just the same," said Cass. "It's like we didn't do a thing." We put the last few pots in the wagons.

Jemmie lifted a limp branch. "They're kind of scraggly."

"They'll grow," said Mr. Webster. "Nature never gives up."

"Want a lift back to Miss Dupree's, Eb?" Aunt Terry asked. It was so late she would have been dropping him off by then anyway. But Eb decided to walk with the rest of us.

As we hauled the last load of trees home we could see lights on in the windows of the houses, TV screens. "I'll take these to my house and water them," said Cass, who was towing one of the wagons. "In the morning we'll have to figure out what to do with one more load of trees."

Chapter Twenty-Two

THE LAST VIEW OF EB

Eb and I went over to Miss Johnette's the next day to see what Justin and Nana Grace had planted in her yard. "Look, Anna," Miss Johnette said. "Look where they put your dogwood."

Justin must have seen the loose soil. Tired of digging, he had planted my tree right on Gregor's grave.

"It's a good place for it." Miss Johnette put her hands on my shoulders. "Dogwoods like a little shade. And now Greg has his marker. A dogwood for the dog, how appropriate." She gave my shoulders a friendly squeeze. "But you probably wanted it planted in Miss Dupree's yard."

"No, I told them to plant it here."

"But, why?"

"Because you'll take care of it. I don't know how long I'll be at Miss Dupree's."

Eb was arranging a handful of acorns in a pattern around the tree on Greg's grave. "Anna's about to get the old heave-ho," he said. "Miss Dupree's engaged all of a sudden."

"Engaged? Who's she engaged to?"

"Mr. Perry." Eb pressed an acorn into the dirt. "He was supposed to be one of her clients. She decided to keep him for herself."

"Anna won't be able to stay?"

"No way," Eb said. "She inhibits things." He pushed another acorn down with his thumb. "Now, how about a snack? I have to eat all the junk I can. My aunt won't buy it. It's against her religion."

What about the cheese popcorn? I thought.

"Help yourself, Eb. You know where I keep it." When I started to follow, she put a hand on my arm. "Don't worry about Miss Dupree, Anna. I'll talk to her. We'll come up with something."

When we went inside, Eb was wolfing down a Little Debbie Zebra Cake and the phone was ringing. "Hello?" said Miss Johnette. "Jonah? Hey!" She smiled, then her face got serious. "Are they putting the fence up?... I see. Figures. What?... Oh, nothing special.... All right, I'd be glad to." Then she hung up. "That was Mr. Webster."

Eb was peeling the icing off his second zebra cake. "No kidding."

"He called to say that they are stringing the fence today, and posting No Trespassing signs. He said we should probably pay attention to the signs. He invited me to go to a bat watch." She swung a leg over a kitchen chair and rested her arms on the back.

Eb rolled the icing into a tube. "You mean he asked you out on a date?"

She rested her cheek on her arm. "A bat watch? I wouldn't call that a date."

"You're right. That's not a date, it's a science fair project." He shoved the icing in his mouth, then held up the piece of cardboard from the package. "See?" he said, dropping the cardboard in the recycle box. "I'm recycling."

"Good for you, Eb. Your children thank you." She reached out and rubbed the top of his head. "Say, Eb, isn't this your big day?"

"Yeah..." He twisted the bottom of his T-shirt with one hand. "...this afternoon."

After lunch he, his aunt and uncle, and Mrs. Riley were supposed to go before the judge. Mrs. Riley was going to recommend that Eb be put in his aunt and uncle's custody. "But that judge has to understand I'm going to live there only for now." Eb reached for another Little Debbie. "That's the main thing."

"Write down what you want to say," Miss Johnette suggested. "That way you won't forget." She gave him a pad and pencil.

"Good idea. I mean, I'll go along with this, but just until Lisa gets her act together. Nobody's going to trick me into getting adopted."

~

When they got back Eb said, "My big day took fifteen minutes."

"But you were gone for three hours."

"Waiting," he said. "We did a whole lot of waiting."

The judge had listened to Mrs. Riley, listened to Aunt Terry, listened to Eb, then found that it was in the best interest of Ebenezer Gramlich to be placed in the temporary custody of his aunt, Teresa Finelli.

It was time for Eb to go.

It wasn't any harder to pack up Eb than it had been to pack Mr. Miller. Eb didn't own much, and most of what he did own was at his aunt's already. Still, his aunt and uncle and Miss Dupree all ran around as if there was a lot to do. Eb and I sat on the white couch and watched them whiz past.

I picked up my explorer's notebook from where Eb had dropped it on the coffee table and held it out. "Here."

He looked at it, even started to reach, then he shook his head. "No, Anna, you're the explorer. You keep it. Besides, you're gonna need it."

Uncle Bill came out of the pink bedroom carrying Eb's battered suitcase. "Let's go, Ebster," he said, heading out the front door.

Eb stood up. "I wish he'd quit trying to sound cool."

I stood too.

Miss Dupree followed Uncle Bill, carrying Eb's dress shoes. "Say good-bye to Anna, Eb. We'll meet you at the car." Aunt Terry followed carrying a half-eaten bag of cheese popcorn.

That left the two of us standing with our arms at our sides. *How do you say good-bye to someone who was almost your brother?* I thought. *Especially someone who doesn't let anyone touch him.*

"So, I guess I'll see you." He took a step backward toward the door.

"I doubt it."

"You're not supposed to say that." He took two steps toward me.

"Why not? It's true."

"I know."

"Listen, Eb, could I give you a hug?"

"A hug?" He sucked his cheeks in for a second while he thought about it. "I guess it'd be okay. But no kissing. I draw the line at kissing."

Eb wasn't much to hug. He was mostly bony spots, prickles, and points, but I hugged him hard enough to squeeze all the air out of him. And then he hugged me back, hard. It only lasted a heartbeat and a half before it was over and we were walking toward the door. We moved stiffly, being careful not to look at each other.

Miss Dupree had to get in a hug too, and a kiss that barely grazed his ear. "No displays of affection," he mumbled, then turned and gave her a quick hug back.

Good-byes are the worst thing. Good-bye is still good-bye even if you drag it out.

Eb didn't look back when the van pulled away. The last I saw of him was the back of his skinny neck and his buzzed head, the same view I had on the day we arrived at Miss Dupree's. I felt terrible. I thought he was gone for good.

But he called me that night. At first we didn't have much to say. After hello, we listened to each other breathe. "What did you guys have for dinner?" he finally asked.

"Spaghetti. You?"

"Pot roast." Another long silence. "And disgusting broccoli."

"Miss Dupree's making me move into your old room. She says it was supposed to be mine, and now I can finally have it."

"You didn't tell her you hate it? Going along with her isn't going to help, you know. She's not gonna let you stay." He wheezed into the receiver. "So, is lover boy there?"

"They're both in the living room." They had totally taken over the couch where the three of us used to sit after dinner.

"Bet they're trading spit," he said.

"Probably."

"Listen, Anna? I'm going to the dentist tomorrow. I've never been before. Does it hurt?"

"He'll give you happy gas. You don't feel a thing." I could hear Miss Dupree and Mr. Perry laughing.

By the time we hung up, the living room was perfectly quiet. Spit trading. I got to the pink room as fast as I could, slid into bed, and pulled the spread all the way over me.

~

After Eb, I didn't belong anywhere. Cass and Jemmie let me hang out with them, but I wasn't a third best friend. I was just something extra. I think they felt sorry for me. I think everyone felt sorry for me. Nana Grace gave me an embroidery lesson. Cass's sister, Lou Anne, told me I had terminal split ends and too much forehead showing. She trimmed my hair and cut me some bangs. "There you go," she said, smiling. "You look good enough to keep." Cass gave her a terrible look. "What? Oh—" She covered her mouth with her hand. "Sorry. I didn't mean anything by that."

At home, Miss Dupree seemed surprised that I was still there. "Oh! Anna!" she'd say. When I was at the house I was always tripping over Mr. Perry. *Doesn't he have a job?* I wondered. Most nights I called Eb just to have someone to talk to. I always knew what he had for supper. I heard all about his five cavities.

I spent a lot of time with Miss Johnette. The Saturday after Eb left, we went on a hike at Torreya State Park with Mr. Webster. The park is one of the only places in the world where the endangered Torreya cedar grows. It was a fairly normal tree—except that it was going extinct.

I felt sorry for that puny little tree, and wondered if I was going extinct myself. When Mr. Perry was at the house I felt myself vanish.

They didn't notice me—which is what going extinct must feel like.

Eb had only been gone for a week and a half when Miss Dupree started talking about wedding gowns and honeymoons and bridal registries. "Would I look silly in white lace? Am I too old?"

"You'd look fine."

"I've always wanted a lace wedding gown, with a train." She had plenty to say about the exact kind of flowers she wanted at the church—calla lilies and ferns—but not much to say about me. She mentioned buying me a new dress, but she had described the whole wedding and was well into the reception and she still hadn't said anything about what would happen after the wedding. Would I still be there, hanging on like the poor old Torreya cedar, or I would be extinct?

I thought of a plan…and a backup plan. Neither one was very good, just the best I could come up with. I waited for Miss Dupree to go out to the grocery store, then I picked up the phone. First I punched the number I'd written on the paper napkin. I heard the click of the phone picking up, then Willie Nelson singing "On the Road Again." "Guess you missed me," my uncle's voice said. "Leave a message at the beep." I hung up and switched to plan B.

Plan B was staying with Eb during the honeymoon, then coming back to the pink room when it was all over. I dialed again. The phone rang for a long time. Finally Aunt Terry answered.

"May I speak to Eb, please?"

"Anna?" Aunt Terry sounded odd. "Anna, I'm afraid you can't talk to him. Eb's gone."

She's probably made him eat brussels sprouts or clean his room or something, I thought. *He'll be back by supper.* "I bet he didn't go far," I said.

"His mother took him away this morning."

I felt like I had swallowed something hard and cold. I remembered what Eb had told me about the last time he left his aunt's. Lisa and Eddie had pulled up, and he had jumped into the car. The bruises on Eb's arm had happened after that. "Was Eddie with her?"

"Thank God, no. She's alone again. That's why she came and got him. I begged her to let him stay. They were gone in half an hour."

I hung up the phone. With Lisa, Eb could end up anywhere: going to the beach instead of school, eating potato chips for supper. Having fun sometimes, sometimes scared.

I kicked the leg of the coffee table, hard, then I kicked it again. On the second kick my sandal left a big black mark. It was the only thing in the room that showed that I had been there. Miss Dupree would spray it with something and wipe it off.

And then I would be gone too.

∼

I knocked at Miss Johnette's door. "Come on in," she called. Her voice sounded far away.

When I went inside she was standing on a ladder. All I could see were her tan knees and army boots and the tops of her purple socks. The rest of her was in the crawl space under the roof. On the floor were dozens of boxes.

"Eb's gone," I told the purple socks. "His mom abducted him."

"That's bad news." She had listened to Eb telling Mr. Miller about Eddie. "I sure hope he'll be all right." Her knees dipped a little. Just by looking at her knees, I could tell she was sad too. Suddenly, I didn't feel so alone.

"What are you doing?"

"Doing?" She pulled her head out of the hole and looked down at me. "I'm hiding everything. Could you hand me that box? I've been going up and down this ladder for hours."

I passed her up a box of birds' nests. "Why are you hiding everything?"

"I have to make the place look normal."

The ladder wiggled as she shoved the boxes around under the eaves. "But you're not normal." I held the ladder steady. "You don't even want to be normal."

She pulled her head back out of the hole again. "Well, of course I don't. I just have to pretend for a little while."

"Why?"

She climbed down. "Come on, Anna, we need to talk." We sat on the edge of the bed in the spare bedroom—we could only sit on the edge because of the *Smithsonian* magazines heaped on the rest of it. "I should've talked to you about this sooner, but I wanted it to be a sure thing first. I mean, the whole thing could blow up in my face."

"What whole thing?"

"I'm being clear as mud, aren't I? I'll start over. When I met you and Eb, I thought, hey, I like kids, maybe I could be a foster mom. All I did was mention it to Mrs. Riley. The next thing I knew, I was in a foster parenting class. I was hoping there might be another Anna in the program—a curious girl who wasn't afraid of every little thing, one with a blue hat." She gave the brim of my hat a quick tug. "When Eb said you were about to get the old heave-ho, I thought, well Johnette, here's your chance to the get the original, so I talked to Miss Dupree about maybe having you move in with me."

"With *you?*" I wanted to hug her. I wanted to dance. "I would love to!"

"Would you? Wow, great!"

"But what did she say?"

"She was relieved, and sad about letting you go. Even though you weren't what she expected when she signed up for a foster daughter, she really likes you, Anna."

"She wanted a girlie girl. One who likes ruffles."

"I guess. But I want one who likes bugs and adventures—a girl exactly like you."

"What about Mrs. Riley? Did she say it would be okay?"

"Mrs. Riley's all for you moving in with me except she says the 'home situation' is a bit problematical."

"What home situation?"

"You know…" She glanced up at the empty wasp's nest that hung over the bed. "It's fine with her because she knows me, but she thinks the others might not see a houseful of skeletons as an ideal setting for an impressionable young girl."

"So, we have to make the place look normal?"

"Right. Normal," she said. "Whatever that is." We looked around the room. It was just the tiny, spare bedroom, but all by itself it could sink our chances. It wasn't just the magazines—at least five years worth—it was the crates of chipped stones that could possibly be Indian artifacts, and the shelf of mud dauber nests, not to mention the eggs from twenty-one species of North Florida birds—plus one from an ostrich. "See what I mean?" she said.

"We can do it."

"All rightee!" She slapped her knees and jumped up. "Let's get going." I jumped up too, then saw her shoulders sag. "Kind of over-whelming, isn't it?" she said.

"Let's start with the magazines."

It took an hour and a half just to stack the magazines in the closet. "We'll be okay," she said, pushing the closet door shut with her shoulder, "as long as they don't open anything."

"If they open that door they'll be killed by the avalanche," I said.

"What do you say, Anna, lemonade break?" When we took our glasses out to the backyard, there was a strange smell in the air. "Something's burning," she said. We turned and saw the smudge of smoke rising in the sky. "No! It's the woods."

I don't know what we thought we could do, but we jumped in her Volkswagen and sped over to Rankin. The woods had already been bulldozed and pushed into heaps. Men were tending smoldering piles, surrounded by a lifeless field of white sand. The two of us hung on the fence. All we could do was go back to the neighborhood and water the small trees we had saved.

We didn't talk about the woods after that. What could we say?

~

It took us three days to get ready for the inspection. There were way too many collections to fit in the attic. We shoved piles and boxes under beds and into closets. We filled every drawer. When we were done, the house looked sad and empty, like nobody lived there. It wasn't a museum anymore, just an old house that needed a coat of paint. "Does this look normal?" she asked.

"Not really."

She shook her head. "I didn't think so."

"Listen, I've lived in some normal houses," I said. "What's missing is stuff."

"Stuff?"

"Knickknacks and whatnots." I remembered my grandmother walking around every Saturday morning with a rag in her hand. "You know, things you have to dust."

Miss Johnette snapped her fingers. "Goodwill."

We hit a bonanza in the fifty-cent bin. Down among the Christmas stockings and giant underpants we found doilies. When I held one up she said, "Creepy little things, aren't they? I had a great-aunt who put them on every chair."

"That's what we'll do. And we can put one on the coffee table with a vase of flowers in the middle." We dug around until we found a dozen of them, all shapes. Then we went looking for vases. I found a china statue of a bullfighter. "We should get this."

She held the bullfighter in one hand. "It's pretty tacky, Anna."

"Which is why it's so perfect. We can donate it back right after the inspection."

We found baskets and a teapot with ducks on it, even a welcome mat that said "*Willkommen!*" which Miss Johnette said was Dutch or German or something. We were waiting to pay when I looked at Miss Johnette. She was wearing her usual army boots, purple socks, and khaki shorts. "What are you going to wear?"

"Clothes."

"You need a dress." We stepped back out of line.

"A dress? Do you think it would help?" We walked over to the rack in the "better dress" department. "I don't have to try them on, do I?"

"You probably should."

There were only two choices in Miss Johnette's size: a long, flow-ered dress and a short one with little bows all over it. She took the flowered dress, which she called "the lesser of two evils," into the dressing room. She wouldn't even touch the one with bows.

I heard her bump into the dressing room wall. "Help! I can't reach the danged zipper." I zipped her, then we stood side by side in front of the mirror. She twisted the waist of the flowered dress and made a face at herself. "What do you think? I'm out of my territory here. Do I look too much like a warthog?"

"You look good. There's just one more thing. Shoes."

Miss Johnette dipped her knees. "Better?" The skirt hung down, but I could still see the toes of her army boots poking out.

"Next stop, the shoe rack."

Chapter Twenty-Three

THE SKELETON
OF THE EARTH

We thought the house looked good, but just to be sure we had Cass and Jemmie walk through. "You need salt and pepper shakers on the table," Cass said, "and a guest towel in the bathroom."

"And a bowl of fruit," Jemmie added. "Cookbooks too." She opened a cupboard, and right in front was a box of Little Debbie Devil Cremes. "This is not good." She hid the box at the back of the freezer. Then she and Cass dashed home to borrow saltshakers and guest towels, fruit bowls and cookbooks.

"We need one more pre-inspection." And Miss Johnette called Miss Dupree, the queen of normal.

"Everything looks just fine." I could tell that Miss Dupree was trying to overlook the china bullfighter and the doilies on the zebra-striped armchair. For a moment she gazed sadly at me instead. "I guess this is really happening isn't it? I'm going to miss you, Anna." I wanted to tell her that I would miss her too, but she was already running for the door. "There's just one more thing. I'll be right back." She returned in fifteen minutes with her arms loaded with canned smells.

"You mean the place smells bad?" Miss Johnette asked.

"No, it smells like nothing. It needs a homey scent—something floral, or maybe pine." We ended up with both. With a can in each hand, she sprayed. She set out bowls of potpourri. She sighed with satisfaction. "My work here is done." Then she gave me a hug. "I'm so happy, Anna. The inspection will go fine. And with you here we can still see each other all the time."

As soon as the door closed behind Miss Dupree, Miss Johnette looked around like, what the heck happened here? "How do people live like this?" she asked. "How did this get to be normal? All these fake natural smells are giving me a headache. Thank God they're coming tomorrow."

Then the phone rang. "The people coming to inspect the house rescheduled for Monday," Miss Johnette said, after she'd hung up.

As she flopped into her zebra chair a doily fluttered to the floor. "These things are driving me crazy," she said. She picked the doily up and put it on her head. "Three days of normalcy's gonna drive me nuts." She crossed her eyes. "Let's get out of here. How about a canoe trip first thing tomorrow morning? What do you say? Would you still like to see the karst?"

I really wanted to go. I'd never been canoeing before. But when I got back to Miss Dupree's, I forgot all about canoeing or the inspection. "We've decided to pass on the big wedding so we can move the date up," she said. "You'll be with Miss Johnette by then, so we'll both be happy."

She sounded so sure. But being normal and pretending to be normal are different things. *Can Miss Johnette pass the test?* I wondered. *Her Goodwill dress doesn't fit all that well. And that bullfighter is really cheesy.*

But that wasn't the real problem. The real problem was Miss Johnette. She was too honest. All she'd have to do was open her mouth and out would pop—the real Miss Johnette.

The next morning I woke up before sunup. I had been dreaming I was on a river choked with ice. I had to step from one chunk to the next. Each time I put my foot down, the ice would bob and I was sure I would slip into the frigid water. Awake, I stared into the darkness. It had to be one of Aunt Eva's omen dreams. Then I remembered that

Miss Johnette had asked if I wanted to see the karst. And maybe that was an omen too. Maybe I was going there to get another memory rock, one to put with the others when I had to move on.

I lay in bed watching the sky go from black to gray through the window of the pink room. I rolled onto my side and looked at my picture. I sure felt sorry for that baby. I flopped onto my back, and my eyes filled with tears, little salty pools that spilled over and ran down my cheeks and into my ears. I wiped my eyes on the sheet and looked at my picture again.

Aunt Eva used to say that an omen didn't tell you what was going to happen, just what was most likely. She said that you could work against an omen. That's what I had to do. I picked my photograph up and wrapped it in a shirt to protect it.

～

Miss Johnette's red canoe, the Lulu II, was already on the roof of her Volkswagen, roped to the bumpers with a few Boy Scout knots. "What do you have there?" she asked, shoving a cooler into the back seat.

"My picture. Can I put it by the bed in the guest room?"

"You mean your room? Sure."

The guest room—my room—was dark except for the early morning light coming through the window. I set the picture down next to the bullfighter on the little table by the bed, and then, just for a minute, I lay down. I looked at the shadows on the wall. *If I get to live here,* I thought, *I probably won't even notice them after a while.* I studied them hard, because if I never got to live here, I wanted to remember.

With the inspection on both of our minds, we didn't talk much on the way to the river. Miss Johnette whistled a little, and drank coffee out of a mug that she held between her thighs.

We pulled into a gravel lot with a boat ramp that went down to the river. "Untie the stern, Anna; I'll get the bow." As I undid the knots I could feel her pulling on the rope at the other end of the canoe.

"We'll go upstream until we get tired," she called, "then we can just drift back. Most people go downstream, but that takes two cars, one here and one at the other end of the run." Then she leaned out until she could see me and grinned. "You can drive the second car once you get your driver's license." I think she said that for the same reason I put my picture by the bed. Sometimes believing helps.

We slid the canoe off the car, each of us taking an end, and walked it down the ramp. The Econfina was a skinny little tea-colored river. A few water lilies floated at the edge along with a whole lot of garbage. Fishermen had left behind plastic bait tubs and beer cans, but Miss Johnette had brought a plastic trash bag. The first thing we did after launching was to nose the canoe around near the landing, picking up junk. Then we were off.

"Choose a side," she said, "then I'll paddle on the other one." When I picked, she said, "Left? Are you a lefty, Anna?"

"Uh-huh."

"Well, what do you know. Me too." We paddled in silence, thinking about the fact that we were both left-handed. It was one more little thread between us.

The river smelled like rain and leaves and sun, nothing like the canned smells from Miss Dupree's cupboard. Sometimes we paddled among lily pads. The bow of the canoe rippled the leaves, turning their purple undersides up. I dragged my hand, combing the water through my fingers. "This river is fed by springs," Miss Johnette said. "That's why it's so cool." I could hear the drops falling off her paddle.

"This is the prettiest day of the world," I said.

"The prettiest," she agreed.

"If I could draw like Eb, I would put the Econfina in my explorer's notebook, so I could keep it forever."

"Keep it by coming back," she said. "Get to know it. That's the only way to keep a river." Small silvery insects skitted across the water. "Look, Anna, water boatmen." The water boatmen were as round and shiny as the heads of screws and they skimmed along on the surface of the water, racing ahead of the boat.

Birds called from the woods along the banks. "Crow," she said. "Pileated woodpecker." She didn't even have to see the birds to name them. "Kingfisher." The kingfisher sounded as if he was laughing, just glad to be alive.

"Do you see the karst?" she asked.

I looked toward the shore. "There?" The banks at the water's edge were not dirt, but stone—the karst—all holey and pitted and as pale as chalk.

She lifted the paddle and let the canoe glide. "The karst is much more than the little bit you see. The karst is under us, storing water like a sponge. We are sitting on top of a giant subterranean river called an aquifer. That's where we get our drinking water from. That's where the rain eventually goes when it soaks into the ground."

I didn't want to need a stone and I didn't want to leave without one. But the karst wasn't like a river rock you could pick up and put in your pocket. The karst was the skeleton of the earth showing through.

It took us a while to find a piece that had broken off. When we did, it was a big chunk, way too big for my suitcase. Miss Johnette didn't hesitate. She paddled over to the bank, rolled her jeans to her knees, climbed out, and wrestled the rock into the canoe. "What do you think? Pretty nice, huh? Look at all those gorgeous holes!"

"It *is* nice. But maybe we should look for a smaller piece. I mean, what if we flunk? Not that we're going to…. Just, what if? I could never take this stone with me."

Miss Johnette blew her bangs back off her forehead. "Why, Anna Casey! This isn't a going-away rock," she said. "It's a staying rock. We're going to put it smack in the middle of the kitchen table as soon as we pass the inspection. Once a month we'll even dust it."

Chapter Twenty-Four

ANNA CASEY'S PLACE IN THE WORLD

Miss Johnette and I had worked it out. My job was to keep my fingers crossed while I waited to hear. Miss Dupree had the same job. The inspectors were coming at two. As soon as they left, Miss Johnette would come right over to Miss Dupree's and tell us the verdict. At two minutes after two someone pounded at the door. My heart sank. It had taken less than no time for them to flunk her.

When I opened the door, Jemmie stood there with her hands on her hips. "Girl," she said, "you want to shoot a few hoops around the corner?" Miss Johnette's was around the corner. I looked out into the street and all the kids were there—Ben and Cody, Clay and Justin, and Cass. Jemmie leaned in and whispered, "They're there. The inspectors. We thought we should keep an eye on things."

I looked over at Miss Dupree. "Go on," she said. "I'd go too, but I don't know how to shoot hoops." I ran over and hugged her. "Good luck," she whispered into my hair.

Walking over, my legs felt rubbery. Like Eb with his asthma, I was having a hard time breathing. The other kids were a blur as they ran, dribbled, and passed the ball. When we came around the corner I could see a brown car parked in the street in front of Miss Johnette's directly across from the basketball hoop.

Clay had the ball. "Slam dunk," he yelled. He jumped up and grabbed the hoop with his one good arm. The hoop was nailed to the telephone pole really low. He looked stupid enough hanging off it. Then suddenly, it gave way, and he smacked into the pole.

"Great," said Ben. "Now you went and busted it."

Straightening the hoop back up was harder than bending it down. While the boys tried to shove it back up, Cass and Jemmie took turns dribbling the ball.

There was a smiley-face bumper sticker on the brown car. HAVE A NICE DAY! *Another omen? Or maybe just another dumb bumper-sticker?*

The ball twanged each time it hit the pavement.

"Ben?" said Jemmie, passing the ball off to Cass. "Girls against boys, okay? Me and Cass and Anna will show you once and for all who's got it."

"Whatever." Ben was sweating, still trying to shove the hoop back up. Clay had stepped back to supervise.

Cody tugged at Jemmie's arm. "Can I be on your side?"

Clay whipped around. "You wanna be a *girl?*"

"I wanna win."

"Smart man," Jemmie said. "Come on, Cody, slap me five." Cody held up a chubby hand. "This boy's with us." While we waited for Ben to fix the hoop she made a square of Cody, Cass, me, and her-self. We bounce-passed the ball. *Twang, twang.* When it was Cody's turn to catch, the ball jumped the curb and rolled across a lawn. "You got to keep your eye on it," Jemmie said, chasing the ball. "You can't go covering your face with your arms. Not if you want to be on the girl's team."

I caught the ball and passed it. I wished I could see what was going on inside Miss Johnette's, but the house hid behind the tall plants of the garden. The windows barely peeked over the tops of the milkweeds. Maybe one of the inspectors had opened a closet door and been crushed. Maybe they had insisted on checking the attic.

Whack! The ball hit me in the side of the head.

"Sorry, sorry, sorry!" said Cass. "I thought you were looking."

"Oh, yeah," said Clay. "You girls are really sharp."

"She's just worried," Cass said. Everyone turned and stared at the house.

"Anna," Cody whispered. "You want me to sneak up and spy?"

I shook my head. "No thanks, Cody."

Ben finally got the hoop straight and we began to play, girls plus Cody against boys. Cody wasn't any good, but at least he was paying attention. I couldn't. My stomach hurt so much I thought I was going to barf in the grass. Even though he had just one good arm, Clay took advantage of me. Every time I had the ball he crowded me, trying to steal it, and I just let him.

Jemmie stamped her foot. "You call yourself a girl? Come on, Anna, this is pitiful."

But Cass walked me over to the curb. "Sit down, Anna. We'll take it from here." She ran back to the middle of the street clapping her hands. "Okay, girls, let's go." Cody made a weak pass to her. Cass turned and shot in one motion. The ball went through the hoop without touching it.

"Nothing but net!" Jemmie crowed, "Way to go, Cass!" Then she sunk a shot of her own.

Across the street at Miss Johnette's the door opened. I could see a little shaking in the tall flowers, then a woman with bluish hair and a man with round eyeglasses emerged. What did they decide? I couldn't tell from their blank faces. They stopped for a moment to look at something on the man's clipboard. The woman laughed, then they got in the car and drove away.

I was still sitting on the curb. Cass plopped down beside me. "Want us to check?"

"No," I said. "I have to do it myself."

Ben's arm hung at his side, the ball tucked against his hip. "Hey, good luck, Anna."

"Yeah, good luck," they all said. I felt their eyes on my back, then I stepped into the flower tunnel. Ahead, I could see the purple door. I realized suddenly that our strategy had been all wrong. It didn't go far enough. We had moved Charlotte, but we should have painted the door some dull color, cut the flowers back. I let myself in. Everything was so quiet.

And then I heard a loud thump from the kitchen. As I rushed in, Miss Johnette gave me a double thumbs-up. Sitting smack in the middle of the table was the chunk of karst we'd picked up on the Econfina River. "I told you this was a staying rock."

~

As soon as the inspectors left Charlotte began a new web. I had to duck it dragging my suitcase up the walk.

I asked for a cat first thing. "I don't know," said Miss Johnette. "To a cat, a birdfeeder is a great big buffet table." I suggested an indoor cat, but she didn't like the idea of cooping an animal up. I thought about it, and decided I didn't either. "Maybe a dog," she said, rehanging the wasp nest over my bed.

"Can we pick an ugly one no one else wants?" I asked.

"Sure," she said. "The uglier the better."

Of the trees we saved that weekend in the heat of summer a few survived: the ones at Mr. Barnett's that the dogs helped water, some in yards that Cass visited every day, the dogwood on Gregor's grave. I wondered about the trees in Aunt Terry's yard, and Eb, too, transplanted somewhere safe I hoped. And how was Mr. Miller? Was he getting along with the other crazy people in Key West?

I, Anna, am doing fine. Very.

I have two pictures by my bed now—my same old family picture, and a new one Jemmie took of me and Miss Johnette. In the picture, the two of us sit on the front step of our house, framed in flowers. If you look carefully, you'll see Charlotte hanging over the path, just like a star.

ABOUT THE AUTHOR

ADRIAN FOGELIN is the author of the award-winning novel, CROSSING JORDAN. She works in a library, writes every day before the sun comes up, and spends her free time at Bluebird, a piece of rural land just outside of Tallahassee, which she, her family, and Tully manage for wildlife. Every fall she tags migrating monarch butterflies.